The Locked Series: Book 1

NOTHING LOST

UNLOCK MORE AT
facebook.com/thelockedseries
@thelockedseries
@gemmalaurenkrebs

GEMMA LAUREN KREBS

Edited by

Jessica Feinberg

Melinda Fraser

Illustrated by

Jessica Feinberg

Cover Design By

Roma Lamor

FIRST EDITION

ISBN:
Paperback ISBN: 978-1-71800-800-7
Hardcover ISBN: 978-1-64370-312-1

The purchase of this book guarantees
$1
will be donated to

One Tree Planted has planting projects all over the world
and, with them,

$$\$1 = 1\,\text{Tree}$$

to find out more go to

onetreeplanted.org

Watch the impact this book makes with
One Tree Planted by visiting

http://onetreeplanted.giv.sh/fundraisers/fnd_cf0537d2f74e2930

How will you save the world?

Dedicated to my favorite tree, Mulberry,
my past self who dreamt of planting trees on the moon,
and those who follow their heart.

Mandala:

A spiritual practice that can involve crafting an intricate sand design. After its laborious and meaningful creation, it is destroyed, its sand scattered ritualistically. Symbolically, it says time and material items are transient.

Nothing is permanent.

1
Great

It began at the light; that bright strip of sun falling across the floor of the dark, earthen tunnel. It drew my gaze and I could hardly keep my feet from dashing forward.

"Shay." A skinny dreadlock fell across my father's face where moist paint glistened. "Remember, shoes off at the light."

I nodded vigorously, "I remember, father."

Reaching the beam of sunlight, I plucked at the ties to my noonyi-skin boots and slid the translucent material from my feet. They drooped slightly as I set them on the flat rock against the wall.

I marveled at the symbols carved into the stone, the same that were scattered across my face in teal paint.

When I scampered impatiently back to my father's side, only one foot was free from his own shoes.

I grinned and tried to be patient, inhaling the fresh smell of soil. My toes dug into soft dirt they now had access to.

Halfway through scratching my face without thinking, I looked down and grimaced at the paint on my fingertips, then smeared it into the pocket of my robe.

My father huffed, standing, finally ready to move

forward.

I straightened.

He stilled himself before the stream of light and slowly inhaled and exhaled. As the Master Gardener, he would go before me. Each day he had to be the first to enter and last to leave the great dome of the Garden. For the last twenty years, he'd been the only one inside besides the Queen.

The appearance of the Garden was still a mystery to me. Grand pictures of lush leaves, pools, and the Great Tree herself were all in my mind; imagined with brilliant colors and little hesitation. These visions had long been fed by the stories and solemnity of the Apprenticeship I was born into.

"Shaylite."

Starting out of my thoughts, I answered haltingly, "Y-yes, father?" He never used my full name.

"Your task begins today. I know you understand the depth of what we do. Take this moment into your memory now, for you cannot go back. From the moment we breach the light, you are no longer my child, you are my Apprentice."

"Yes, fath—Master." Settling myself with a breath, I did my best to shift my mind into the elevated state I'd worked so long to achieve.

To be worthy of tending the Garden and able to understand the behavior of the plants, I'd gone through years of frustrating meditation. Even recognizing what that mindset felt like had taken longer than I would have wanted. Now though, I could more easily find the way to click my brain into that soft, quiet space that always waited.

"Then let us move forward." My father's voice usually seemed too big for the spaces it occupied, deep and rumbling. But here, surrounded on all sides by earth, it was swallowed whole.

I couldn't help but think we were both very small.

Carefully pressing his feet into the soil before us, my father stepped onward. The sunlight shifted over his large frame, then over my own scrawny one as we crossed onto the hallowed ground.

The smell of water swelled the air at the entrance.

My father lifted a chain around his neck, revealing a small, golden key. The same gold as the gate before us.

A soft click, an oiled swing of metal, and we were finally in the Garden.

Dark hedges stood tall on either side of a narrow path. I couldn't see anything ahead, but the rich, silvery-grey material of my father's robe. I looked up and marveled at the light coming through the panes of stained glass making up the dome. I'd only ever seen them from the outside, muted and dark. Here though, where the sun could shine through, they spoke vibrantly.

I knew the Great Tree wasn't far ahead. Excitement filled each of my limbs. My life so far had led to this moment.

At the end of the high sentry hedges, my father stepped aside. The Garden lay before me.

There was nothing else like it in our world...but I was still disappointed.

Trim shrubs wound along paths of rich soil in intricate designs. Orange, red, pink, yellow, and purple flowers spiked up and exploded from many of the plants. Between these were clear, jewel-bright pools arranged artistically.

The Great Tree, set at the center though, did not live up to her name.

To be sure, the Tree was interesting. Unlike the plants covering our island, she was long and bare for the most part. The large chunk of wood making up her stem was light grey with shadowy lines crisscrossing upward. A spray of leaves shot out from the ends of each branch and were a bright, almost luminous, green. They wavered slowly, though the air seemed still around us.

The Tree was beautiful, but only slightly taller than myself. To have been called 'Great', I expected her to tower to the stained-glass ceiling above.

Light shone down in brilliant streaks of golds and blues, spearing into the pools as purples and teals splayed over soil. There were a few places in the dome above left without panes to allow fresh air and pure sunlight into the space.

Small roots at the base of the Tree sprawled and bumped across the floor, seeming to seek out water, but they could not yet reach.

"So here it is, Shaylite." My father's voice rose up, "Here, at ten years of age, you are allowed access to the Garden we must protect. What do you think?"

I paused, not knowing how to express what I was feeling. It came out as a disappointed question, "This is the Great Tree, Master?"

He gazed forward to the Tree, "No."

I almost laughed in relief. Of course, this couldn't be her. Perhaps there was a more secret chamber where she was hidden away. This was a decoy to fool...someone. Maybe.

"This, Shaylite, is the Tree of the Fallen—"

He didn't pause, but I interrupted, "Why are there two Trees? I thought she was the only—"

His words cut me off swiftly, "Shaylite. The Great Tree is no more."

My mouth clamped shut.

"The Tree of the Fallen is the only remnant of what she once was." A quiet rage seemed to build up inside him, but the only sign was a slight movement of the hand hanging by his side.

"Did—did she die?" I asked cautiously, not sure if I was ready to hear the answer. Ready to hear how our family might have failed its task as Keepers of the Garden.

The anger seemed to wash out of my father, his words

empty. "Yes, but not in a natural way. She was destroyed. We don't know who did it and we don't know why, but the Great Tree was cut down and her seeds stolen."

A hole opened inside me; an emptiness where my bright, new life had been. Then a thought struck, "But how did you grow the Tree of the Fallen if all the seeds were stolen?"

He let out an extended breath. "I had long noticed that each branch of the Tree looked quite like a small tree. Our last hope was to take one of those branches from her, plant it, and hope it would flourish anew. We were lucky. I'm not sure it would ever work again. I believe it was the power of the Garden that did it. But the Tree of the Fallen has grown since then and she will become the new Great Tree."

He turned to me, his lined eyes hard, "Shaylite, besides protecting the Tree and tending the Garden, our family's task is to guard this secret. Only you, I, and the Queen know. The Prince will learn eventually, as will his wife when he gains one. Anyone else knowing could cause a panic, do you understand?"

I nodded solemnly.

"Good. At your next visit we will perform the bonding ceremony and vow of non-violence required for your Apprenticeship. Today I simply want you to explore the Garden, learning the placement of each plant and noting how they are to be cared for."

"Yes, Master," I said, bowing to him, trying to remember the Garden etiquette I'd studied.

After nodding, he left me for the Garden alcove to get his tools and begin his own work.

I stepped gently along the path before me. The bright red of 'Glory's Lips' smiled up and I knelt down to softly nudge the flower.

Though I tried to enjoy finally being in the Garden, I felt the presence behind me.

A streak of purple light illuminated the Tree of the Fallen when I looked back to her hesitantly. Sighing, I stood once more and walked to her. She was so much smaller and plainer than I thought she'd be.

Whether she could truly protect our ring of islands, I didn't know.

Would she be enough?

I almost started laughing at myself but held it in as I heard my father return to water the Garden.

The Tree of the Fallen was not for me to judge. How many people had doubted my sparring and athletic talents because I was young or smaller than some of the other boys. Even with those setbacks, they were hard-pressed to beat me. This included the Crown Prince who was two years older than me.

My shoulders seemed to loosen. Perhaps the Tree was small, perhaps she wasn't the original Tree, but that was no reason to doubt her.

I reached out a hand and lightly brushed her rough bark.

The only way to know if she was strong enough was to wait and see.

It seemed this was the only Tree we had. One day I would be her only protector. Her, the Garden and, through them, the kingdom. I would not fail in my task to keep them safe.

Who though, would have cut down the Great Tree in the first place? If there were people out there that wanted to destroy her, would I have to protect her from them as well? At least I was training in swordsmanship. I could do it if need be.

Before moving again through the richly green leaves of the Garden, I gave the Tree one last solemn touch.

Though I was still worried, for now I would trust that the Tree of the Fallen, the Great Tree now, would do her duty. I would try to do mine.

A gathering of 'Reaping Sunlight' lay at my feet, the skinny flowers bright yellow. How very large this task seemed; to protect all that lay before me.

2
Brash

Severed, straw heads littered the training ground.

Derrif, the Weapon Master, was supposed to be teaching us a new sword strike, but he hadn't shown up. He often left us to train the Royal Guard.

Only allowed to enter the Garden every two weeks, I'd had to go back to my regular daily routine.

My best friend, Jevin, wasn't even here to train with me today.

I sighed, set myself again in front of my straw dummy, and struck my sword stance before darting forward, dealing a swift stab to where the dummy's heart would be. Then I turned to the side to avoid any further attack.

I stopped. This just wasn't interesting. I looked over to where some of the boys had gathered and were sitting, talking to each other instead of practicing.

One thing I knew, if I practiced, at least I would be more prepared if someone did come to kill the Tree again.

Huffing at the boys just lazing around, I turned back to my dummy, its straw face staring blankly.

After three more successful strikes, the last one felling the dummy's head, I was near finishing for the day.

Hearing high gasps from the side, I looked over. A few

girls seemed to be on break from their lessons and were watching us practice over the barrier. Among them was Princess Neeren, the little sister of Crown Prince Fedrid. A small hand covered her mouth as she whispered to the girl next to her.

I looked over to Fedrid and saw that he'd grudgingly gotten up from sitting around with the other boys.

Fedrid, two years older than me, was hard to get along with. When I beat him for the first time in foot-racing, he'd stepped on my foot afterwards. There'd been no repercussions for him. He was the Crown Prince.

One of the servant boys running around had brought a new dummy to replace the one I'd defeated. I nodded my thanks.

I felt a sharp nudge as Fedrid drew up beside me, sword in hand.

"I'll take over from here," he said.

I'd been wanting to leave soon, but somehow Fedrid always rubbed me the wrong way and I didn't want to let him win today.

"There are other dummies, Crown Prince. Use one of them, if you will."

He turned to me, his blue eyes flashing, "You dare talk back to your Crown Prince?"

I did dare. He wasn't being fair and as the Apprentice Gardener, I had nearly as much say in palace rules as him. I found myself itching for something more challenging than be-heading a straw figure. "Shall we spar for it, then? The one who wins can stay here."

He looked back toward the dummy, "There's no need to fight you. I'd win. Listen to your Crown Prince." I saw tension lining his body.

Anger swelled within me. "Are you afraid I'll bruise your cheek like last time? I promise I'll be more careful. I know you don't get around to practicing much." I got such satisfaction as he reeled around, his mouth twitching downward.

His free fist rose, and his nose nearly touched mine as he leaned forward, sneering, "I'm better than you'll ever be, Apprentice Gardener. Go water the plants and stay where you're meant to be." He laughed.

I found that laugh far too infuriating. He turned away, but I'd dropped my sword, reached out and grabbed his shoulder and, before I knew it, Fedrid had let out a squeal of pain as I knocked that laugh from his face.

The girls on the sideline squeaked in horror.

"How dare you—" Fedrid clutched at his cheek, tears streaming from his eyes.

Before he could finish, or I could reply he deserved it, my throat was cinched by my tunic's collar.

"You little—if there's one thing not to do here, it's harm your future King." Derrif's breath was hot in my ear, "Where's your father?"

∝∞∝

Not fifteen minutes later, Derrif had nearly thrown me at the Queen.

Her manicured hand gripped my shoulder tightly as she escorted me down the tunnel to the Garden.

At the gate she yelled, "Master Gardener! Please make your way here."

A few minutes later, she'd explained what I'd done, my father had apologized profusely, and I was left standing alone with him in the near-darkness.

"Shaylite," he said, after nearly three minutes of silence. "Though you haven't taken the vow of non-violence yet, you should know better."

"Yes, father." I felt my face still scrunched in anger.

"I don't think you understand." My father's voice had turned to a deadly whisper, and I timidly raised my face to him. "If you act like this, you cannot be a Gardener. Our role is to protect, and you clearly have no regard for that."

"I'm to protect the Tree, father. Fedrid insulted me, so I hit him. What's wrong with defending myself?"

"The Tree protects everyone. You need to respect that. Clearly I've failed in your lessons if you cannot even comprehend that much."

"Father, I—"

"No!" He sounded angry, almost yelling the word at me. My father was not to show emotion ever, his voice scared me, "How dare you. Your mother died giving birth to you and this is how you live your life? You need to be living in a way that she would find honorable. Here, as you are now, acting on every selfish whim? Better that she had lived and you'd died."

I'd been about to plead my case, but the words disappeared as a void opened within me. I had always known that my father didn't like me very much. That I was at least partially to blame, most definitely in his eyes, for the death of my mother.

Never though, had he said it out loud to me. I thought I must have physically shrunk. It might have been better if he'd struck me. My eyes burned with unshed tears.

I'd always tried to be as much like my father as possible and as little like how I thought my mother might have been, so I wouldn't remind him of her.

I saw now, that I was failing in that.

"I'm sorry, father." The words were barely words. Only shame spilled from my mouth, "I won't do it again."

"Of course you won't," said my father, already turning back to the Garden. "If you did, you'd be nothing to me."

I clutched at myself as he left me alone in the darkness.

This had happened because I'd let myself be weak. I'd struck when Fedrid had only taunted me.

My father was strong. He never acted on his emotions. He did his job and little else, protecting our land.

I had to be like him. I had to stop myself and think about what I was doing. Thoughtless emotions would drive my father from me. He was all I had.

❦

Rushing down the hall back to my room, trying not to let any tears fall, I nearly bowled over Princess Neeren.

"Apprentice Gardener." She nodded her greeting to me, "Are you alright? My brother—"

"Forgive me, Princess, I'm fine," I said, avoiding looking at her and hoping she wouldn't see the tears about to fall. I gazed at the stone walls surrounding us and willed my tears back into my eyes.

"My brother seems to have acted inappropriately. You cannot pay heed to him."

"I acted inappropriately, Princess." I looked at her, trying to speak normally.

Her face filled with anger, "You are the better man than him. I'm sure he must have said something terrible to you. I would not have wanted to stand for it."

"Thank you, Princess." I was hardly hearing her, still thinking of what my father had said.

The echo of footsteps came down the hallway and Jevin joined in our conversation, smiling and bowing to the Princess, "Your highness."

"Jevin." She said, nodding back.

"I must borrow Shay from you, if you would be so kind."

The Princess looked hesitant, but finally nodded, "Of course." Then she bowed and left us.

I started walking again, wanting to get back to my room and Jevin came along.

"I heard you hit the Prince. Everything alright?" His light voice came from my side, but I didn't look at him.

"I lost my temper."

"Well, we know he's never liked you much. I'm sure you had good reason."

I shook my head. Thinking back, it hadn't even been a good reason. "It doesn't matter. My father got angry at me because I used violence. We're not allowed to as Gardeners."

"Ah. Sorry."

We had reached my door. Jevin shuffled his feet. He was a year older than me, but I was still a little taller than him.

He smiled slyly, "Next time call me over and I'll use violence for you."

Jevin could always cheer me up and I relented, slightly, thanking him before entering my room.

$$\infty\!\infty$$

That night, I promised myself I'd do everything I could to be the best Master Gardener. I'd never give my father another reason to hate me.

I knew I could do better.

3
Shay

Steam rose from my brown skin as I pulled up and out of the hot-spring pool in my washroom.

After spending half the day restoring washed-away soil beneath plants, I'd needed a bath. My lips twitched as I realized it had now been more than six years since first entering the Garden.

Every two weeks I went and worked with my father, yet still I had much to learn. I was sixteen now and, in just four years, I'd have to know the complex Garden rituals, how to trim the Tree from the platform swing, and how to burn excess branches and seeds.

Water, running down my body, pooled on the dark blue tile.

The drying cloth was still on my bed.

Taking careful steps across the tile, I froze when meeting an unexpected pair of eyes in my room.

Princess Neeren's smile faltered, quivering, her eyes broke from mine and shifted down to my chest in confusion. She looked up and back a few times, "You— you're—"

A dull knock sounded as her elbow hit against the clay door. She stumbled out of my room backwards then whirled around, her long braids swishing behind her down the hallway of the palace.

I stood in place, unthinking. Then I remembered myself, wrapped the drying cloth around my unclothed body, sprinted to the door, and slammed it shut.

A nervous laugh broke from me before I ran a palm over my shaved head grimly. I felt the short, black hairs beginning to grow out again.

Everyone had always assumed I was a boy. I'd never lied outright or purposely concealed that I was a girl. Looking down to my chest, now covered with the drying cloth, I knew it would have been impossible for it to go unnoticed forever.

Seawater splashed slightly against the stone weights of the time-watcher. I needed to leave if I was going to meet Jevin at the beach. I'd worry about Neeren when next seeing her.

Drawing an undershirt, light tunic, and shortened leggings from my wardrobe to swim in, I quickly dressed and left the room.

At the west entrance of the rounded palace, Jevin extended his long arm upward, eyes crinkling into a smile.

"Apprentice Gardener," a clear voice called.

Veler, the Queen's Chief Royal Aide shuffled at me abruptly, halting before Jevin and I, "The Queen requests your presence in the throne room." Instead of meeting my eyes, he looked only at my nose.

Before I fully processed the order, he'd swept past, the edge of his deep red robe brushing my ankles.

"What could that be about?" Jevin asked, a laugh bubbling in his question. I looked up to see a wrinkle appearing between his dark eyebrows.

Neeren must have told her mother what she'd just seen.

Jevin's head tilted in question. He'd find out soon that I was not the boy he'd known all his life, though I was still me. There shouldn't be any reason he wouldn't understand.

Jevin had asked to sit next to me at a meal one afternoon when I was six years old. I'd nearly beaten him in swordplay just before. Since then we caused trouble, sparred in combat training, and sat together at meals when we could. He was my best friend.

Had I not been a boy, at least in most eyes, I would not have been able to be with him like that. Girls were never allowed to set foot on the training grounds.

I'd tell him myself. Jevin would accept it.

He crossed his arms.

"I—Jevin, I..." I had to believe nothing would change, "...am a girl."

His grey eyes went wide, and his mouth opened and closed before making a sound, "You're...what? No, you're not." His full lips twitched, ready to laugh when I admitted I was joking.

The words tumbled from me, "I didn't mean to hide it. No one asked. They just thought I was a boy. I'm sorry." Looking down the hallway to my room, I took a step back. "I know it's a surprise, but nothing is different. I have to change into a nicer robe and get to the throne room...sorry."

His eyes shifted back and forth as if trying to remember our times together.

I smiled, attempting to lighten the situation, "We'll talk more of it later. Alright?"

He let out a short breath, nodding slightly. I nodded back and turned toward my room.

Jevin stayed where he was.

∞∞∞

Dressed in one of my nicer robes, a silvery rope-belt cinched around my waist, and only the slightest feeling of dread coating my stomach, I rose from a bow to meet the eyes of the Royal Family.

The Queen, her back stick-straight as she sat in her

throne, Princess Neeren on her left, and Prince Fedrid on her right.

Four guards stood stoically around the room, but otherwise, we were alone.

The skin around Princess Neeren's eyes looked slightly swollen.

Clearing her throat smoothly, the Queen drew my attention, "Apprentice Gardener." She ran a thumb over the glazed arm of her throne, "The Princess has come to me with an interesting story."

Her tone was neutral. I wondered if she believed what Neeren had seen.

"Yes, your majesty," I said, not sure if I should wait to be asked.

She didn't wait for me to decide, but flashed her eyes up to mine, "Is it true, then? Are you a woman?"

Breaking her gaze for a mere moment, I looked to Fedrid. He wouldn't take this well, "Yes. I am, your majesty."

Fedrid's jaw tightened.

The Queen folded her hands slowly. "And," she finally continued, "why have you never chosen to share this information?"

"No—no one asked me, your majesty." I had nothing else to say.

The Queen's eyes narrowed. It didn't seem like she thought this was reason enough, but before she could pry further Neeren stood, her whole body shaking and unshed tears glistening in her eyes, "You deliberately hid it! You said your name was Shay! That isn't a female name! Why are you lying?" The tears started to fall freely.

"No. It is my name!" I protested, indignant, "I—it just isn't my whole name. I'm Shaylite."

The Princess' face contracted, a few more tears squeezing from her eyes before she stormed out through the door behind the thrones.

Fedrid seemed to be attempting to bore through my skull with his eyes.

The Queen rubbed her temple, "You realize you were meant to have your Matching Ceremony at fifteen? It has been nearly two years since. You might have brought it up then."

Somehow, I had thought I'd be notified when it was time for my Matching Ceremony. I didn't think it was my responsibility. When it passed unnoticed, I hadn't complained. Boys were still matched at nineteen. Fifteen always seemed too early to pair girls with their future husbands, "Perhaps I should have, your majesty. Forgive me."

"Really, it should have been your father informing us of this. He hasn't talked of anything, but the business of the Garden since your mother passed."

"Yes, your majesty." That much was true. I hardly ever saw him apart from our time tending the Tree.

"I thought to call him here, but Neeren's tale seemed ridiculous."

I chose to say nothing.

"Well," the Queen fixed me again with narrowed eyes, "Shaylite, then." A small wrinkle appeared next to her nose, "It seems we have a Matching Ceremony to perform. Your position is too important to leave you unmatched any longer. Let us have it in two-days' time at mid-morning. I will inform your father."

"Yes. Thank you, your majesty." The words stuck in my throat.

She tilted her immaculate, crowned head slightly to me.

Fedrid bled spite in his glare as I bowed to him as well, then left the throne room.

The night before the Matching Ceremony nervous energy coursed through me, all I could think to do to calm myself was train.

Swarms of stars encroached on the moon and I spun under them, fending off imagined foes.

The dirt of the training ground scraped beneath my boots as I led my limbs through well-worn steps.

Right block. Left knee; extend to kick and fend off. Turn, turn. Forearm then elbow. Extend back kick to defend against imaginary attacker coming from behind. Duck, cross right fist, but stop before impact to distract. Step forward, left hammer-fist to jaw, knocking out my opponent.

The steps were easy. Too easy.

My thoughts continued to well-up and spill over.

In the past day, hardly anyone had looked me in the eyes, though several had turned to talk with each other in disgust.

This was not the way to go into a Matching Ceremony.

I stopped my practice, panting.

Giving myself wholly over to worry wouldn't help, but it appeared it wouldn't be worked away with sweat and exertion.

Letting out a breath at the distant moon, I thought it must be well-past midnight. The silence of the palace grounds enveloped me as I stilled. My own exhalations were not enough to drown the deep hush filling the star-addled night.

Sheer light glinted off the stained-glass dome sunken into the middle of the upper gardens. Though a way off, I could smell 'Night-blooming Tresses', the deep-blue flowers signaling the beginning days of summer.

In the past I'd sometimes stay out until sun-up, simply breathing in the scent of plants, the heady rush of newly-flowered blooms filling the air as seasons changed.

Though the upper gardens were not my responsibility, I still enjoyed being with the greenery under open sky.

My position as a Keeper of the Garden had always guided me forward with such certainty; perhaps I'd neglected other parts of my life.

Because of how others would now see me, it was obvious that things would change.

Granules of dirt skidded beneath me as I slumped to the packed ground.

I, myself, had thought I was a boy until the age of eight. I was 'Shay', a strong male name here on the island of Cresstalan. Shay wore tunics rather than dresses, had a shaved head, and was one of the best of the youth at swordsmanship. A smile twitched my lip.

I'd never seen a reason to correct people, not even when I learned the truth about myself.

The actuality of my gender had been revealed to me when I contracted the red-striped fever and was tended to by the Castle Physician. He'd exclaimed audibly when applying a cooling-salve and discovering my less-than man-like genitalia.

I'd been lucky to even survive that ordeal. That was what I took from the experience rather than the newfound truth about myself.

About a day after I'd been treated, the Physician himself had passed away, having caught the disease. It affected adults much more severely.

I thought of the accusatory glares I'd been receiving. The truth seemed to matter to everyone else more than it had to me.

Being a girl, something I'd never even thought about, suddenly seemed wrong and shameful.

I'd heard nothing from my father. He usually kept to himself, but I wondered if he'd known that everyone thought I was a boy. Perhaps not.

I think it had been different once. I had never known the sharp-witted champion of sparring practice, though I was told of him at times. That part of my father seemed to have withdrawn after my mother died giving birth to me.

My throat clenched as I thought of his harsh words to me so long ago, "Better that she had lived and you'd died." I shook my head. I'd done nothing wrong since then...and he'd hardly seen me to know.

He looked after his duties as the Master Gardener in a way that kept him from daily palace life.

As soon as I could eat and wash-up alone, I'd been moved to the youth wing, free to live how I pleased.

Circling my thoughts back to the problem at hand, I gritted my teeth. I knew why it was important to be matched. Eventually I'd be expected to produce an heir to the Keepers of the Garden. Though I didn't like to think on it, I knew I had to.

In the last day I'd realized there was only one person I wouldn't mind having to spend the rest of my life with. Jevin. I was lucky he still remained unmatched. Hopefully the Court Reader would say that Jevin and I were meant to be.

We'd talked briefly after I had revealed myself.

I'd asked if he was alright.

His smile had turned slightly sadder, but he didn't look away, "You're still the best friend I have, Shay. I think it is, indeed, strange that you didn't tell us you weren't a boy. You're right that we just assumed, so I suppose I don't blame you."

My feelings had been beyond relief to hear that and things seemed to be normal between us again.

I was fearful, I realized, of being matched with anyone besides Jevin. It was unlikely another soul in the palace would want to wed me.

A yawn cracked my jaw as I released it. Finally, sleep was tugging.

Hoisting myself into a standing position, I re-entered the palace.

Two guards stood on either side of the door. I knew they wouldn't acknowledge me. Unless there was danger, they were not to move.

Tonight was different though. The guard to the right met my eye for the briefest moment and I would have sworn he gave me a sneering look before resuming his stillness.

I focused my gaze on the ground as I brushed past them into the palace.

4
Wild Soul

After the time-watcher had shown I was nearly late the
morning of the Matching Ceremony, I hastily tossed my
tunic and leggings aside and entered my washroom. I'd
fallen into bed last night and still stunk from training.

Hot springs on the island were so plentiful that we were
able to divert their warm water to the baths of the palace.
Not all rooms had them, but most did.

There were no steps into the fairly-deep water. I hissed,
lowering myself into the steaming pool. Sighing as heat
seeped into my skin, I dipped my head beneath the water,
rubbing my face and scalp to remove sweat. I scooped a
handful of soap flakes from their golden bowl at the pool's
edge. After scrubbing down quickly, I basked in the
soothing water for just a moment more, then forced myself
out and tore a robe from my closet, dressing.

The dark grey material slid smoothly over my head and
I cinched a rope-belt around my waist. My noonyi boots
were a few years old, but the skin they were made from
never dirtied and they were suitable for all occasions.
I laced them up.

Because I'd spent most of the last day and a half outside
training, when I quickly checked my reflection in the

looking glass above the wash-basin, I saw the sun had changed my complexion slightly to a deep, earthy brown. I smoothed a hand over my cheek and smiled. I'd always loved that my skin was almost the same color as the rich soil of the Garden.

Trepidation surged in the pit of my gut as I again thought about the marriage-reading. I closed my eyes, trying to ease the tension, then looked my reflection straight-on, my green eyes resolute. I focused and set my jaw, my features a façade of bravery.

"It will be fine," I said softly.

I took a breath and deemed myself presentable.

As I rushed down the curved corridor of the palace, I spotted Jevin's tall form leaning against a wall. He shook his head, jokingly reprimanding me for my near-lateness.

The strain I felt relieved slightly. I didn't have time to stop, so settled for sticking my tongue out at him then grinning apprehensively as I passed.

I hoped it would be him.

At the arched entrance to the throne room, I slowed. My father was there, waiting to go in. He glanced up. The waist-length, black dreadlocks that hung from his head were tidy. Usually one or two would hang in front of his face, but they didn't today. He wore a robe of deep blue instead of the silver one worn as Master Gardener.

His face was set in neutrality. This, combined with the absence of painted, teal symbols covering his sharp cheeks and wrinkled forehead, made him strangely dull.

I walked the remaining distance, gulping. My mouth seemed too dry.

The whole of the Court was inside the hall. I'd long underestimated the importance of being matched. The Apprentice Gardener was almost level, status-wise, with the Prince or Princess, both of whom were sitting at the far end of the hall behind the Court Reader, looking bored.

The Prince was slouching in his chair and the Princess uninterestedly examined the embroidery snaking over her violet dress. Their mother sat between them, her golden crown shining atop smoothed, midnight-black hair. She was still until she spotted me, then she sat up straighter and stared unflinchingly. Her glistening, tawny eyes urged me to the Reader's table. I guessed she was anxious for the reading to begin.

Whomever I was matched with today would become a part of our family, not becoming a Keeper of the Garden themselves, but allowed to learn many of the secrets held within.

Whispers and mumbles died away as I made my way to the center table. The Court Reader was on the other side, poised on a low, cylindrical stool.

My father faded away from my side into the crowd.

No one except immediate family would normally come to these readings, but my fate would affect the well-being of us all.

If the Great Tree of the Garden wasn't properly cared for and nourished, it could wreak havoc on Cresstalan, perhaps further. It was believed that the Great Tree was the heart of the ring of islands that comprised our kingdom, it protected us from all devastation and ill-luck.

The Keepers of the Garden were as important and powerful as the Queen or King; and the Court Reader, in front of me now, was the final authority concerning palace decisions. Everyone worked together to lead our country.

I eyed the gathered crowd, finding craning necks and squinting eyes. I guessed they were trying to spot my feminine features.

Then there was Jevin's resolute face, his lips pulled tighter than usual. His presence helped me continue forward to the Court Reader.

I set my shoulders back, walking boldly to the low table the Reader sat behind, then kneeled and bowed my head.

"Shaylite." The Court Reader spoke with a rasp.

I raised my eyes to him. Wisps of white hair and sagging, dull skin swathed and softened the protruding bones of his face. He wore a silver-blue robe loosely.

Notched sticks were lined up on the table between us, each one representing an eligible bachelor. The number for each boy had been drawn at random before the ceremony.

The Court Reader motioned for me to come to his side. I rose and obeyed.

"Please kneel."

I did, and he raised a thin hand to my forehead. It felt cool, dry, and smelled slightly of pastry, perhaps from his breakfast.

Lowering his head, he began to move the sticks on the table, eyes closed. Finally, his hand stopped above one and he nodded vigorously. The other hand dropped from my forehead and motioned for me to take my seat.

I did so, descending toward a stool identical to his own and nearly missed it, anxious for the answer that would shape the rest of my life.

Gazing at the stick, his eyes widened slightly at the number of notches. It had three. Of course, because the numbers were matched with people at random, the number, itself, had no meaning.

Who was it? I gulped and glanced at the Prince. He was one of the boys still unmatched. It must not be him. I wouldn't stand for it if it was him.

The Court Reader raised the stick above his head, "The Apprentice Gardener, Shaylite, has been matched." Everyone was deadly silent. The Reader waited a few moments.

"Shaylite is matched with...no one."

My stomach dropped away.

The room fell, somehow, into a deeper, stunned silence.

"She has been deemed," the Court Reader continued, "a Wild Soul and will not be matched with anyone."

My heart seemed to soar upwards, the heavy weight of apprehension melting away.

I didn't have to marry anyone. I liked Jevin, but if I was honest in my heart, I didn't want to marry him.

Muttering started up around me now, angry and confused. The Queen rose and swept coolly over to the table, her pearlescent dress skimming the floor.

"You must do the reading again," she said softly to the Reader. "She needs to be matched. Without a match, her family will end and so will the Garden."

The Court Reader ignored her, stood up, and walked out of the hall. He knew his job and that had been done. It was forbidden to do a reading twice.

I didn't know that not being matched had been an option. I was free, but it would certainly cause trouble.

Searching the crowd gathered to my right, I found my father. He was staring angrily downward. I'd certainly disappointed him.

The Queen's face was at a loss as she watched the Court Reader exit. I'm sure she had known I couldn't be re-read. Her eyes stirred agitatedly in thought though and, a moment later, I could see that she had an answer.

She cleared her throat, "So; Shaylite, the Apprentice Gardener, has been deemed a Wild Soul. This cannot be changed, but the Keepers of the Garden must live on after her. Therefore, we must appoint another Apprentice in the hope their offspring will continue the Garden's lineage."

Unease crept back in and I felt my brow gather worriedly. Another Apprentice?

The voices around me rose. No one outside of our family had ever been allowed to be a Keeper of the Garden. It was passed down the same way as the kingdom. We were born to tend the Garden and keep its secrets. I didn't know what would happen if we deferred from tradition.

The Queen made her way back to her throne, deep in thought, as those surrounding me began to murmur.

My father had left. I couldn't find him amongst the gathered Court. He would most likely go to the Garden.

Perhaps I should talk to him about what had happened. I used that thought as a reason to excuse myself without a word, returning to my room.

I donned my bright green Apprentice robe and painted the symbols of the Garden onto my face.

Dipping my fingers into the pot of paint, my mind drifted to the new Apprentice. Who would it be? Was there protocol for this situation?

I stared into my own eyes reflected in the mirror. My duties in the Garden would certainly change. I supposed I would become a bit of a Master myself, training the new Apprentice. Perhaps this wasn't a bad thing.

∞∞∞

Voices echoed up the hallway as I left my room and I soon ran into the Prince and a group of boys accompanying him. They paused in the middle of the hallway and ceased talking when they spotted me.

I veered to the farthest side of the walkway, wanting to avoid him.

It seemed Fedrid was looking to stir up a fight. He slinked across to me, blocking the way forward. I didn't meet eyes but tried to move to his left. He dove back in front of me.

I looked up, angered, "Fedrid, if you would be so kind as to move, I'm needed in the Garden."

His eyes danced. "You won't be needed there much longer."

Idiot. "Fedrid. Move."

He swept back elegantly and dropped into a low bow, "As you wish my...lady, was it?" He raised his head, demonic blue eyes glinting, "I'm sorry. It's just not easy to tell."

What was his problem? I knew punching him in the face wasn't the answer, but it didn't stop me from thinking how satisfying it would be.

No. I'd learned my lesson about acting that way.

Clenching my jaw, I tried to continue.

Fedrid stood back up quickly and shoved his shoulder into mine.

Jeering rose behind me, but I kept moving.

I never did make it to the Garden that day, meeting people on the way who, through spiteful looks or laughter, made me realize I wasn't ready to face the inevitable shame that would come with seeing my father.

I'd gone to the Garden just a few days before, a time that seemed so long ago now, so I didn't have to be back for almost two weeks.

Instead, I chose to go where I could restore myself. The ocean.

❧❧❧

The muted sweeping of the waves coursed through the air as the sun shone enthusiastically on white sands. I felt my stress flee immediately. Exhaling, I lay down on the powdery beach and took a moment to close my eyes and focus on my breath. I hadn't meditated at all today and that always interrupted any calm I could have hoped for. On a day like today, with so many unexpected happenings, that had certainly been a mistake.

Calming energy infused my tired body and I felt the retreat and roll of the waters before me. The measured rhythm was soothing.

Feeling a little better, I sat up and focused on the clear, gem-like water. A velvety breeze tangled around me, upsetting the heat of the sun which seemed determined to seep into my skin. The strip of sand to my left was deserted. In the distance I could see silhouettes of ships floating in the harbor.

"Shay!" A call came from my right and I turned to see Jevin walking through the waves, toiling back toward shore in a drenched tunic.

I raised a hand to him. I wasn't really feeling up to talking to anyone, but at least it was him.

"So." He sat next to me, "No one?"

I shrugged and tried to smile, "I'm a Wild Soul, Jevin, not to be tied down."

Rivulets of water skimmed down his deeply brown skin and were nestled in the short dreadlocks covering his head, they glistened in the sun, "I wouldn't have expected a new Apprentice to be the solution."

"I'm the heir of our family. If I can't continue the line, there's really no other solution. I can't think of another answer."

Jevin nodded, "That is true."

I rubbed my hands over my face and fixed my eyes on the horizon in front of us.

Jevin shifted beside me, "Who do you think it will be?"

I paused, thinking, "The rules for this type of situation haven't been used. I know it's written down how to choose the new Apprentice if it must be done, but I don't remember how." I sighed, "My father will be taking care of it, I'm sure."

Jevin pulled his knees close to his chest.

"I'm glad I wasn't matched though." I scooped a handful of sand into my palm and shifted it unconcernedly, "With everyone just now realizing I'm a girl, I think it would have been difficult for me and a prospective match to overcome that."

Time sifted by slowly, then Jevin asked a hesitating question, "Why didn't you tell any of us?"

I let the rest of the sand seep out through my fingers. "Honestly, I didn't think it mattered. I'm not going to change anything. It was easier to live as a boy and more fun. All of the girls do embroidery, have long, heavy hair, wear uncomfortable-looking clothes, and are shut up inside for most of the day." A breeze skittered across the sand before us. "I used to think they liked it and I was just different in wanting to do what the boys did. I wonder though, if they are unhappy with their circumstances?" I brushed my hands together, "Why does this small part of ourselves determine how we have to live our whole lives?"

Jevin didn't answer. I suspected there wasn't one.

I lay down on the beach and closed my eyes, listening to the waves brush the sand. My thoughts were too dense to sort through, so I let them wash away.

Jevin stayed quietly beside me for a while, but then headed back to the palace. As one of the assistants to the Royal Family, he would have to help them get ready for dinner.

I wasn't usually required to be at the evening meal in the banquet hall, so I went to the kitchen pantry after resting for a while and snagged some smoked fish, sea greens, and a small jug of spiel-fruit tea to eat in my room.

Save the guards, I didn't meet a soul as I rambled down the corridor.

Most of my food was gone by the time I got to the room. I sat at the desk against my wall, finished the small meal, then went to the book shelf to look for a particular tome.

I did wonder how the new Apprentice would be chosen. There were many people in the palace that would be wrong for the position.

The stout volume was bound in glazed and stitched leaves. I pulled it from its place and cracked it open. 'Tree Care'...'Ritual Watering'...no. I flipped through the pages. I remembered the section, it was somewhere in the second half of the book.

Finally, I found the heading I needed, 'Tradition and Choosing from Beyond the Keepers'. A couple pages over was the section I needed. I skimmed it quickly.

With the cease of the original Keepers,
Either through death or an inability to continue the line,
The newest Keeper will be chosen as follows:
All orphans from the age of ten to twenty-five residing in the palace, either noble or servant, shall be gathered and counted.
The Reader of the Court shall follow the practice of a traditional Matching Ceremony.
In place of a woman, they will use the Great Tree herself.
In place of the bachelors, the orphans.
Whichever one is matched as being bound with the Tree shall follow in the footsteps of previous Keepers and continue the line as long as they and their offspring are able.

It always came down to the Court Reader. Chance had the greatest power in Court, it seemed. I assumed the new Apprentice would be chosen soon.

There were a few people whom I knew now were out of the running because their parents were alive and well. That was some consolation.

I placed the book back on its shelf and went to the washroom. A smile stretched my face as I caught my reflection in the looking glass. I still had the teal, painted symbols on my face.

Pouring a stream of water from a pitcher into the clay wash-basin before me, I scrubbed until the hushed, deep tones of my face gleamed in the lamp light of the washroom and the water was tinted a greenish-blue.

The liquid in the clay bowl swirled and attempted escape as I brought it to the window, tipping the colored water onto some wildflowers growing below.

I closed my eyes and stood still for a moment, breathing in the fragrant evening air. It was almost summer, and the coastal breeze mingled harmoniously with the scent of flowers and fresh leaves.

In the distance I heard the steady rush of waves, then the soft beat of wings as a bird hurried home. The sky was a rusted orange near its base where the sun had gone down not long ago, and the first white pin-pricks of stars were appearing out of nowhere, without commotion.

It had been warm today, so I decided to leave the window open, letting the delicate sounds and soothing smells accompany my sleep.

Slumber took me as soon as I lay down.

5
Apprentice

Out of the darkness came a sharp knock. Someone was pounding on my door. The eagerness of my visitor suggested they'd been knocking for a while now.

I rose from bed, slipped on a pair of leggings to present myself half-decently, and opened my door the smallest amount.

"Ye—" I cleared my throat, "Yes?" I said, trying to keep my eyes from closing.

It was the servant girl, Heyda, who cleaned my room every few days, "Um...miss?" She curtsied. Dark curls sprung haphazardly from the blue cap she wore. It looked as if she'd been hastily awoken as well.

I nodded, encouraging her to continue with her message so I could continue with my rest.

"Apprentice, the Master Gardener has sent me to fetch you. You're needed in the Garden at once."

Why would I be needed in the Garden at this hour? There wouldn't be any light to see by. I blinked and forced myself to begin thinking coherently.

"He also says that you must come in full array and to hurry."

"Ah. Thank you, Heyda." I rubbed my face bleakly,

"I'll be there soon."

She bobbed down again, and I shut the door.

Full array? Then I'd have to don the ceremonial pieces of my Apprentice uniform. What was happening? Could it be that we were choosing the new Keeper tonight? The book hadn't said that it needed to be done at night, but my copy was only a glimpse of the true Garden Handbook. That was kept in the alcove of the Garden itself.

Sprinting to the washroom, I lit a couple lamps along the way, then sketched the symbols chaotically onto my face, realizing belatedly that I should have put on my robe first. Too late now.

I carefully pulled off my tunic, making sure not to smear the paint, and painstakingly drew on the green Apprentice robe. A small spot of paint got on the inside of the neckline.

The wicker cupboard near the window gave a dull squeak when I opened it. Gold pieces of my ceremonial armor glistened dimly inside. Slipping the smooth chest plate over my head, I adjusted it onto the upper part of my torso then tied the gold mail skirt around my waist. Finally, I removed the enameled green and gold headpiece. It was a helmet with leaves that were crafted so delicately it seemed as if they stirred in the wind. When finished dressing, I exited the room.

I reached the break in the wall that was the entrance to the Garden. Though it was supposedly a secret passage, everyone knew it was there.

Rushing through, I walked swiftly down the tunnel. There were a few lamps lit along the way so I could see my path. Ahead was my father and, what was most definitely the Queen.

"Master. Your majesty." I bowed to each as I reached them, holding my headpiece as I did, so it wouldn't fall off. "What is the news?" I asked, rising quickly. "What's happened?"

I looked from one to the other. My father wore his full array as well, identical to mine, but with more leaves on the helm and an abstract tree engraved into the chest plate. The Queen wore her crown as usual and had her hands tucked tightly together.

My father moved his mouth to speak, but the Queen beat him, "We have chosen the new Apprentice."

I stared, then shifted my eyes to my father, questioningly. Why had I not been included in the ceremony, "Already?"

They nodded.

"Wh—who is the new Apprentice, Master?"

"He will be here momentarily. It is—ah, here."

I looked behind me to where he now gazed.

The new Apprentice walked forward, their green robe beginning to show in the lamp light. The figure drew close and I felt my eyes widen, beginning to smile back as he grinned conspiratorially.

Of course. It was Jevin.

∞∞∞

My father bowed to Jevin as he stepped forward to join us. I did the same, but was having difficulty not laughing out loud, the hesitation inside me dissipating.

Jevin, though his eyes were lit up, scuffed one of his feet in the soil and was clenching his robes in a fist.

The Queen swept in front of us, standing between my father and I and Jevin.

Her voice strode through the silence, "Jevin. The fate of our kingdom shall now become your responsibility. I hope you will not take it lightly. You must train diligently to care for the Garden. Are you up for the task?"

Jevin bowed low to the Queen, his hand releasing his robe's material, "I will do my very best, your majesty."

I felt a slight nudge near my shoulder blade as my

father pushed me forward, next to the Queen. He posted himself on the opposite side.

"So," my father's low voice began, "you have been selected for what may be the most important task in this world." He let out a great sigh, "To care for the Garden and the Great Tree within is not a simple task."

My father turned to me, "Shaylite, you will begin Jevin's training tomorrow. We must lose as little time as possible. Teach him the meditative strategy, the basic care of plants, and explain the Great Tree as I did before you entered the Garden."

"Yes, Master." When I rose from my bow, I found myself bouncing ever-so-slightly on my toes. I had always ached to share the secrets of the Garden with Jevin. Now it was my duty to do so.

The explanation continued. "You will gain the full array of your Apprentice uniform, as we are wearing--" my father gestured to the decorated metal we both wore, "when the basic training is complete, and you've learned to properly take care of the Garden. Until you finish the initial training with Shaylite, you will not enter the Garden, nor will you take the vows solidifying your apprenticeship."

Jevin bowed to my father, "Yes, Master."

I caught myself before I let out a laugh at hearing Jevin call my father 'Master'. Of course, to the rest of the palace he was known as 'Master Gardener', I'd heard Jevin call him that once. It had been strange then as well.

"Very well." My father shifted, light playing across his chest plate. "The hour is late, and I am sure you will both wish to begin training early. Shaylite, I will give you two weeks with Jevin. Afterward, come to me to relate how he is progressing." I nodded my response. "Then," he let out a breath, "let us leave now and get some much-needed rest."

"Jevin," said the Queen, "one more thing. I'm sure you have guessed, but your usual duties as the Royal Family's attendant will be taken over by someone else. I expect you to devote all your time and energy to learning about the Garden. Understood?"

"Of course. Thank you, your majesty."

She nodded sternly.

The three of us bowed to the Queen, allowing her to exit before us. My father followed, and Jevin and I walked behind him together.

I elbowed Jevin's arm and widened my eyes, trying to convey how very excellent this all was. His mouth opened in a silent laugh before he snapped it shut, still smiling, and pressed a finger to his lips.

At the end of the tunnel, my father and the Queen went one way and Jevin and I went the other to the youth wing.

We burst out laughing as soon as it seemed we wouldn't be heard, quickly silencing ourselves as a guard came in sight, patrolling the hallway.

Coming to my room, I couldn't help but usher Jevin in, shut the door, and exclaim, "Jevin! How could you have wrangled that? The new Apprentice?" I sat down hard on my chair, "I couldn't have chosen any better."

He was laughing now, "I can't believe it myself. After dinner your father, the Queen, and the Court Reader seemed to have met. They must have chosen me, and I was notified a few hours later when the Master Gardener came to my door with this robe." He picked at the robe and sat down onto the ground. "We'll begin training tomorrow, won't we?" He turned his face up to me and his fists clenched and unclenched excitedly, "Then you can tell me all of those secrets you've been keeping."

Removing my headpiece, I relished the weight leaving my head. "Of course I can't wait until you learn them, but first you have to go through the basic training." The luck of this situation still astounded me, "I'll have to find a spot for us to train, but let's meet for breakfast first. We'll need food."

I looked to the time-watcher, alight in a streak of moonlight. Dawn was not far off.

"How early can we start?"

Although I was as eager as Jevin, I knew that without a few more hours of sleep I'd be useless.

I smiled, "Meet me in the dining hall at mid-morning. We'll need plenty of rest for our first tasks."

"Alright." Jevin was nearly vibrating with enthusiasm, "Can't you tell me just one secret now though? No one else is here."

Glad he wanted to learn, I laughed, but knew I couldn't alter the course of his training.

I set my headpiece down on a shelf, took Jevin by the shoulders, and turned him to the door, pushing him out, "Goodnight." He stumbled for a couple steps, then looked back, his untamed smile making him look so young, "My pupil." I stifled another laugh.

He began to protest, but I shut the door, my mouth stretched into a smile.

After readying once again for bed, unbridled joy coursed through me. Being able to work and share the secrets of the Garden with my best friend was more than I would have hoped for.

I flopped onto my bed, pounding my fists and feet onto the mattress to expel some pent-up excitement, then realized I'd forgotten to put out my lamps.

Thinking of what Jevin would learn tomorrow, I sat up, let out a long breath, and moved my hand slightly downward, motioning toward each lamp in turn. The flames went out one by one, replaced by moonlight.

I laid back, laughing heartily.

Sleep came to me late, put off by my racing mind and heart.

6
Exercise

An uncomfortable heat woke me. Attempting to make my way over to close the window, eyes closed, I stepped heavily onto the ground only to hiss when a prickling pain lanced through my foot. I drew it back up to the bed hurriedly.

My eyes opened, and a stunted breath escaped me. Taking my foot in my hand, I gently turned it over to see blisters beginning to form.

I looked over the edge of the mattress to see small, scale-like shapes covering the sea-grass rugs.

My hands kneaded my face as I flopped back. Flake fungus. Fast-growing and extremely irritable to human flesh. A small creak came from my open window swinging in the breeze.

Limping to the washroom, groaning, I grasped a handful of soap flakes before submerging my foot in the steaming water.

It throbbed heatedly. Washing would help, but my foot would be uncomfortable for a few days.

When what sounded like a desperate knock met my door, going on far too long, I grunted and rose, hopping over.

"I'm coming!" I yelled as the knocking continued. It stopped abruptly.

Jevin, eyes wide and...wearing no shirt, was there when I opened the door.

I let out a burst of laughter, setting my foot on the ground without realizing, and grimaced as I brought it back up. "What are you doing? Are you alright?" I asked him.

He looked sleepy and dazed.

"I'm late!" He said, eyes going wide.

I looked to the time-watcher. It was already early afternoon.

"Looks as if I am as well," I sighed.

Jevin pressed his forehead to the door, wincing, "My first day doing the most interesting job at the palace and I'm already messing it up."

"I just woke up, myself," I confessed.

He looked up past me, "What's that on your rug?"

"It's nothing," I said, closing the door slightly. "Flake fungus. Probably just some bullying. No one is exactly friendly with me at the moment." I smiled, though it felt pained. I nodded to Jevin, "Besides you, of course."

Jevin put his hand on the door above my head and pushed it open, stepping inside, examining the fungus.

"Still, it shouldn't be to that extent, Shay. It isn't as if you actually did something wrong."

I shut the door after a moment. "Thank you," I thought I was the only one who believed that. "I'm sure it will pass soon. People get tired of one thing and move onto the next. I just have to bear with it until then."

He turned back to me, and met my eyes, "Again, you shouldn't have to. You need to do something about this."

Folding my arms, I laughed, "And what would that be? Tell someone? Find the culprit and beat them?" I shook my head. "No one will care. This is the first instance. And as for violence, you know I can't. In fact," I recalled Jevin's new position, "neither of us can now. You'll take the vow of non-violence as well when you enter the Garden."

Jevin's shoulders drooped. Did he realize he'd been in the hallway without a shirt on? I focused on his face, his brows were drawn together.

"I never quite understood that. Why do you train if you can't ever use your fighting skills?"

"I am allowed if it is a life or death situation," I shrugged. "It's good for exercise and, of course, I like training with you." My foot felt better, and I was able to set it fully on the ground. "I never expected to use my abilities for anything else."

"Fine. But why must Gardeners take a vow of non-violence at all?" Jevin's eyes narrowed.

"Jevin..." This didn't feel like the right time to explain. He had no context of the ideas of the Garden yet. "You'll learn more about it when you've been properly trained, but what you must realize is you're a protector now." I felt my heart start to beat faster as the words poured out, remembering my father explaining it to me when I hadn't understood, "A protector of the Great Tree, the Garden and, like it or not, every single person on the islands; maybe even the world. Everyone. People who are nice to you, as well as those who bully."

He rolled his eyes, unconvinced.

I felt myself deflate slightly at his reaction, but I would teach him. "I'm serious, Jevin. This is one of the most important things to learn. When you take the vow, you must remember. You need to find a way to deal with people no matter what they do to you. It cannot be with violence unless there is truly no other choice."

He brought his hands up to grip his own elbows, frowning at the floor.

It was too soon to go into this fully. "Come on now," I patted his shoulder, "you don't have to worry over it, just keep it in mind. We'll talk more later, but let's get food and start your training." I sighed, ready to move forward with the day, "I'm starving."

Jevin lowered his arms and nodded, seeming slightly more relaxed.

"We'll still have plenty of time," I opened the door again and stepped to the side so he could leave, "but...we should both get dressed."

Jevin looked down, seeming to realize for the first time he didn't have a shirt on, his cheeks folded back as he smiled, "Right. Sorry."

I tried not to laugh and said, "Meet me in the dining hall, alright?"

Jevin did laugh and started walking swiftly down the hall, throwing one look back to me as he went.

On our way to eat, we came across Heyda.

"Just a moment," I said to Jevin.

He halted.

"Heyda."

She jumped slightly when I called her, and her eyes looked glazed, most likely she hadn't had the luxury of sleeping in after being woken in the middle of the night.

"Sorry to trouble you, but someone seems to have snuck flake fungus into my room last night. Be careful if you go to clean. I'll take care of it tonight if I can get there first."

She nodded, seeming uncomfortable. "No need, Apprentice. I'll take care of it shortly."

"Thank you, be wary of it though. I was already stung this morning."

She dipped a curtsy and hurried away.

I watched as she moved so quickly. Perhaps she, like the rest of the palace, was still uncomfortable with the recent reveal of my gender. I sighed, making my way back to Jevin and rubbed my face tiredly.

"Are you sure you're alright?" Jevin asked.

"I will be." I started walking again. "Let's go eat."

∞∞∞

During our quick meal, I'd remembered a perfect place for Jevin and I to practice the Garden teachings.

We climbed the last few stone steps to the tower room.

The space before us held stacks of unused tapestries, bedding, and random, tarnished decorations, no longer needed. There was room in the middle that was just large enough for what I wanted to teach.

A small cluster of stout candles drew my attention and I collected three of them, breaking a spider web and forcing its resident to flee.

"Candles?"

I gathered them close. "Yes. Go ahead and sit down, Jevin."

As he did, I placed a candle before each of us and the last one off to the side.

"As Keepers of the Garden," I said, reaching into the pocket of my robe for a tinder stick, "our most essential skill is not knowing how to care for plants, though it is important. That's as far as gardeners not of our order will get. We, however," I gripped the stick in my hand, "work to first master the practice of meditation."

I rose once more, leaning out into the hallway to light the tinder stick from a lamp. When each candle was lit, I shook the stick to put it out then laid it aside.

Sitting once more, I crossed my legs and Jevin listened intently.

Normally I would have the lightened the mood with a joke, and I felt a strong urge to do so. Jevin though, was not just my best friend now, he was my pupil. I had to teach him the ways of the Garden.

I took a deep breath to put myself into the proper mindset.

"When you work in the Garden, you must connect and commune with the plants. In order to do so, you must match the energy in your own body to theirs. Plants are calm for the most-part. They look at the world slowly and without the prejudice humans accumulate as they go through life."

I recalled my father giving me the same speech when I was five years old. I'd hardly understood it then.

Jevin looked confused but still payed attention.

"When you settle into the correct mindset, you know it, though it is difficult to remain there for an extended period of time. First, you need to know how it feels. That's what we'll learn today."

I closed my eyes and took another deep breath. "When your mind goes into the right spot, it will feel perfectly clear. For that split second of a moment, you will be thinking of nothing at all, but your mind won't be empty. Within the feeling of nothing, there blossoms a knowing. Deeply, you will know that you are open to what is before you. My father says that with that knowing, anything is possible." I hadn't found this to be true, but I didn't want to taint Jevin's lesson with my own thoughts and observations quite yet.

"To get your mind into that place," I said, opening my eyes once more, "we will put a candle out just by moving our hand a small amount."

Jevin had been excited before, but I saw now that I'd lost him as his eyes narrowed warily. "We are to put out a candle by moving a hand at it?"

"Not exactly that, but in a sense, yes. When I do it, I will put my candle out from a couple feet away, but first I'd like you to try."

Jevin looked confused, "What do you mean?"

"Drop your hand just a little, in a way you think would

put out the candle. I want to show what happens when you aren't in the proper mindset."

An eyebrow raised, he did so, and the flame hardly moved.

"Good. My turn."

He looked at me, doubtful.

I shifted into the mindset before backing away from the candle a good distance, then gently moved my hand downward.

The candle went out immediately with a faint crackling from the wick.

Jevin seemed dubious.

"Isn't there some sort of trick you're doing?"

"That's what I thought when this was first demonstrated to me. You'll see the difference is the mindset when you do it yourself. The candle will only go out when your mind is perfectly clear and not before."

Jevin swiped his hand down again to put out the candle. Then did it a few times. Each time he seemed to be trying harder. The flame wavered a little more than it had the first time, but stayed resolutely lit.

"So how do I make it go out?" Jevin asked, discouraged.

"You must relax and avoid focusing on the candle. In fact, you will see when you succeed, you won't be focusing on anything. You can't make it go out. That's using too much effort and it won't work. Instead, allow it to go out. The moment the flame disappears, your mind will be perfectly empty."

I sat back, "A good way to start out is to count down from twenty to one, moving your hand up and down at each number, breathing slowly in-time. When you reach zero, let your hand drop down." I demonstrated it quickly. "That will help you concentrate less on the candle."

Jevin nodded, then held his hand near his forehead, beginning to move it down and up slowly. I could see him start to count silently in his head.

Twenty seconds later, he brought his hand down, and the candle still didn't go out. He sighed harshly.

"It takes some time," I said encouragingly. "It took me hours to get it out when I first learned. Once you do though, it gets much easier."

Jevin closed his eyes and took a deep breath as I'd done, then tried again with the same results.

I thought it might be easier for him if I wasn't overtly staring, so I relit my own candle.

When Jevin was trying to learn something new, his sense of competition helped him to master whatever it was more quickly. He seemed more focused and intent as my candle repeatedly hissed out and was relit.

We went along like this for a few hours. Jevin hardly spoke a word, only pausing to ask a question, usually one whose answer was unhelpful. I didn't know exactly how to teach this part successfully. My father had let me figure it out by myself, for the most part.

Perhaps Jevin needed to learn it differently though.

The difficulty was that you could only truly understand the meaning of the mindset when you'd reached it.

Jevin seemed to grow increasingly frustrated and the flame moved fewer and fewer times. After three hours of this, I decided that was enough for the first day.

"Alright, it's no good trying to concentrate for this long. Let's do something else. We'll try again tomorrow."

Jevin just stared stoically at the candle. "You go. I'm going to keep trying."

I admired his dedication, but if he continued like this, it wouldn't help him and could perhaps hurt him in the end.

I stood up. "No." Jevin looked up at me. "As your instructor, I insist you take a break or you won't make any progress. You're too tense right now." I held out my hand to him, "Come on. Let's go."

His shoulders released, and he smiled a little. "Yes, Master," he said reluctantly, grasping my hand. We worked together to pull him up from the floor.

He sucked in a breath, "Ow, my legs are nearly numb."

"I'm not surprised." I grinned. "Maybe we need to move a bit. We haven't practiced our swordplay together for a while, do you want to spar?"

"Alright. Shall we change into training clothes and meet at the grounds in a few minutes?"

"Perfect."

We left the small tower space and headed to our own rooms. I changed, then stopped by the armory to grab the sword I used to practice.

Because of the rule of non-violence, I wasn't allowed to own weapons, but the palace had many I could use.

I entered the armory. Derrif sat in the corner, polishing a sword and mumbling to himself. He usually wasn't too friendly, so I went to where my sword was kept to grab it and leave quickly.

It was not in its place.

I'd have to ask Derrif. It's not that I couldn't use another sword, but that one, out of all the others, had the best balance for me.

"Derrif?"

There was a moment of silence, then, "Mm," He grunted.

"Do you know, by any chance, where this sword is?" I pointed to the empty space on the wall.

He left out an aggravated sigh and waved the sword he had in his hand over his head.

I recognized it as the one I was looking for.

"Oh, sorry, were you polishing it?"

He grumbled, "Only because I came in to find it covered with honey. It's taken me hours to get it back to its rightful state."

"Honey? But why..." I knew why. The flake fungus this morning; now this. I supposed these little pranks would go on for a couple weeks until whomever was taking so much amusement in them found something else to occupy their attention. I didn't want to explain the situation to Derrif. "Well, if it's alright now, can I use it to spar?"

"I should say not."

I looked to him, surprised.

He finally met my eyes and continued, "You. All this time pretending to be a man and doing things indecent for your sex. I won't have it. You're not welcome in here anymore." He huffed and went back to polishing, clearly done talking to me.

I felt like I'd been struck a blow to the gut. It took me a moment to process his words. I wanted to fight back, to protest, but nothing would come out.

People didn't like what I'd done, I knew this by now, but to have privileges taken away seemed extreme.

Unable to argue, I left.

Entering the training grounds, I spotted Jevin to the side, stretching and circling his arms to warm up. I took a step toward him to explain what had happened, then heard a burst of laughter from behind me. I knew who it was.

Fedrid and his friends again. No doubt the ones who'd been making my day as difficult as possible. I didn't turn to look at them. It wouldn't lead anywhere good and all their efforts were most definitely aimed at getting a rise from me. I would do my best to disappoint them.

Before I reached Jevin, he'd looked up at the sound of laughter. I caught his eye, motioned toward the beach, and turned that way, not wanting to spend any more time near my tormentors than I had to.

I got to the beach, sat down, and didn't even have to wait two seconds before Jevin showed up and seated himself next to me.

"What's going on?"

I closed my eyes and shook my head, "Well, firstly, I've been denied weapons because apparently using them isn't appropriate for my sex. But it wouldn't have done much good anyway because my sword was covered in honey, and my foot still hurts from stumbling into the bed of flake fungus earlier." I rubbed my face. "I think it's mostly Fedrid and his boys, which I can handle, but to have Derrif ban me from the armory and any use of weapons was more than I had anticipated." I stared at the rolling waves before me.

"You're banned from the armory? Because you're a girl?"

I nodded solemnly.

"Here." I heard metal clinking and looked to see Jevin unbuckling his sword from his side. He held it out to me.

I didn't take it. "Jevin, you know I can't own weaponry."

He looked down at the sword, "Well, I can't either now, right?"

I sighed, "Yes, that's right. You'll take the vow of non-violence when you're a full Apprentice."

"Well, I still want to spar and you're the best partner I have." He seemed to be thinking for a moment. "We'll just keep it somewhere. You won't own it, but use it to spar and I'll borrow from the armory. Fair?"

Grudgingly, I relented. "That's not a bad plan. Do you think your sword will work for me though?"

"It's not much heavier than the one you're used to using. A little practice and you'll master it. Here." He set it on my folded arms. "Try it."

"I'm not to use weaponry outside of the arena."

"You're not using it, you're weighing it."

I sighed and raised myself onto my feet, pulling the sword from its scabbard. The silver hilt was sculpted into the likeness of a Fainian Peal-Digger, a mythical creature said to have once been known to live in the sands of Fainia, the island across the ring from Cresstalan.

The Peal-Digger was supposed to have a comical face and would bring luck if it found you and you laughed instead of screaming at its monstrous size, vivid colors, and habit of popping out of the sand in less than a second.

There was also a small, pale green sapphire embedded in the tip of the sword's pommel. I'd seen the weapon come at me a thousand times while practicing with Jevin.

I started to swing it around, dancing the steps of an easy footwork drill and slicing the air around me. Jevin was right, it was heavier than I was used to, but I could handle it. With only a bit of training I'd be able to use it easily.

I stopped and slid the sword back into the scabbard, sitting down once again. "Thank you. I'm glad you, at least, are on my side."

The sun was nearly down now, and my appetite had been lost to anger. I faced Jevin. A smile warmed his features. "I'm going to bed early, but let's meet at the ruins tomorrow. Be there at sunrise. We'll learn another meditation technique."

He stood as well, brushing sand from his calves. "Right, bright and early. I'll walk back up with you. Did you want to eat dinner first?"

I sighed, "No." Sand ground beneath my boots as I began walking to the palace.

Jevin fell into step beside me. His own boots were dangling from his hand.

"I don't really feel hungry. I just need a bit of time to myself. I'll feel better after more sleep too." I smiled, then looked down at my own hand, to the sword I gripped. "Are you sure it's alright I use your sword? You've had it since I met you."

"It's not forever, Shay, and it isn't as if it'll be far away." He shrugged.

We made our way along the white and blue stone walls of the palace, the shadows long now. The intricate clay doors at the south entrance stood open, guards on either side. Going through together, Jevin would go right to get to the dining hall and I left to return to the youth wing.

"Thank you again, Jevin."

I held the sword close to my side, hiding it as much as possible.

He nodded his head toward it, "I hope you can find a good place for it to be kept."

"I'll figure it out."

We waved a quick goodbye and went our separate ways.

The door clicked closed behind me and I sighed, leaning against it.

Today had been...interesting. Jevin being made Apprentice, I'd taught him, there was more bullying, and now I had a sword.

Thankfully, it seemed Heyda had gotten rid of the flake fungus. That was one less thing to think about.

I had to figure out where to keep Jevin's sword. Raising it in front of my face, I squeezed the soft, translucent fish skin of the scabbard and the metal rings making up the detailing jingled. The Fainian Peal-Digger on the hilt seemed to laugh at me, its mouth and eyes wide.

I laid the sword carefully on my bed and lit a tinder stick from the ever-lit flame in the bathroom, then lit the lamps of my bedroom. I shook out the stick and looked around.

Where would I keep the sword? I supposed if I just shoved it deep into my wardrobe behind something I didn't wear often, it would be fine.

It wasn't my sword though and I didn't know if that would be disrespectful.

My eye caught the wicker cupboard in the corner. Neither Heyda nor anyone else, besides my father of course, was allowed access to this cupboard. I slid it open and the ceremonial armor reflected candle light.

The empty bottom shelf would be perfect.

I placed the sword in its new home.

After hardly sleeping the night before, I was ready for bed even this early, and I lay down heavily.

Through the night though, dreams plagued me, filled with visions of my feet on fire or having to swim through oceans of honey.

7
Extinguish

A plate of steaming renn-berry tarts sat alone. They leaked shining, poppy-colored fruit from between flaky pastry. I swallowed so my mouth would stop watering. Sticking my head through the doorway from the pantry to the kitchen and seeing no one, I shuffled quickly to the woven table where they lay. Four were mine in a mere moment, though I hissed as the oven-fresh tarts' heat bled into my fingers.

High-pitched laughter came from the direction of the kitchen gardens and I tucked my plunder closer to my chest, rushing back to the pantry and through the outer door to the outside of the palace.

Stars still hung in the sky. There was only a faint tinge of light from the coming sunrise. I breathed in the slightly cool air and the fresh smell of sleeping plants.

As I took a bite of pastry, I delighted in the tart stickiness.

There was a large rock ahead of me, sitting amongst low, fragrant bushes. I let myself down onto it and finished my breakfast, saving two of the pastries for Jevin.

The world around me was silent, but for the soft brush

of wind against leaves. I closed my eyes and began to focus on my breath.

Today I wanted to be prepared. If I was going to help Jevin calm his mind, mine needed to be tranquil. I sat still and allowed the sound of the wind, the smell of our island, and the lingering taste of sweetened renn-berries to fill me. For the first time in days I could feel a glimmer of true calm.

I didn't stay for more than a quarter of an hour, but it was enough. The sun would be here soon. Rising from the stone as quietly as possible so as not to disturb my calm, I grabbed the remaining pastries and went to the ruins.

There wasn't a lot left of the ruins and their story had been lost to the ages. They stood, made of chalky, white stone, weathered and broken. There might have been worn decoration on them, but it was too far gone to make out.

When I got to the crumbling stones, Jevin was already there, sitting on a tall piece with his legs dangling over the side.

"Ready for another day of training," he said as I came close. His voice sounded like a croak.

I gave him a hesitant grin back, something seemed strange. "Alright, well come down here and we'll get started."

He leapt down from the pale stone and sat down next to me on a broken platform that could have once been a giant pillar as easily as a table.

I showed him how to cross his legs properly, with feet on top. Our combat training always included a lot of stretching exercises, so he didn't have any trouble getting into position.

"This morning I'll show you the proper way we meditate." A slight breeze rose between us. "When excessive noise clouds our minds, it helps to calm it through meditation." I rested my hands on my knees. "Half of meditation is getting the proper mindset, which is what the candle exercise is for, but we'll learn the other half of what you'll need today."

"Is there really much to learn? Can't we just continue on with the candle exercise?" Jevin asked it nicely, but still seemed agitated.

"Jevin, were you trying to put out the candle on your own last night?" That seemed to be the most obvious explanation for his tiredness and irritability.

He didn't meet my eyes, but said, "I thought I might get farther if I practiced more."

"And, I suppose that didn't help?" I asked.

He shook his head tensely.

I sighed, smiling, "I know you just want to learn it, and you will, but first you need to quiet your mind. I think what I'm going to show you will help." I sat up straight. "There's a bit more than you may think to meditation, and it will enhance all work you do with the Garden."

Jevin let out a terse breath, "I understand. Sorry, everything is just taking so long." He yawned.

I wondered if this type of training was more difficult to learn for Jevin at the age of eighteen than it had been for me as a child. I didn't remember being so frustrated.

If we continued though, I knew Jevin would succeed.

"Here's something that should help you feel a little better." I reached behind me and took out the renn-berry pastries, handing them to Jevin whose eyes seemed touched with a bit of a smile at this.

"Breakfast." I placed the tarts into his hands and he started eating them, cheering up as he devoured them. He finished, not five minutes later, licking his fingers with enjoyment.

"Good?"

"Yes," he acknowledged. He still looked quite weary.

"Then let's begin. First, close your eyes."

He did.

"Let your breath begin to slow and focus on how it fills you and then empties you. Don't force it in and out, simply notice it. Just do this for a few moments." We did that, then I began again, "Now take several deep breaths, in...and out...in...and out."

After doing that a few times, I continued. "Now, this exercise is also needed to help you to connect to the Garden and the Great Tree herself—"

Jevin's eyes opened just a little, "*Herself?*"

"Yes, the tree is female, and we always refer to her that way." I smiled a little, "Now close your eyes."

He did, and I continued, "Picture the Garden. It doesn't matter that you haven't seen it for yourself yet. Just let an image of what it may look like come to you."

I gave him a couple minutes to build it in his mind. "Can you see the Great Tree?"

"I still have no idea what the Tree is supposed to look like."

"That's why this practice can be fun before you enter the Garden. The Tree can look however you wish it to. Just let a picture of her grow in your mind without judging it."

He still didn't look quite convinced, but after a moment he relented, "Alright, I've got it."

What did Jevin's version of the Tree look like? Mine had been far off. I thought there would be more color and, of course, I'd also pictured it larger than it was. How would Jevin react to the secret of the Tree?

"Good, keep breathing deeply and walk over to the Tree and put your hand on her, closing your eyes. Feel the water she is drinking flow up through her. See if you can feel any consciousness within her." I allowed Jevin to stay with those thoughts.

"Now, sit down with your back to her and try to connect. Observe the Garden as she does. View the other plants as she would." I heard him exhale a long breath, "Good. We'll sit here for a little while. If your thoughts drift from the scene of the Garden, gently bring them back."

We sat there in silence for half an hour. I let myself slip into the Garden mindset and connected to the Tree and the Garden myself.

I heard Jevin shift quite a few times during our meditation. I wondered if he opened his eyes, peeking, at all. I had nearly the whole time during my first meditation.

I kept my own eyes resolutely closed.

When enough time had passed, I told Jevin to come back, "Now, let the Garden go and return to yourself. Begin moving your fingers and feet; open your eyes when you're ready." I opened my own.

Jevin stared back, his grey eyes thoughtful.

"So?" I said. "What do you think? Did you see anything interesting?"

He shrugged, "I don't think so. I'm not sure I did it right."

"There's no way to do it wrong. Your connection to the Garden will get clearer with time, I promise." I took a deep breath. "Do you feel calmer?"

Jevin nodded, his shoulders lowered as he seemed to relax even more.

The sun was up now. The ruins overlooked a small meadow filled with yellow grass and, beyond that, the sharp blue line of the ocean touching the sky.

Slim, dusk-purple flowers swayed in the breezes of the meadow. They hadn't been here when I'd come a few weeks ago.

I didn't know how to proceed next, but the world was waking up and the sun warmed us.

Jevin's eyes were closed again, he seemed to be drinking

in the day. Though it was entirely possible he was just exhausted.

He'd worked so hard to put out the candle, even attempting to go about it on his own.

I looked around, summer seemed eager. On the air was the fragrance of drying grass, the hum of insects, and the sound of wind through ruined stone.

"Jevin," I said, suddenly having a thought.

He kept his eyes closed and made a small noise of query.

I went on, "Keep your eyes closed. Don't worry about what you're thinking, just stay calm. I want you to fully embody yourself. Instead of being the Tree, be you now. Try to reach out and connect to the world around you as yourself. Don't judge it, just notice."

He took a deep breath and simply nodded. I closed my own eyes and let myself fall into a deep meditation, hardly aware of the stone supporting me after only a few breaths.

I could feel the world around me, but as I did, I felt myself melding with it. For the briefest time I was not separate from my environment. I was the laughing breeze, the thirsty grass, the flustered insects, the rushing water, the joyous sun. And it was all me.

The feeling faded quickly. I thought I should come back to myself.

I placed a hand on Jevin's shoulder to rouse him and he slowly opened his eyes.

They went wide, "I think I might have felt it that time. The thing I'm supposed to feel, almost an emptiness, but powerful."

I grinned, "Did you? I mean, there's nothing you have to feel. The mindset simply allows you to connect with yourself. Do you think it worked?"

"It might have. Can we go back and practice putting out the candles in one of our rooms?" asked Jevin. "I feel a bit stuffy in the tower room. A familiar area might help."

I nodded, "We can go to my room."

"Let's do that," he agreed eagerly.

We started picking our way between the large pieces of rubble at the edge of the ruins, heading back to the palace. Though I felt at peace, more than I had since the day I'd been found out, I felt something strange as I left the ruins; almost as if the ancient stones themselves watched us leave.

∞∞∞

Back in my room with the candles set up, Jevin was having trouble again, his teeth clenched in concentration.

"Why can't I do it?" He waved his hand at the candle frantically.

I grabbed his hand and held it still. He looked up at me, eyes wide and questioning.

"Jevin. You can do it. Just use what you learned. Imagine yourself back at the ruins and remember what you felt." I let go of his hand.

"I'll try." He seemed to retreat. He closed his eyes and breathed slowly on his own, deeply settling.

After a minute, he nodded, opened his eyes, and extended his hand once more, but gently this time.

Moving his hand in a more relaxed way than I'd seen him try before, it took Jevin merely ten tries before he finally dispelled the flame.

He moved his hand downward and the flame was gone in one soft sputter.

Jevin still held his hand where it had stopped, his eyes glazed as if he couldn't believe it went out and, perhaps worried that if he moved his hand the flame would jump back to life.

"I did it," he looked up at me, meeting eyes, "Shay, I felt it. Or...didn't feel it. It was as if, for the moment the flame went out, I wasn't thinking anything at all and I just let it happen."

My smile was cheek to cheek, "That was great! I knew you could." I was so glad it had worked. "Now," I lit the tinder stick from my own candle and replaced Jevin's flame, "do it again."

Jevin lowered his hand finally, and brought it back to rub his forehead, laughing heartily.

8
Lovestruck

The time I had with Jevin flew by.

Tomorrow was the day my father would evaluate what he'd learned. It was a difficult task trying to squeeze ten years of knowledge into two weeks.

Today Jevin and I would go to the upper gardens and I'd check how he looked after those plants. Though there were special varieties in the true Garden, their care was essentially the same.

We had planned to meditate in Jevin's room before we went to the gardens. I raised a fist to knock on his door, but halted when I heard someone crying...a girl.

Thinking I might have been mistaken, I pressed an ear to the door. The crying quieted and I realized I shouldn't be listening like this.

Instead, I knocked. Low voices spoke for a moment then Jevin opened the door, but not widely.

"Good morning, Shay," he said. "Where are we meeting today?"

"Oh."

Clearly, he'd forgotten the plans we made the day before. It seemed he wasn't going to let me into his room.

"I was going to eat breakfast. Then I thought we would

train at the upper gardens. We'll test your skills in plant care before going to my father tomorrow."

Jevin nodded once. "Then I'll meet you at the upper garden in, what, half an hour? Will that work?"

"Sure," I said, unsure, trying to slyly look past Jevin into his room.

Before I could see anything though, he had shut the door.

A part of me wanted to wait down the hall and see if anyone exited his room when he did, but I decided to simply ask him about the crying girl later.

I picked at the food on my plate, mashing the rubble-tubers with the back of my spoon. Instead of eating, I was thinking about Jevin. He'd seemed more distant, diving deeply into his study and training. Though I was the one teaching him, he was always lost in thought, miles away. And now besides that, it appeared he was keeping something from me.

I left the dining hall, deciding to meditate in the upper garden before Jevin arrived.

The sun had risen not long ago and was making many of the flowers glow softly. I sat, staring at a 'Coral Bloom', the orange-red of it lit like fire in the morning light, when I heard footsteps behind me. I looked around, expecting to see Jevin.

However, it was Princess Neeren. The few times I had seen her recently, she'd turned and avoided me, yet now she approached defiantly.

I rose and bowed, "Princess."

Her hair was pulled back into a braid, though some loose hairs were broken from it.

"Why did you do it?" she said, nearly shaking with anger.

I hadn't had a chance to apologize to her, and she clearly needed one, "I'm sorry if I hurt you in some way, Princess. I..."

"Why did you do it?" She folded her arms, clutching at herself.

It seemed she was only after a straight-forward answer. I braced myself and did my best, "I didn't think it mattered if I was a boy or a girl. I just did what I wanted to do and dressed in a way that made me comfortable. I'm sorry to have hurt you. I'm not sure what I did wrong, but—"

The impact and burning on my cheek came before I realized what had happened. Then Neeren was gone.

"Ow," I whispered, feeling a tear sting the edge of my eye.

I'd been hit many times before, but only as a training exercise. There had never really been any malice in it. There was in Princess Neeren's slap though.

Perhaps it would do some good, provide some closure for her, for whatever reason she was suffering.

We had been friendly before. Not best friends, nothing like what I had with Jevin, but we'd gotten along well. I doubted we could go back to that.

"You realize she was in love with you, right?"

I turned around to see Jevin. "Jev—," what he had said reached me. "What?"

"When she thought you were a boy, she was in love with you." He stood with his arms crossed.

"L-love?" What? I looked away, how could that be? Was it true? "I-I don't think so."

Jevin reached out a hand to graze my cheek, pain still pulsed across my skin. He must have seen Neeren slap me.

Pulling back his hand, he said, "She told me, Shay. She was in my room this morning. I think she wanted to talk with you without really talking to you. She knows how close we are."

I dropped my hands to my sides.

"She'll need time to get over it. It was a huge shock and, you know, when you were a boy," he looked side to side, perhaps unsure that was the right way to phrase it, he sighed, "there was little chance that the two of you would have been matched anyway. I think she still held out hope though. You know her Matching Ceremony will be in several weeks, right?"

I did know that. Neeren had brought it up a lot when we were last talking. Now I knew why.

Jevin continued, "She knew there was only a slight chance and, when she went to your room and...found you...she was going to tell you how she felt." Jevin's eyes met mine, glowing silver in the early sunlight. "She's quite shaken. More than anyone else, I believe."

I tore my eyes away, sitting down and rubbing my face. "I didn't know."

"Of course, you didn't." He sat next to me, "You wouldn't have considered it."

I didn't want to speak of this anymore. My chest was starting to tighten. I didn't like thinking of romance. I had never felt close enough to anyone to think in that way.

I looked up to Jevin. "I'm sorry you had to deal with it," I said, "thank you for your help."

I shook my head, trying to force myself into the mindset to continue Jevin's training. "We should do a meditation," I said.

"Are you okay?" Jevin stayed where he was.

"I'm fine. It's—we need to meditate." I didn't want to talk. Jevin was the person I was closest to, no question, but I found myself resistant to discuss it even with him.

Shame flooded my body. "Close your eyes."

Jevin's eyes didn't close, but found mine once again, so I closed my own and started speaking, beginning the meditation.

We didn't talk of Neeren again.

After meditating I felt better, at least calmer, and all

I had to do was follow Jevin around as he explained care for each plant to me.

He did well enough that I wasn't too worried to bring him before my father tomorrow.

At the end of the day Jevin and I parted ways, perhaps more tensely than usual. I dropped him off at his room to study.

I was proud of Jevin. I thought my father would approve of how I'd taught him.

When I lay down in the darkness though, Neeren's face rose in my thoughts. I felt terrible for having led her on, but I'd never shown particular interest in her. She had allowed herself to see me as a man and a potential partner. I'd only seen her as a friend.

I rolled over, letting out a groan. I had no idea what to do. Perhaps if I gave her time to get over it, things would be alright again. She would have her Matching Ceremony soon and an actual partner to return her feelings. It would be alright.

9
The Garden

Jevin and I met at the entrance to the Garden tunnel at mid-morning. The green of our Apprentice robes shone starkly in the dim lighting of the palace.

"Ready?" I asked, smiling.

Jevin nodded avidly, but there was a small wrinkle between his brows.

"You've been doing quite well with your training. I'm sure it will be fine."

"Thanks, Shay." He let out a breath. "Ready."

I tilted my head toward the hidden break in the wall, "Let's go."

We sidled through the narrow walkway leading to the tunnel. Firelight flickered warmly, the lamps already lit for the day.

We met my father before the line of sunlight dividing the tunnel, it cast a faint glow around him as he stood.

We bowed to him and he nodded back, one cord of hair coming loose to his shoulder.

"Good morning, Master," I said.

"Shaylite. Jevin," he greeted us, eyes resting on Jevin, then turned to me. "You have been training him? How has he taken to the ways of the Garden?"

I had worked all morning on how to present the information to my father, he didn't like to waste time.

"Very well, Master. He was able to put out the candle and has done so every day within a few attempts after he first achieved it on his second day of training. He is doing well with meditation and is making progress using the mindset in his meditation. Yesterday I took him to the upper gardens to assess his skill with plants. We have gotten through eight of the twenty-five chapters of the small handbook and he has memorized nearly all of that. I believe he is well on his way to becoming a fine Apprentice."

Jevin shuffled his feet. I doubted he was used to being assessed so resolutely.

"Good. Jevin, how do you feel your training is going? Are you getting to a point where you can commune and understand the plant life around you?"

Jevin clenched a fist. "I believe I have gotten glimpses of what it means to communicate with the plants. I've been able to extend the mindset that puts out the candle and practice often."

My father seemed to retreat into thought, "Very well. Neither of you have taken your duties lightly." He stepped back, I saw his shoes were already removed. "The Queen has asked me to allow you to enter the Garden as soon as possible. I was hesitant, as typically we wait ten years before letting an Apprentice enter the Garden. However, this circumstance is quite different. In just two years you will need to be working full-time in the Garden alongside me."

I held my breath, waiting for the decision.

"It seems to me that you are even further along in your studies than I could have hoped. At this rate, I believe you will be able to learn the rest quite quickly. The most important part of the training, besides the beginning mindset, is caring for the Great Tree. You must learn about her, how to protect the Tree and the plants that surround her."

Jevin nodded, seeming a little dazed.

"Therefore," continued my father, shoulders dropping the smallest amount, "I want you to enter the Garden tomorrow."

Neither Jevin nor I said anything. My mind went blank for the slightest second. Tomorrow? Truly?

"Shaylite." I shook myself mentally, striving to pay attention. "I know you haven't gotten to the procedures to enter the Garden, so I expect you to go over those with Jevin for the rest of the day. Make sure he can apply the face-paint himself and instruct him as to what the symbols mean. I want both of you here tomorrow at mid-morning, ready to go into the Garden."

I bowed, "Yes, Master." Tomorrow.

"Thank you, Master." This was Jevin. He had surely been shocked before, but now a slight smile was coming over him.

"I will see the two of you tomorrow." My father met eyes with each of us, his face more serious than I'd ever seen. "Now go finish the training I have assigned. I must go care for the Garden." His silver robe swiveled around him as he turned down the dark walkway.

Jevin and I turned as well but didn't start walking.

He was beaming now, "Can you believe it, Shay? I'll be allowed to enter the Garden tomorrow! Your training payed off more than I could have guessed!"

I smiled, though it took more effort than I would have liked. "You did well, Jevin. You worked really hard." I let out a sigh. "We have a lot to learn for tomorrow though. Let's go back to my room to study. I have the materials I need there.

"Right," said Jevin.

The rest of the day was non-stop. I didn't let it stop.

I gave Jevin as much information as I could about the symbols of the Garden, how to mix and apply the bright teal face-paint, the significance of the stone where we placed our shoes, the importance of entering the Garden with only bare feet, and the resonance you would feel in the Garden if you kept your thoughts in the correct mindset. Jevin was more eager to learn today than ever before.

I left him late. He was reading the handbook, nose-deep, when we walked to his room. Though he was so serious about learning, he almost seemed to lift off the ground as he walked. I smiled softly as I left him, glad he was so excited.

After returning to my room, I closed the door and stood with arms crossed.

Though I'd known Jevin was older than I when I started my training and that his would be accelerated, I had to admit it was painful knowing he was going into the Garden after merely two weeks.

Opening the cupboard that held my full array, I ran a finger over the golden chest plate.

I had done a good job. That was why Jevin was able to enter so soon. I should be happy. We would be able to share in the secrets of the Garden even sooner now. I'd be able to discuss things about the Garden that I would never speak of with my father.

A soft breeze came from my open window. I walked to it, dropping my arms to look outside, there were the stars. More than I could ever count. I lost myself for a while in looking at them. They seemed to draw me in. They moved ever so slowly if you watched and I realized the longer I looked, the more stars I could see. They appeared from what had surely been black a moment before.

Things could get better. I just had to keep looking for better things. My chest felt looser and swelled as I drew in a breath of plant-perfumed wind.

I wasn't hungry the next morning. My hand had been inches away from Jevin's door, but something stopped me from knocking.

I wanted to be alone.

The tunnel was dark when I entered, the lamps unlit as it was almost an hour too early, but I'd been unwilling to stay in my room.

I plunged into the darkness of the walkway, staying in the middle so as not to run into either wall.

Somehow, in the complete black, I felt almost weightless. My boots were silent on the soft soil.

Though I hardly knew where to place my feet with each step, I noticed that I felt strangely comfortable. I'd been down this tunnel many times before, but in its darkness by myself, I didn't have to think about how other people saw me or even how I saw myself. I felt safe walking through the unknown.

I smiled as I came to the bar of sunlight lying across the ground, one end touching the east side of the tunnel, the other making its way to the west.

My eyes fell onto the flat stone set by the wall. It had symbols carved smoothly into it. My version of the handbook hardly said anything of the stone, but that it was where we were to place our shoes.

The carvings on the rock were similar to the symbols on our faces, but they were much more harmonious than our painted symbols, blending together seamlessly.

As I gazed at the stone, I felt as though I were trying to remember something that could not be remembered. The markings seemed like they belonged to something else as well.

I waited silently for my father and Jevin, straightening as lamps lit up one by one ahead of me.

My father stopped, eyes wide, when he saw me. "Shaylite."

I bowed. "Good morning, Master."

He looked behind me. "Where is Jevin?"

"He should be here soon."

My father lit a final lamp and we stood in silence.

Not a minute later, the soft padding of boots reached our ears as Jevin came into view, his robe and face-paint perfect.

We said our hellos. Jevin smiled brightly to me, and I returned it as I saw how eager he truly was.

I may have been wrong to feel uncomfortable about Jevin entering the Garden today.

After our shoes were removed, my father stepped ahead of us until he was standing just before the light. He took a deep breath. "Jevin."

In the back of my mind there echoed a "Shaylite." The way my father had said it my own first day in the Garden.

Jevin and I stood side by side, my robed shoulder touching the soft green fabric over his upper arm.

"Today you will enter the Garden," my father continued, his low voice resonating within him, "You will leave behind whatever life you saw for yourself and move forward in your knowledge to become the Master Keeper of the Garden." The three of us were all perfectly still, "You must understand the depth of this. From the moment you breach the light, your task is to protect the Great Tree."

"Of course, Master," said Jevin, not missing a beat.

We removed our shoes and the light slid over my father as he broke through it first. After taking a breath and settling into the mindset, I was next.

I heard Jevin letting out a long breath behind me. I hoped he would fall into the mindset easily this morning.

When he caught up to my side, we followed my father together to the antechamber of the Garden.

The colored light of the stained-glass windows slanted through the gold gate. The key clicked as my father turned it in its lock.

I heard Jevin's breath catch.

"Shaylite." My father spoke, "Jevin needs to see the Garden clearly the first time he enters it, so he will enter after me."

I felt the slightest twinge near my heart, but I understood.

Jevin winked as he sidled past me. He seemed so happy. I wanted him to have a clear view of the Garden when he saw it.

Jevin's dreadlocks tilted backward the slightest bit as we crossed into the Garden and he looked up at the stained-glass ceiling. The light stained him brilliantly. I looked down at myself, watching the teals, purples, and golds slide over my robes and feet. As the light shifted, I felt the changes in color.

My father moved out of the way as we reached the end of the tall hedges, then Jevin was centered, in full view of the Garden.

A small noise of awe escaped him, then I saw his shoulders droop. He moved to the side to let me through, locking eyes as I drew beside him.

I nodded toward my father. He was in charge if Jevin's training now. And, especially with the Tree of the Fallen, he would be the one to explain.

"Master," began Jevin, "the Great Tree, she...she is smaller than I would have thought."

"This is not the Great Tree," the Master said, gazing forward.

I realized he wasn't upset as he'd been when relaying the news to me. He was almost relaxed.

"The Great Tree was killed many years ago."

Jevin turned to me once more, I held his eyes this time.

Again, my father didn't seem ashamed as he told the

rest of the story, about the people whom had destroyed the Great Tree and her seeds. Jevin listened in earnest.

My father allowed no time for Jevin to ask questions but started taking him around the Garden and showing him the different plants, explaining aspects of them.

As Jevin crouched, absorbed while my father explained that this plant, 'Steps of Wrath', needed a specially-made fertilizer, I realized I wouldn't be given further instruction.

My duties were waiting to be done, and I determined I'd do a few my father might not have time for while training Jevin.

I worked, feeling separate from the Master and his new Apprentice.

⚬⚬⚬⚬

When our day was over, and our shoes were back on, my father turned to Jevin and I. "You have done well with Jevin's initial training, Shaylite, now however, I will be taking over."

I nodded, that much had been clear from the day's duties, but I felt a small swell of pride in my father telling me that I'd done well.

"You won't need to be back in the Garden for another two weeks, as usual." He then looked to Jevin. "You, Jevin, I want in the Garden every day. We must get started on all you have to learn as soon as possible."

My insides deflated once more. I kept getting disappointed with how much Jevin was allowed to learn but said nothing. Jevin needed this training. He would be the Master Gardener eventually. I would not...I would not.

When Jevin and I left, there were many people in the hallways preparing to go to the evening meal. We got to my bedroom door and, because there were a few children shouting and running by, he said nothing, but his wide eyes and raised brows made it clear that he wanted to talk.

For one streak of time, I considered pretending I hadn't understood. A wash of what might have been jealousy or inadequacy was starting to surge in the pit of my stomach.

That wasn't Jevin's fault though and I instead held the door open slightly for him to walk into my room. There was another part of myself eager to talk about the Tree of the Fallen with my best friend.

I thought the washroom might be the best place to speak. I doubted anyone would hear us there and we could wash off our face-paint.

As I seated myself next to the steaming pool, Jevin dropped down heavily next to me. The door was shut, and he spoke reverently, "So. The Great Tree. I never expected that."

"I know," I had long wanted to share this burden with him, "when I first saw it I was so disheartened. I'd expected the Tree to be as tall as the stained-glass dome. It's hard to believe the Great Tree was destroyed."

"Truly. And now there's a new Tree. The Tree of the Fallen, was it?"

I sighed, "Yes. Sometimes I wonder if it's right that we keep it secret. My father says people would be afraid if they knew. As long as it protects them, I suppose there's no harm in it."

Jevin nodded, solemn.

I swirled my feet in the water as Jevin scooped some into his hands and leaned forward to remove his paint. Blue-green droplets trailed down his fingers, sending small clouds of color into the water below. I rolled up my sleeves to begin removing my own. Jevin grabbed at a drying cloth and patted his face.

"Is it all off?" He asked, pulling his face from the cloth.

I laughed. He still had faint teal streaks running down his cheeks. I took a handful of soap flakes, scooting closer to place them into his cupped hands. "Here. Sometimes it's difficult to remove the paint because of the oils it contains."

He took the soap and went back to scrubbing.

"What did you think of the Garden?" I was almost afraid to know.

He held up a finger, soap in his eyes, then rinsed and dried his face once again. It was back to its original color now and glowed in the lamplight. Water slid down the sides of his face. "The Garden," he said, "I thought it was wonderful. The pools almost seemed to glow and there were so may plants I had never seen before."

"Good." I smiled.

"I just...can't believe the Great Tree was destroyed," he said, sliding his eyes back to me. "You really don't know who did it?"

"No." I sighed and shook my head, "I wonder who it could have been all the time. The Great Tree protects everyone, so who would have wanted to cut it down?"

"It is strange. And the Master Gardener; it's amazing he was able to grow a new Tree."

"It is. I have no idea what I would have done in that situation, can you imagine? But he found a way." I ran my hands over the steaming water, warming them. "The thing you're supposed to care for, suddenly destroyed. Not knowing how or why."

"Indeed." Jevin stared at the wall unseeingly.

"Hopefully we won't ever have to deal with something like that." I filled my hands with water, beginning to remove the paint from my face, grabbing soap flakes to finish, and rinsed. I felt the drying cloth touch my hands, "Thank you."

"What are you going to do for the next two weeks while I'm in the Garden?" Jevin asked as if he wasn't too interested. I wondered if he realized I was feeling uncomfortable.

I could have told the truth. I didn't know what I was going to do. I would try to train, try to do...something. He was my only companion these days though, so I would be by myself. Before any of this, I never would have minded.

Tomorrow though, Jevin would be in the Garden and I...wouldn't. I would only ever be an Apprentice now. Jevin would go and learn the things only meant for Masters.

"Probably work on training. I haven't been able to train properly lately." I don't know why a smile crossed my face as I said it. I don't know why I pushed those feelings aside and didn't tell him. But I did know he could do nothing to change any of it.

"That sounds like a good plan." He leaned back.

We left soon after that, satisfied in sharing the secrets of the Garden.

10
Exile

When I woke, I felt flattened. I'd tossed and turned for most of the night and it was now late morning.

Dust motes sailed softly through beams of sunlight. Unwilling to move, I watched them.

Jevin was probably in the Garden with my father. Usually I had things I wanted to do when I wasn't in the Garden, but I seemed unable to remember them. I had no friends to talk to, but the one currently bound to the Garden.

If Jevin was with me, we could spar at the training grounds.

I sat up a little. I could still go train.

Pushing up off the bed, I steadied myself. I could do this. It was fine. I could go practice my swordplay.

Opening the cupboard where I'd been keeping Jevin's sword, I saw that the bottom shelf was empty.

For a moment, I thought the sword had been stolen, but remembered that Jevin had taken it back to his room to polish. I had forgotten to ask him to return it.

His was the only sword I had access to, the only one I was allowed to use. Digging my toes into the warm rug,

I contemplated what to do. I changed into a comfortable tunic and laced up my boots.

Jevin usually kept his window open. I doubted the sword would be difficult to find or that he'd mind if I took it back to practice. He had given it to me after all.

I smiled as I contemplated the small adventure. The day was already balmy as I flung open the window. Moist, heated breeze tumbled into my room.

Jevin's window was just two over from mine. I pressed myself up onto my own window sill until I sat on it. Closing my eyes and leaning into the warm air, I listened to leaves shifting. I jumped down, landing just past the flowers growing below.

The day was clear as crystal, the sky wide and cloudless. I stretched out my arms to feel the sunlight.

The sun glinted off Jevin's window. When I pressed on the glass pane, it slid open. I peeked into his room. The oil lamps were out, the room empty. His window was higher up than mine had been from the inside.

I scanned the area around me, making sure I was alone. There were only standing stones and bushes as witness. It took two tries to get onto the sill.

I landed hard on his seagrass rugs and stood still for a moment, hoping no one had heard.

There was the sword, lying flat on Jevin's desk, covering scattered papers.

At the desk, I saw briefly that the papers were notes on the Garden. I smiled. Truly, I was proud of Jevin for being whole-hearted in his learning. He was retaining information so quickly.

I picked up the sword but knocked a few of the papers to the floor. Bending to pick them up, I stopped when I saw what exactly was written on them.

They were indeed notes on his studies...but this was too much. There were detailed drawings of the Garden. At least the basic shape of pools and plant placements, many of them labeled.

If anyone found this...I had to talk to Jevin. Information like this wasn't ever meant to leave the Garden. I didn't want to leave it here but couldn't think of a safe place to keep it otherwise.

The only option I could see was to burn it. I had to memorize these things about the Garden by being in the Garden. Jevin should have to do the same.

I went back to the desk and moved the papers around, checking each in turn. Most were Jevin's notes on my version of the Garden Handbook. These were fine, though I wished they weren't out in the open. I slid those papers into the top drawer of his desk.

There was one other paper where Jevin had started noting information on taking care of the plants surrounding the Tree. I took that one too.

Perhaps it would be fine leaving these here for the day, but I didn't want to risk it. Hopefully Jevin would understand why I'd burned them when I brought it up to him later.

The main oil lamp in his washroom was still lit and I dipped a corner of both papers into the flame. Holding them over Jevin's wash-basin, the curling, grey parchment fell.

When the last parts dropped away, I filled the basin with water, swirled it around to get the pieces loose, and poured the remnants out the window.

The basin went back in its place and I picked up the sword, belted it around my waist, then leaped back out into the bright day.

Jevin still had so much to learn. He was doing well, but I had to make sure he understood all aspects of his position. Secrecy was essential.

I decided I would meditate before training to get into the proper state of mind.

The ruins would be fit for this. Perhaps it was me missing the Garden or the fact that sweat was already beginning to coat my feet, but I took off my boots and carried them as I made my way to the ruins.

I was still concerned about Jevin, but once again began to truly enjoy the day.

There was life everywhere. Birds rushing here and there, filling the air with song, insects zipping in every direction, and a half-hearted breeze starting to pick up.

Near the ruin site, I spotted Henn and Mety, two boys I was barely acquainted with. I was close enough that they had already seen me.

Not wanting to meditate with other people around, I nodded in their direction then walked past the ruins.

Henn yelled over, "Oy, Shaylite. What are you wearing there? Where's your dress? And...shoes?"

I lowered my head, quickening my steps.

I heard Mety say quietly, "Henn. Don't."

"And, hey, isn't that Jevin's sword?" Henn continued, ignoring Mety.

"He probably let...uh...her...use it," Mety said.

"Don't know about that."

I sped out of earshot and was glad when they didn't follow.

I'd almost forgotten the issues I had been having with everyone in the palace, too focused on training Jevin lately. I couldn't retaliate though. I wouldn't give them fuel and it was pointless to start something up.

From here I could see the peak of Cresstalan. The dormant volcano. There was a spot not far from it where I could train instead, only half an hour's walk.

The day was beautiful. I still held my shoes, so I was having to be more aware where I placed my feet, avoiding pebbles.

Somehow though, I was comfortable. Having my feet free put me in the mindset of the Garden. The sand or soil shifting beneath me gave a deep sense of connection. I felt on-level with the land.

As wind wrapped around me and insects whizzing by, I thought of nothing else, and was simply held in the moment.

Before long, I was breaking through dense greenery into an open area. Somehow, I always forgot about this place. It was a little further from the palace than I cared to wander, so I didn't visit often.

A fall of clear water came down large panes of rock into a pond. Colored stones sat at the bottom of the pool and water plants waved beneath the surface.

I closed my eyes, listening to the rushing fall, drowning out all other sound.

Soft lush grass grew beside the water and I lowered myself into its sweet scent. I crossed my legs, closed my eyes, and began to breathe, lengthening each breath as I went. Tension released. As it did, I felt a tear roll down my cheek.

Breathing, letting myself come back to me, soon sound was lost. My hands and heart-center began to tingle, feeling less pressured. I didn't try to think of anything specific.

I finished the meditation and opened my eyes, rising, it took little effort. I felt quiet within.

My mind clicked into the knowing mindset, a ringing emptiness that somehow always felt as if it overflowed.

Before returning to the training grounds, I found I wanted to do some warm-up exercises...in the mindset. Once or twice I had unexpectedly fallen into it to spar. Today it felt right.

I drew the sword and began a simple exercise. Without thought.

It was almost as if the sword swung itself, jabbing, withdrawing, cutting through. The enemies weren't invisible this time. They were nothing at all.

My breath grew heavy long after it usually would have and only when I was panting did I stop, realizing what I'd been doing.

The mindset made everything different. Today's exercise had been better than ever. I'd felt at peace.

I looked at my fingers gently holding the sword, the Fainian Peal-Digger smiling widely, and I released it back into its scabbard, dropping down into the grass.

∞∞∞

The training grounds were mostly deserted when I arrived. Five off-duty guards trained on the far side, but there was no reason that should interfere with my training.

I began by running in loops around a good half of the grounds, staying out of the guards' way.

After warming up my body, I stretched it out carefully then began drills of punches, kicks, and a few more complicated moves I favored, arm blocks, knee jabs, and dodges. I was impressed with my speed and was smiling as I finished when I heard a voice behind me.

"You're the one who's a girl, aren't you?"

I turned around, panting slightly, to find three guards standing there watching me.

"Yes," I said.

"You're quite fast." This was a guard standing a little farther forward than the other two.

"I try."

"You probably shouldn't be training anymore though."

"Ain't proper," said one of the other ones.

I did my best not to roll my eyes at this. Here we were again.

"I won't stop training simply because you know I'm a girl now," I said, keeping my voice polite, "I was a girl this whole time."

I tried to continue my exercises, thinking on the sword moves I wanted to practice.

"Yeah, we heard about that."

"Shouldn't have been training at all then, should you? Ladies can't fight."

I knew I should have turned away and ignored them, but I found I wasn't able to. Anger and indignation rose within me. I said, before I'd realized, "Well, come and spar with me then. I'll show you ladies can fight."

Two of the guards looked appalled at this.

"Can't fight a lady," said the front one.

The third guard let out a short laugh, his teeth sharp with his mouth open.

The last guard, who hadn't yet spoken backed away, but the one who had scoffed said, "We're trained guards. You can't go up against us. Lady or not, you're just a member of the palace staff. Haven't even trained properly."

I shrugged, "Then spar with me." Perhaps I was going to have to start proving that I should be here at the palace.

"No."

"Can't"

"Alright then."

The three of them spoke at the same time, the sharp-toothed one agreeing to my challenge.

I used to spar with other boys every day. I had never, however, sparred with a guard who was fully trained. I hoped I could at least show that I was a semi-decent fighter. I was rarely beaten when I trained with other boys.

The guard began to remove his sword belt, it seemed we were going hand-to-hand.

One of the other guards took it for him and seemed to be trying to talk him out of it, glancing over at me with disgust.

"I'm going to show her," my opponent said, smiling cuttingly.

Hoping I wouldn't embarrass myself, I rolled my neck to loosen it.

Then I remembered how easy it had been to swing my sword when I'd purposely been in the mindset. Should I use it against this guard? I truly didn't know my chances against him, I now realized. I didn't often watch the guards train. Still, I would take on this trial.

I was tired of being underestimated, of others trying to decide how I should act or dress, and of losing.

I decided to use the mindset, use everything in my power to put up a good fight and hope I came out the other end in a somewhat better place.

Taking a breath, I felt my mind empty. Calm coursed through my body, flooding the areas that had been too tense without my realizing.

The guard came to his place across from me. "You have no chance. I'll show you that a girl cannot pretend to be a man. There's no place for your kind here."

I didn't know what he meant by 'my kind', but I didn't get angry. His voice seemed to roll off me and I just stood, ready.

The other two guards seemed to be making comments as well, but I found it easy to ignore them.

"If I win," he said, "you can't train here anymore. In fact, you can't practice combat at all." He grinned nastily.

"I won't promise any of that."

His face contorted towards anger.

I focused as he brought his hands up, fists tight. I went looser, almost relaxing my hands completely and lowered my weight into my legs.

The guard came at me, but I dodged and spun around him, catching his shin with a hook of my leg, setting him off-balance.

"Blasted—," he let out.

He came at me with a series of punches. They seemed rather slow, however, and I blocked each one. I decided to move to the offensive as his last punch went just far enough to leave an opening.

I elbowed him in the side of his ribs then came up around him, under an arm, to place my hands on his back and push him forward and away.

He was fast to recover and spun around with a kick. The heel of his boot just clipped my ear. It fizzed with pain, but I relaxed further into the mindset to continue.

Before he snapped his leg back, I grabbed his knee, slamming it down to the ground. This left him no choice but to put his hands out to catch himself and stop his face from hitting the ground.

"Bit—" I didn't give him a chance to finish his thought. He'd turned onto his back again and shot his legs forward forcefully to drive me off. I had already moved above where he could reach me though, and my hand was flat against his throat.

This was how sparring matches ended, so I got up after a second, standing back. I had won. The guard was still on the ground, his face seething.

The other two guards were silent.

"I can fight," I said, hoping that was obvious by now, but wanting to say it clearly. I didn't want to spend any more time with these guards. "May I go back to practicing now?"

The guard pushed himself to his feet, grunting, and said, "As if I would use my full strength on you, girl. Lucky."

I almost laughed, but decided not to, staying still.

The other two guards came and gave the third his sword.

"If I had been using this," he yanked the sword back and raised it to my face, "you'd be dead."

I seized up as he suddenly spat on me. It landed on my cheek and he walked away, laughing.

I wiped the spit harshly with the sleeve of my tunic.

Even in winning, I couldn't win.

My mindset was gone, the training ground was empty,
I let out an enraged yell.

11
Scavengers

I'd left the training ground dripping in sweat.

After my sparring match, I trained. Hard. I put on weights and practiced swordplay to strengthen my arms further. Other boys drifted in and out of the grounds, but they all ignored me.

∞∞∞

Back in my room, I placed Jevin's sword back onto its shelf, and quickly changed, heading to the dining hall for an early dinner. I hoped Jevin would be there, so I could tell him about having to burn his notes.

Jevin wasn't in the dining hall, but I sat in our usual spot, piling a steaming piece of fish and browned splay-mushrooms onto my plate. I took a hearty slice too from a fresh loaf of root bread on the table. My stomach ached for food and I ate as fast as I could.

Taking a long draught of spiel-fruit tea when I was finally, partially satiated, I nearly dropped it when shouts started ringing through the hallway outside.

Everyone rose as one and went to see what the noise was about.

There was a small crowd outside the throne room and shouting coming from inside, but I couldn't see why.

I squeezed through the swarm of people, hardly noticed as everyone's eyes were fixed on the commotion ahead, when I came to a place where I had a clear view. Two guards stood in front of the three thrones populated by the Royal Family. The guards stood on either side of what looked to be a girl in a maid's uniform.

The queen was speaking to her, "There is no chance you will be forgiven."

I heard stuttering sobs coming from the girl who seemed to be in trouble for something.

"Take her," said the Queen, waving a hand lithely.

"No!" the girl shouted.

I knew that voice. Standing up onto my toes, I saw her struggling against the guards trying to take her through a door to the side. I gasped as I saw who it was. Heyda.

What could she have done?

A sheen of tears lay on her face and spit dripped from her mouth as she wept angrily.

The Queen had already gotten to her feet and Fedrid and Neeren followed, they watched as Heyda was taken away.

I wanted to stop what was happening, but I had no information. What would warrant this kind of treatment?

Heyda was now shouting, pulling back on the guards with every ounce of strength she had. "YOU HAVE NO RIGHT TO BE HERE AND YOU MAY HAVE GOTTEN ME, BUT I'M NOT THE END!"

One of the guards clapped a hand over her mouth, but I could still hear her muffled shrieks.

A roar filled the hall as Heyda seemed to have bitten the guard's hand, giving her a small window to shout one last thing.

"SCAVENGERS!"

The door shut as Heyda was dragged through and other guards began pushing us out of the throne room. The Royal Family was already gone.

⨺⨺⨺

I was shocked by what had just happened and allowed myself to be driven from the great room.

Had Heyda been arrested? What could it possibly have been for? And what did she mean by calling the Royal Family 'scavengers'?

I felt a hand on my shoulder and looked around to find I'd wandered toward the Garden entrance. Jevin stood next to me.

"Shaylite? Are you okay?"

I couldn't remember Jevin ever calling me Shaylite.

"I heard shouting," Jevin said, turning toward the throne room, "What's going on? You look sick."

Indeed, my stomach had started to churn. "I'm fine." I said, "Heyda..." At the mention of Heyda, Jevin met my eyes in surprise, probably not expecting it to be about her. My stomach let out a shallow moan and I suddenly felt nauseous.

"Heyda...? Never mind, you don't look well. Let's go to your room." His hand cautiously grasped my far shoulder. I flinched slightly when I felt his arm along my back.

⨺⨺⨺

We got back to my room and I immediately ran for the washroom and emptied my evening meal into the wash-basin, hanging over it for a moment after I was finished, panting, tears leaking from my eyes.

Jevin was hanging back in my room. "Shay. Are you alright?"

Slumping down to the tiled floor, I closed my eyes, feeling better that I'd at least gotten everything out.

I heard Jevin walk near me and it sounded like he took the wash-basin away. I was grateful for that. The smell had been threatening to make me sick again.

Mixed within that, however, was a strange scent. I knew it.

Temne root. I thought back to dinner and realized there hadn't been root bread on anyone else's table. Someone must have mixed it into the loaf.

There were patches of temne root scattered about the island. It wasn't poisonous, but would make you sick.

I let out a moan. More bullying. I had something worse to think of now though. Heyda.

Opening my eyes, I saw Jevin hovering in the entranceway.

"Do you need me to get you something?" he asked.

I shook my head, scooping a bit of water from the pool next to me and sloshing it around my mouth to remove the foul taste. I leaned and spat into the chamber pot.

That was better.

Jevin sat down next to me, raising a hand to rub my upper back a couple times, trying to comfort me, I supposed. It didn't really work, but he lowered it a moment later.

"What was that about?"

I let out a sigh, unwilling to explain everything.

"Something bad at dinner."

"Ah. Sorry," he said.

I was feeling better every second, and I thought I should continue from earlier, "Jevin, I think Heyda was arrested."

He was silent, and when I looked up at him, his jaw clenched tightly. "What do you mean? Your maid?"

I nodded, "They were yelling so I went to the throne room and she was there in front of the Queen. They told her she wouldn't be forgiven, and they were taking her away somewhere. She was really upset and told the Royal Family they didn't belong here. She said it didn't matter that they'd gotten rid of her because she wasn't the end. She called them scavengers before she was dragged away."

"Scavengers?" Jevin was thoughtful.

"I've never known Heyda to break any rules. I'm not sure what she could have done to warrant any of that. Where will they take her?"

"I'm not sure," said Jevin. "That is all very strange."

"I know. What do you think she did?"

"I've seen the Queen be quite cruel at times," said Jevin, "Heyda may have done something small and gotten punished more than was deserved."

"That seems too much, even for the Queen," I said.

Jevin shook his head, "I really couldn't tell you, Shay. Perhaps we'll find out in the next few days. I assume everyone will be talking about it if it was that public."

"You're probably right."

"Are you feeling better?" He tilted his face to me and I was transfixed at the teal symbols upon it. I wondered what he was learning in the Garden.

The Garden. I almost forgot I had to tell Jevin about his notes. "Jevin, there's something else."

"What?" His eyes widened worriedly.

"I trained today and had to get your sword from your room."

"What did you do, go in through the window?"

I smiled. "Of course."

He laughed.

I continued, "But the sword was on your desk, surrounded by papers. I knocked some of them down and noticed they were notes on the Garden."

"Right," he said, listening closely now.

"Jevin," I met his eyes now, "You can't leave those lying out in the open. If anyone found them...notes on the small handbook are one thing, as long as you keep them out of sight. Some of your notes were on more secret parts of the Garden though. You had a detailed map." I didn't want to sound like I was blaming him.

"I need to learn it. I need to learn it quickly." His eyes were steeped with an anger I didn't often see, gleaming like his sword.

"I know. I...sorry, I should have said something earlier. We've been going over so much, I suppose I neglected the secrecy parts." I sighed. "I am sorry, but you can't make maps of the Garden or take notes on the plants there, most of those are secret as well. Many are special varieties."

Jevin looked down at his knees. "I...I suppose I understand."

"Jevin, I had to burn them. Sorry, I couldn't have anyone finding them."

He seemed slightly shocked at this, meeting my eyes again, then resigned. "I understand. I should have realized."

"And I should have told you. It's my fault."

Jevin was silent for a couple minutes at this.

I was still feeling a bit weak, but I mustered up my strength to ask, "How are you? Are you alright?"

Jevin's long fingers flexed. "There's just so much to learn." He said it almost to himself. "Today was overwhelming. We began to talk of how to care for the Tree. I had no idea it took so much work."

I nodded. "It's the only one for a reason. At times I think she probably wasn't meant to grow on an island like ours. We have to take great care, so she can thrive."

"And the rituals. We learned one today."

"Oh?"

"It was quite complicated."

This time I didn't speak, though I don't think Jevin realized. I had only learned small, simple rituals. I would have been taught the full ones when I became a full-time Gardener at twenty, but Jevin was learning them already?

"I suppose I'll learn it all soon enough. It's more difficult when I can't write it down."

"I'm sure it is." Jevin seemed like he needed help. "I suppose you could ask my father to study the Garden Handbook inside the Garden. You may even be able to take notes and keep them there if that would help."

Jevin yawned and said quietly, "I think he did mention that at some point, actually. I'll try asking tomorrow."

My hands were clasped in my lap and I stared at the firelight dancing over them.

Jevin was quiet and, a moment later, his head fell sideways onto my shoulder. He'd fallen asleep.

His dreadlocks brushed my face gently and I smiled. I looked around his head to his face. Lines stood out clear under his eyes and his face looked worried. It was clear he hadn't been sleeping much.

It would do him no good to sleep here though. I shook my shoulder slowly to wake him.

He let out a groan and raised his eyes up to me, disoriented, "What?"

"You were asleep."

He hesitated a moment, then closed his eyes again. "You should have left me."

I leaned back, drawing my shoulder out from under his head, which dipped for a moment before he brought it back up, sighing.

"You need to go to your room and sleep."

He moaned, "Fine."

He shook his head and I leaned forward again to sit next to him.

"All these years I thought you were just watering plants, but there's so much to being a Keeper of the Garden."

"I hope you're still up to the job," I said, half-joking.

"Me too," he said seriously.

"I'm going to go to bed too. I need sleep."

Jevin rose up from the floor and reached out a hand to help me up. I took it and he pulled me towards him.

I let go of his hand and stood on my own.

"You'll figure it out." I said, pushing him toward the door out to the hallway. "Goodnight."

He didn't look back but waved as he walked.

I lay down in my bed.

Jevin was learning the rituals now. I didn't want to admit it, but I was feeling worse and worse about him being in the Garden. Why had I been chosen as a Wild Soul? If I'd been matched at least I would still have been a Master Gardener.

Now I would be an Apprentice forever, going around and helping Jevin when he was the Master. He would surpass me, learning things I would never be allowed to learn.

I let out a breath, convincing myself to relax.

I had to take things one at a time. Why was I worrying? I'd be back in the Garden soon and all would be fine. I was still a part of the Garden and I wouldn't let my jealousy stop me from doing my own duties as a Keeper.

Smoothing my brow, I did my best to sleep.

12
Back Again

I'd felt isolated outside the Garden and hadn't seen Jevin since we'd spoken of Heyda.

Though I tried to distract myself by listening in to different conversations talking about her, there was never more information on what exactly happened.

Today though, the two weeks were finally done and I would re-enter the Garden, happy to return to my father's and Jevin's company.

Eager to start, I immediately slipped into my Apprentice robe, cinching the belt with vigor. It was still early so I took time painting my face, lingering over the sweet earthy smell of the paint and crafting each symbol carefully. I couldn't wait to be back in the peace of the Garden.

At mid-morning I arrived at the carved stone in the tunnel. Jevin and my father were already there.

"Master. Jevin," I said, bowing.

Jevin bowed back and my father nodded.

"Let us enter the Garden," said my father.

When we went to cross the light, there was the slightest confusion as I attempted to go before Jevin. I quickly realized though, that Jevin going first would have to be the new way of things.

Jevin looked a little sorry as he went before me. I did my best to be unconcerned with it and simply thought of the Tree and pools, looking forward to seeing them.

Though it was usual for me to go to the Garden only every two weeks, these had felt longer than the others.

As we passed through the gold gate and moved between the flourishing plants, I began to breathe easily. This was right. This was where I was meant to be.

"Shaylite," said my father, the three of us now gathered around the Tree.

"Yes, Master?"

"Today your task is to log all progress the plants have made this year. You know what to do."

I looked at him, confused, "Master, don't we usually wait until summer has ended?"

"I have decided to move it up this year. While you take care of that, I will teach Jevin which plants need specific fertilizers."

"Yes, Master."

Jevin smiled at me, possibly trying to lighten the situation. I gave him a small one back and went to the alcove where the records of the Garden were kept.

The large Handbook, nearly as big as half the alcove itself, lay open on its gilded stand.

Twenty smaller volumes populating a large shelf contained records of the Garden. Tomes filled the rest of the shelf as well, but they were empty, waiting to be filled.

The only information kept was measurements and health of plants in the Garden, updated each year. I always wished there was more. Names of past Keepers, history of the Garden, and other information was not to be found.

I had seen a lot of the true Handbook and, though it said the Garden had been alive for multiple centuries, the records only went back barely a hundred years.

I'd never had the courage to ask my father what had happened to those other records, fearing they'd been stolen along with the seeds of the Great Tree when it had been destroyed.

The Handbook also didn't seem to have information on how the Garden began or where the Tree had come from in the first place. I supposed this was because of the last thing stated in the book, the cardinal rule of the Garden, "There is never to be another Great Tree. Destroy the seeds she produces."

I picked up the logbook we'd been filling for the last four years. This year's recordings would finish it.

Picking out a glass pen and gilt measuring stick, I went back to the Garden.

The soft sounds of slowly moving water filled the air. Though I would be doing the most monotonous task of the Garden today, it was nice to be back.

'Apex of Time' was the first to be logged and I knelt beside it. I measured the heights of the pointed, blue flowers, leaves, blossoms, and width of the plant. This one had grown by three inches. There were no dead leaves and its color was healthy. Not too much to note. I went to the next plant and continued.

At one point, my father started his other tasks while Jevin was left to fertilize the plants he knew. He was spreading the thick mixture around the plant I was to log, 'Candle's Note'.

"How are you doing?" I asked quietly.

"Well," he said, spreading more fertilizer over the soil. "I feel like I'm finally able to retain most of what the Master teaches. It's getting easier."

"I'm glad to hear it," I said, truly glad.

Jevin lowered his voice further, "Have you heard anything more about Heyda?"

I shook my head. "No one seems to know what she did or where she was taken. Of course, I haven't talked to anyone who might know anything of note."

"How odd," said Jevin, finishing and brushing the soil and fertilizer from his hands.

I nodded, writing down the height of a wavering orange flower.

"Let me know if you hear anything else though," he said, moving on to the next plant.

"I will."

In the late afternoon, my father came to check on my work. "How have the plants changed this year?"

"They're doing well," I said. "Most have grown and are healthy. Of course, you know we lost a few of the 'Lady's Belt' in winter, but I've noted it and many of them have revived."

"Yes, they have. Good." He walked away. "Go on and log the Tree next."

This was the part I'd been looking forward to. My father had shown me the process last year, but I had never been allowed to do it on my own.

The gilded platform swing hung next to the Tree, swaying slightly as I stepped onto it, clutching tightly. When I pulled at the metal cord nearby, the platform jolted, starting to rise. I was elated as it drew me to the top of the Tree.

Jevin's mouth hung open as he watched my ascent. I let out a long breath, holding tight to the cord.

The Garden spread out beneath me and I could see it in whole for the first time. Though I knew its design from pictures in the Garden Handbook, I'd never seen it in its living form and it was stunning, splayed colors vibrant.

Looking back to the Tree, I noted the place we'd measured last year and calculated how much the Tree had grown. It was several feet taller. I brushed a few of the leaves gingerly.

Several suspended cords allowed me to maneuver sideways and circle the Tree to see it at different angles.

I watched the Garden as I soared over it, the afternoon light shifting through the bright pools and still plants, over Jevin and my father who'd gone back to their work, over the tall hedges near the entrance, and the glint of the golden gate beyond them. It left me full of wonder and content.

Soon though, the day was done, and I had lowered myself back to the ground. We left the Garden for the evening.

My father turned toward his room as we entered the hallway, saying, "Shaylite, we will see you in another two weeks."

I felt slightly crestfallen as I realized I wasn't invited back until then. Jevin turned, and he and I went back to the youth wing together.

We walked in silence until Jevin broke it, "I—I'm sorry, Shaylite. I think your father wants to teach me more of the rituals and...I suppose you're not allowed to learn them." He didn't look at me.

"No problem," I said, brushing it off. I changed the subject, "Are you hungry? I was going to raid the pantry for a meal." I didn't want to tell him I hadn't trusted the food of the dining hall lately.

He sighed, "I need to clean up. I haven't been able to since the other day, but food does sound good."

"That's fine," I said. "How about I get something and bring it back to eat in your room?"

He nodded, "That will work. Though I won't be able to be with you for too long. I want to go over what I learned today and get some rest."

"Of course," I said. I hadn't been planning on staying for too much time, but I let it lie.

"See you soon," said Jevin, his tall form entering the room.

In my own bedroom, I changed into casual clothes and washed my face.

Grabbing an array of food from the pantry afterwards, I returned to the youth wing. However, I saw Fedrid there, speaking to a couple guards.

I decided to avoid anything that situation might turn into and backtracked outside, leaving out the south entrance and making my way around the palace. I'd enter through Jevin's window.

It was thrown open when I got there. I was about to call through to him but stopped on hearing voices inside.

The low timbre of my father floated out to me. "You are the new Apprentice," he spoke. "You will have to learn to manage the Garden on your own. There cannot be two Masters. You are the one who is chosen now, not Shaylite."

My heart seemed suspended. I had known I couldn't be the Master, but I realized I'd been clinging to a faint wisp of hope that perhaps, somehow, I would still be allowed to learn all that the Garden held.

"Shay can. I don't see any reason to. After all the time she has been there. She can work with me until there is another Apprentice, can't she?"

"Perhaps after my death, if need be. That will not be for a long time, however, and your nineteenth birthday is nigh. Soon your marriage reading will match you with a wife and you will have a child." He seemed to sigh and shift. "I will not give her more hope than she should have. This is the reality she must face. The sooner she does, the better it will be."

"You could step down when you've taught me what I need and—"

"I will do no such thing. I'll observe you for as long as possible. Shaylite is not trained as you must be. There should only be two Keepers at a time and this has gone on long enough."

Not wanting to hear any more, I sped to my own window, dropped the food into the room, then clambered inside.

I drifted over and sat numbly in the chair at my desk, blankly staring at nothing.

Then my brain started murmuring again.

I wouldn't be allowed to continue working in the Garden at all. I couldn't even stay on as an Apprentice.

It had been foolish to not think it through. This was what made sense, but then...what was I to do? I had no skills to pursue anything else. What would I do with my life?

Perhaps an answer would leap at me from my dimming room.

It didn't.

I'd be forced out of the Garden.

Before that happened, I needed to figure out where to go instead.

I sat longer, not truly thinking, just letting the knowledge sink in. Still, no answers found me.

When I looked around again, it was dark. Food was scattered on the floor, but I had no desire to eat it or move it.

Perhaps I should speak to someone about this. But whom?

What would my options be? Now that everyone knew I was a girl, would I have to do something that only girls could do? That left few options. I wouldn't even be allowed to learn a trade as a woman.

My father seemed set on turning me out with little warning. I didn't want to speak to him about it.

Jevin would be the one taking my place, so he wasn't the one to ask either.

I'd worked so hard all these years to become a Gardener.

Now I would have to find a new way.

13
A Way

There was perhaps one person I could speak with about what to do next.

I walked down the curved hallway of the second floor to someone everyone asked advice from.

It was late, but the Court Reader usually gave out readings far into the night.

I lifted the enameled metal knocker and struck the door three times.

A faint voice called, "Enter."

After fortifying myself, I opened the left of the two clay doors.

Candles lined the walls of the large room, the myriad of flames reflecting in the large windows, now black with the night. These were some of the grandest windows I'd ever seen, and they sat directly behind the Court Reader. He may have been dozing, for he stared at me with half-lidded eyes, seeming slightly disoriented.

My feet moved forward of their own accord and I found myself standing in front of the wizened Reader and bowing.

I had no answers myself. The course of my future seemed murky, but clearing away that unknowing was what the Reader was here for.

His eyes widened slightly upon looking at me now he seemed to realize I was present.

"Court Reader." I nodded solemnly to him.

He'd said I was a Wild Soul. That had broken me from my path toward becoming a Master Gardener. His reading had placed Jevin there instead. Perhaps he could inform me what I was to do now.

"Ah," said the Court Reader with a rasp, "Shaylite. The Wild Soul." Though there were many candles, the lighting in the room still seemed quite dim. The Reader's pupils were dilated, only black, depthless pools set into his withered head. The shadows and unsteady candle light only helped to accentuate this.

"Yes. May I ask to receive a reading?"

"As that is what I am here for," he said, gesturing for me to sit with a wavering hand, "I shall give you a reading."

The chair moved slightly, whining as I sat.

"What is it you wish to ask?" His eyes were again nearly closed, but he seemed to be listening.

I thought for a moment, and said, "I need to know how to proceed into my future. Things have changed and I'm unsure of the way forward."

I wasn't exactly sure how readings like this worked. I knew of the official readings, marriage readings and the ones parents got for their newborn children to know their future. I had never had one of these. My future had been set when I was born.

Now I needed one.

The Court Reader gave a shaking nod that lasted merely a second. "I see."

He bent sideways to open a drawer in the desk we sat at, pulling out a plate of confections. I remembered the smell of pastry on his fingers from my Matching Ceremony. A small waft of the same sweetness came from these. He must be partial to them.

I hoped he would eat one and wake up a bit. I wanted him to be alert. Though he may do this kind of thing every day for countless people, this could decide the course my life would take.

He pulled out two plates from the same drawer, setting one of those and then a biscuit before each of us.

He took a bite right away and chewed contentedly, nodding at me to do the same.

I lifted mine, unsure, but as my stomach growled I took a large bite. After swallowing, I prepared to take another, but the Reader's hand appeared over my own, halting me.

"Wait," he said, meeting my eyes. "Put it down now."

I hesitated, but he didn't look away and I obediently set the pastry down, a few crumbs falling.

The Court Reader sat back into his seat, contented, and finished the last bite of his own. Brushing his fingers against each other, removing crumbs, he moved his plate out of the way.

I simply sat still.

He lifted my plate and drew it to himself, examining the pastry.

Was there something wrong with it? Why had he stopped me from finishing it when he'd finished his own? My stomach rumbled softly at having the food taken away when I was still hungry.

The Court Reader was staring intently at the few crumbs littering the plate. After two minutes of this, I realized this must be the reading itself, so I stayed silent.

Another minute went by and then he moved the plate off to the side and looked at me once again.

"I have seen," he said, "that your future does not rest on this island."

The Court Reader always seemed to have answers

I never expected.

"My...not on Cresstalan?" I asked.

"That is right. I see no future for you here."

Was he going to give me more information than this? "Then where does it lie?"

He made a small, high sound. "It could be anywhere. It is not told here."

"Do you see anything else?" Only this much was unhelpful.

"The future is not what you thought it would be."

This I knew. It was becoming clearer with each passing day. "Then what shall I do? Am I to leave?"

"Do not worry over that," the Reader said, waving his hands absently. "It will come about of its own accord."

This was even less help. "Then I'm to do nothing?"

"No," he said, picking a piece of my remaining sweet and placing it into his mouth. "Do things as you would normally, and you will fall into what the future plans for you without trouble."

Perhaps he could tell me one more thing, even if he seemed determined to give me as little information as possible.

"Will it turn out well? Is my future to be fortunate?"

At this he tilted his head back and forth a few times. "That...depends on how you wish to see it, but I think...no."

My heart sank.

He seemed to have realized what he had just said and met my eyes. "Of course, there will be good things that happen. The future is always, ultimately, in the hands of the one living the life. Things change with the flow of time, but for now, what I see is not what I would call fortunate."

"What do you see then?" I said, slightly desperate to know.

"Oh," he said. "Nothing clear. Just feelings of what could happen, but I think it is best to simply live your life and follow where events lead. That is all." He lifted my plate and began eating the rest of the pastry, waving a hand for me to exit.

I didn't know what else to do. It seemed he would not give more information, if he even had any.

So, I left. I walked back to my room, mind blank. What was I to do now?

I entered my room and sat on the low bed.

For much of the night, I simply stared at the walls as they shifted with moonlight.

COⱭO

I must have fallen asleep eventually, because I woke when the sun was high, half my body hanging on the floor rather than the mattress.

I felt nearly nothing. I didn't want to meditate. I didn't want to do anything.

My stomach growled loudly, and I looked to the food still resting on the floor from last night. Sitting, I slowly picked at the dried seaweed, fruit, and tuik nuts.

Afterwards I relieved myself in the washroom, but what would I do next? With a nebulous idea of going for a walk, I went into the hallway.

I stumbled a bit when exiting. Though I was so tired, I felt no urge to try and sleep.

Dazedly walking up the hallway, I vaguely noticed a lack of guards.

Hands grabbed me from behind, covering my mouth swiftly, and dragged me into a nearby room.

Friends of Fedrid; at least five.

Fedrid stood in front of a window, the noonday sun shining behind him, his nearly-shaved head harshly lit.

Still trying to wrap my mind around what was happening, I hadn't tried to fight back.

Fedrid's arms were crossed and he grinned mercilessly.

The boy's hand covering my mouth smelled like rancid seaweed.

My mind began racing, trying to find a technique that could throw all five boys from me. Though, I realized, this wasn't a life-or-death situation.

Truly, I couldn't fight against them without breaking my vow of non-violence. I wouldn't make that mistake again.

"I've been trying to get you to act the way you should," began Fedrid, his voice like poisoned honey, "I tried to stop you from swordsmanship training, yet you show up to the grounds with a borrowed sword. I've tried to be subtle, having Heyda steal your razors so your hair would grow and trade your clothes for those more appropriate. Of course," he said, closing his eyes angrily for a moment, "I didn't know she was in league with our enemies then, so who knows what she actually did."

His blue eyes appeared once again. "Then I tried to make you sick, but you seem to have avoided that. So here I am now, saying it straight to your face." He tapped my face lightly with the palm of his hand.

I would have bared my teeth at him, had they been exposed.

Fedrid was cruel and quick to anger, had always been. Now I was finding out just how far he'd go. And for what? To make me act like a girl?

A thought crossed my mind then that hadn't before, did he know how much Neeren had liked me? Perhaps...just maybe...he was trying to protect her.

"Be a girl. That's what you are, so act like it. You can try it now, I'm sure it's better than you think."

Another boy came up from behind him holding a dress and what seemed to be a long, stringy mass of seaweed. The seaweed was arranged a bit like how a lady would wear her hair.

What was this? They were going to force me to dress like a girl? To an extent, anyway.

Why did it matter so much to them? Neeren knew what I was now, she would move on soon. Me dressing like a girl or boy was of no consequence.

"All this time," said Fedrid, frowning cruelly, "you were training in defense, shaving your head, dressing like a man, and running wild. You should never have done any of it."

The boys holding me were starting to move. I tried to shift but couldn't.

"You're not wanted here as a boy, Shay-*lite*. Though, I doubt anyone will want you as a girl either."

I grunted, pulling at my arms, but it didn't drown out what Fedrid said next.

I felt one of the boys begin to tug at the belt around my tunic. "Actually, you're not wanted here at all, are you? Not even as a Gardener."

Something inside me broke. I almost felt it physically, as if everything inside me, blood, bones, organs, were gone. I was empty, replaced with a seething pain.

I heard myself give a visceral yell behind the hand holding me and bit it. Hard. That boy flew from me, screaming and holding his hand. The other four boys backed away. It didn't stop me from kicking and punching soft flesh without discrimination.

Screams filled the room until the boys were laid out on the floor, clutching limbs and faces.

Fedrid, eyes filling with fear finally came at me, fist pulled to strike.

I brought my palm up first and buried it into his nose.

Blood began pouring out, washing over my hand. He backed away, his nose dripping blood into his mouth and staining his teeth red. There was a rushing in my ears and I thought he was yelling at me, but I couldn't hear it.

I looked down to my hand, covered in his blood.

"—dare you?" Fedrid's voice came back and he brought his fist back once more. He was always so slow. I ducked his blow easily.

I felt my anger now, a boiling rage coursing through my body.

But what had I done? With that rage came a sudden clarity of thought. This hadn't been a life-threatening situation. I had broken the code of non-violence.

Yet still I felt I wanted to rip Fedrid's face in half.

My fingers tightened, and for the briefest moment, I pictured myself pinning Fedrid down, my foot on his chest, him gasping.

What was I doing? I backed out of the room, nearly stumbling over the other boys. Away.

Back to my room. Back to myself. If I stayed, I would do something I'd regret even more.

I rushed into my room, slamming the door, and propped myself up against it. My vision was hazy, and I shook.

"Argggggggh!" I let out the pained noise. It was the most coherent expression I was capable of. What had I done? What had they made me do?

My fingernails scraped the door behind me.

I was the same person. Why did they hate me so much? I did the same things, though more of those were being taken away every day.

I was wrong to have thought this would all go away quickly.

A deep breath didn't help the shaking, but it did make the room before me a little clearer.

I walked slowly to the washroom. As I glimpsed my reflection in the mirror, I saw a haunted face. I ignored that and looked at my hair. It hadn't been shaved recently. I looked for the razor beside my wash-basin, but it was gone. I hadn't even realized Fedrid had taken it, but there was another stashed in my closet.

Finding it, I went back to the mirror, staring at myself. At my skin, the deep brown of it so close to that of the Garden's soil which I was seeing less and less of these days. An upturned nose and mouth that was curved to smile, but at the moment was only pinched in hurt and anger and...and confusion. I looked down at my hands, still shaking slightly.

Maybe if I focused on a normal task, I could calm myself.

I held the rounded razor in my palm and brought it to my scalp, the familiar movement stilling my hand.

I'd shaved my own head since I was five years old. I paused and glanced again at my reflection, thinking of the way other girls wore their hair. Long, usually braided. It looked fine, but it wasn't me. This was me and I wasn't going to change for any of them. I liked me.

I gave myself a determined look and started cutting the small hairs from my head, back down to the way I was supposed to look. I calmed for a moment, before I realized the hand holding the razor was still glazed red. It started to shiver once more and, before I knew, a bright slice of pain shot through me.

A drip of my own blood slid down my face, I'd just barely cut myself. I threw the razor across the washroom, hissing in pain.

It was too much. I couldn't handle even this additional small wound when I felt like I'd been shredded to pieces by accusations, stares, harassment, and my own actions.

I had to get out of here.

∞∞∞

That decision steadied me. I wouldn't leave forever, but I had to get away. Just do something...else.

I walked to the razor where it had slid to one of the walls, bringing it back to the looking glass. I washed my hands thoroughly and splashed water over my face, wiping away the blood and cleaning the cut, which had already clotted.

With practiced movements, I finished shaving, then pulled my dingiest practice tunic and pants from the closet and dressed.

Burrowing further into my closet, I found a small pack I kept treasured belongings in. I poured them out. An earring of my mother's. A stone from the beach that Jevin and I had found, and he'd let me keep. It shone with multiple colors when wet but was dull now. Last was a dead leaf I had taken from one of the plants in the Garden the first day I'd gone in. I hid these behind the clothes of my wardrobe and stuffed an extra tunic, pants, underclothes, razor, a small bag of coins, and a cloak into the pack.

After closing the pack, I sat. Where would I go? I felt my body starting to grow tense, shame trying to fill me.

No. I had to keep ahead of this. Where?

Sunlight glowed on the seagrass rugs covering my floor. The salty, earthy smell of them rose in the warmth. I stared at them, not thinking.

Then, I knew.

The sea.

There were ships that traveled only a little way to move supplies to and from islands nearby.

I stood, decided.

There was a good chance I could catch a ship this very day. I wanted to board one before I lost the nerve.

I tied on a belt, fumbling slightly as my fingers tried to shake again, but I steadied them.

Should I bring Jevin's sword? A picture of the boys I'd just fought, bloody, rose in my mind. And I discarded the thought.

No. No weapons. I had already disgraced myself enough.

If I was ever in real danger, I had my razor, but my bare hands would do as well.

I swallowed painfully, but continued, slinging my pack over a shoulder.

I left the room out my window, allowing it to sway open in the summer breeze.

My father had said I could come back to the Garden in two weeks. Perhaps that was when he would tell me I was no longer welcome there, but I still had those two weeks that I wasn't allowed in. Two weeks where my father would be teaching Jevin the things that should have been mine to learn, but that I'd soon be banned from contemplating.

For now, I would go. And for the first time in far too long, I felt I was headed in the right direction.

14
The Sea

The first thing I noticed about the docks was the sheer amount of people. The second was the strong, lingering scent of fish.

An impatient wind wound its way through the harbor, rattling sails. Because clay was the most readily available and versatile material, it was used to craft most things, including ships. Studying the hushed, grey tone of the vessels, I remembered learning there was a protective coating brushed over the clay to make it waterproof and sturdy.

I knew, as a woman, it would be difficult to board a ship. The fact that I looked like a boy was my only hope at passage. It had worked for sixteen years; now though, I would use it on purpose.

In awe, I looked from one to the next and was immediately drawn to a vessel whose mast and accents were carved with intricate designs. Its name, painted upon it in scrolling script, was 'The Truth Cleaver'. A bit dramatic, but it certainly garnered my attention.

The crew loaded supplies. I was transfixed at how smoothly they passed cargo from one pair of arms to the next. The large men laughed, making rude jokes as they worked.

So absorbed, I nearly leapt from my skin when someone placed a hand on my shoulder.

"You alright there?" It was a boy whose black eyes were beginning to crinkle, amused. He might have been near my own age. He doubled over and began to laugh hysterically. "Scaring you wasn't what I was meaning to do, but you nearly took flight, you jumped so high!" He slapped his knee and straightened up, wiping tears. "I thought you were sick or getting ready to turn into a statue, you stood so still!"

I relaxed from my scare and tried to grin, but found I was a bit thrown-off this stranger had approached me at all. "Ah. I was looking for passage on this ship. Do you know whom I might ask?"

The boy scratched at his hairline, his hair was pulled tightly at the back of his head and braided close to his scalp at either temple. He flung my question away with a wave of his hand, "The Truth Cleaver? Are you headed their way, then?"

I looked back to the ship. "I'm not sure. I simply want to leave Cresstalan for a little while."

"Ey, you don't want a ship like that, then. They cross the rough seas to other lands, much of the time. The crew there's even rougher; unfriendly, you know? What would your name be?"

"My name? It's...Shay."

"Well then, Shay," he tacked his fists onto his hips, "the ship you want is mine!" He slung an arm around my neck and steered me toward the opposite end of the harbor.

We pushed through the thick crowd of people milling from ship to ship. Sailors shouted orders and harsh replies to one another and market stalls called out their wares.

Meanwhile, the boy talked non-stop, pointing to random things on the way. At a vendor selling colorful eels,

"Those ones are to be avoided, I can't stomach 'em myself."

I nodded, wondering if I should still be going along with him. "You know, if money is what you want, I don't have much with me."

He started laughing again, "Me and my crew aren't much for treasure." He stopped and turned me to look straight at him, a mischievous gleam dancing through his eyes. "If honesty's what you're after, here's all. I saw right away you didn't belong here and I thought I knew ye'. Your name what's confirmed it, surely." His smile was wry. "I know you're from the palace and I know what you've done. Gossip's what we got here on the docks and we were here a few weeks ago when your story made the rounds."

Then why did he want me?

"You are, right? You're Shay! The one who's lookin' after the Garden!" He laughed, holding his gut as if it would run away. "You really had 'em going, ey? Such a ruckus they made. I knew I wanted to befriend you there and then! Now you're here, looking for passage on a ship, and I've got one. Can't get more perfect if you're asking!"

My shoulders sagged in relief, perhaps it was a trick, but at least he already knew I was a girl. "I...don't have many friends at the moment, so I won't turn you down. What's your name?"

"Ah, Jet! Jet's what they call me!" He put his arm back around my neck. "Now enough talk! We're setting off too soon and I don't want to be left behind again. Be quick, Shay!"

I was quick and, after squeezing through the remainder of the crowd, we came upon Jet's ship.

I almost left right then. The ship was painted a sour green color and pieces of it were crumbling, scratched, or even broken away. Barnacles coated its hull farther up than I thought they should possibly go and seaweed hung on clotheslines, stretching from the mast to random spots around the deck, perhaps to be eaten later.

The sun on the harsh green paint gave off a sickly glow. None of the other ships had color as this did.

The ship also seemed to be deserted.

Jet finally released my neck and slapped both arms down to his sides. "Now where've they gone?"

At this point I was sure this ship wasn't for me, as outgoing and persistent as Jet was, and I began to sidle away from him, "If they're not here, it's alright. I can find another ship, but thank you, just the same. Perhaps we'll meet again."

Before I could dash away though, he started speaking again, not having heard one word I'd said, "I suppose since it's near high noon they went to get some food. Good idea as we'll be at sea for the next weeks on this venture." He turned to me, wrinkling his nose in disgust. "Between you and me, the next island we'll be visiting isn't too appealing if food's in question." He sighed then straightened up. "Let's you and I go get ourselves something as well, then we'll come back and be off!"

"No need, I reall—"

He began dragging me back toward the food stalls before I could finish my protest.

"Don't worry, I've got coin for the both of us!"

That wasn't the issue and I started to tell him so when he let out a whoop near my ear, startling me into silence.

He waved over near one of the vendors where fillets of smoked fish and golden slices of kira-fruit glistened in the afternoon sun. Around it was a strange group of what must have been sailors as they raised their hands between bites of food to wave back at Jet.

"There's the crew!" he said, grinning widely. "I told you we'd find 'em before long!"

He turned back and started pointing to me enthusiastically. The crew took a minute, squinting in the sunlight, then seemed to recognize me. Looking between themselves, they gestured widely for us to come sit, most wearing friendly smiles.

As Jet brought me forward to them, I wondered what to do in a situation like this. I'd never received such a welcome, not even before the whole of the palace was ignoring me completely.

One of the crew members, a man with shaggy, greying hair reaching to his waist and a round, clean-shaven face, was handing a large portion of fish to Jet who waved me over and pointed animatedly to the food.

I was not in the mood to pass up a free meal. It had been hours since my small, half-hearted breakfast.

Jet patted the bench next to him and motioned for me to sit. After I had, he turned to the man next to him, "Clare, this is Shay. Shay, Clare." Without another word he tore into his piece of fish.

I nodded to Clare, unsure of what to say, but he began talking quickly, "You are the girl who pretended she was a boy for so long, are you not?"

Even though I hadn't exactly been pretending, I didn't want to go into it and simply nodded, beginning to eat the piece of fish Jet had torn for me from his own.

"Ah. That was an interesting story, I grant you. I don't know why you did it, but if it was to be interesting, you certainly succeeded in your goal," Clare continued.

I hurried to swallow my fish and coughed out a "Thank you." It came out quiet. Clare's comment seemed a strange one to make.

A woman with violet eyes and braids cropped to her shoulders jumped into the conversation, "So was Jet, here, walking you around the marketplace and showing you our ship and all? He's been wandering the docks every time we stopped at this port for weeks, hoping to run into you. Says you ought to be friends."

I turned to look at Jet who let out a small groan, then continued to eat his fish as though nothing had happened.

"My name is Mercully," the woman said, extending a calloused hand for me to shake. "I'm the captain of 'The Sea's Ribbon'."

I shook her hand. Not only a woman sailor, a woman captain.

"Sorry, 'The Sea's Ribbon'?" I was missing something, "What is that?"

Jet shoved me in the shoulder, "Shay, that's our ship, don't tell me you didn't even look at the name. I went and painted it myself!"

I'd been too distracted by the green coat of paint to notice the ship's title, but I just nodded. "Good to meet you, Captain. Jet said I might be able to gain passage aboard your ship. Is that possible?"

Captain Mercully narrowed her eyes at Jet as the rest of the crew looked to her warily. "We'd have a might load of work for you, should you do that. Gold isn't something I need, but extra hands are welcome. We leave within the hour if you're set on it."

I thought again of Fedrid's bloodied nose. This seemed my best option.

"That won't be a problem."

She shifted her eyes from side to side, seeming to hesitate for a second, but then, "Very well, Shay. Welcome to the crew."

I smiled, small at first, then grinned widely. I remembered how the Court Reader had said my fate would come to me easily.

Jet swallowed the last bite of his meal then grabbed me by the shoulders and shook me back and forth, welcoming me with the others. Even Jevin was not this familiar with me. I felt my cheeks warm at the crew's instant acceptance. I was still wary, it was hard to believe they could be sincere when almost everyone else I knew had been shunning me for weeks.

I snuck looks around the table every now and then as I ate, this group of people seemed an odd mix. A number of ages, though Jet seemed the youngest. There was even another woman. She didn't seem to talk as much as the other members of the crew.

When we finished our meal, Captain Mercully stood, slapped her hands on the table, and barked out, "Let's move, crew!" She turned and set off towards the ship.

Everyone stood, stretching and rubbing their stomachs after the meal, then followed Mercully to the ship. I stuck close to Jet.

He laughed a little, "Mercully was right, I'd been searching for you for weeks. But see then, we did become fast friends! You coming on as part of the crew for a spell was more than I'd measured though. Couldn't have worked out better!"

He was smiling wider than I thought was possible. His enthusiasm sincerely caught me off guard.

I nodded. "Do you know how long this expedition is supposed to last?"

"Ey, it's a short one. Not more than a fortnight, only meeting four islands of the ring. Not to worry!"

Arriving back at 'The Sea's Ribbon', I stretched to look at the putrid-colored ship, noticing her name painted in what attempted to be fancy lettering along the back. I pulled the straps of my pack up, preparing to travel further than I'd ever gone.

Something that felt akin to laughter shimmered inside me and I started after Jet who was running forward, already halfway up the gangplank.

15
Sickness

Two hours into the journey and I was rethinking my eagerness. The wind blew with malice against the sea, kneading it mercilessly. My stomach seemed to be outraged at the sea's mistreatment and emptied my lunch in protest.

I clung to the edge of the ship, watching the small black mass that was Cresstalan fade into the distance. I hoped its stillness would still my sickness. More spit pooled under my tongue however, and peace was not mine just yet.

Every few minutes one of the crew members would come over to pat my back, laughing and telling of how they first got sick on a ship. They would then return to their duties. I wasn't well enough to dwell upon distinguishing them and time flew by.

Finally, it grew dark and the sea became calm. I wasn't entirely better, but as I had nothing in my stomach left to lose, everything settled down. I'd set myself against the railing of the ship on the deck and was blandly staring at nothing when two bare feet appeared in front of me.

I looked up to see Jet grinning too grandly for how terrible I was feeling.

"Good first day?" he asked, handing me a small cup of water.

I took it with both hands, holding onto it as though it were the most precious thing in this world, and drank the tiniest sip. My insides didn't object so I took another and quietly rasped out a, "Thank you."

Jet laughed and plopped down next to me, letting out a sigh. "Ey, don't worry too much though. Most of us started off on the ship as you were today. Of course, it goes on its way and soon you like the waves more than the dirt of the land, to be sure."

I nodded slightly, still not feeling that I should talk too much.

"Why, I was sick three weeks before things settled, nearly got off at each and every port. 'Course, I had nowhere else to go."

I nodded again, trying to keep listening as he talked. My head seemed to stretch side-to-side.

"Perhaps you should go and get to sleep."

I shook my head. Although I was feeling a little better, I didn't want to go beneath the deck. I thought it might provoke further sickness.

Jet got up and walked away. I didn't know how I could have offended him, but another wave of nausea washed over me, and I buried my forehead into my arm, hoping to steady myself.

A couple minutes later I felt a soft, warm blanket being thrown over me. I looked up at Jet.

"I'm sure you don't want to listen to me prattle on while your insides are squirming about, so I'll leave you with this and be on my way."

I smiled a little and Jet began walking, then turned back once more, "The sickness will pass, and there's where the adventure begins! You'll live."

I let out a laugh that sounded more like a croak then rested my cheek against the blanket which, though it smelled slightly musty, kept the chilling air from me and stilled my stomach once again.

✆✆✆

I woke to a sky just beginning to light up in the east. Grey dawn chasing away the deep black and blue of the night sky.

My knees were pulled to my chest as I huddled under the blanket, staring at the stars slowly winking out as a blush rose where the sun neared.

Somewhere below the deck a clanging bell rang out, causing a series of what sounded like muffled curses.

I began to stir, careful to move slowly. The ship's rocking was hardly noticeable now, though I still felt fairly weak. I folded the blanket, setting it to the side to return to Jet, and gazed out to the open sea.

Orange blazed in the distance, lighting the clouds across the sky and, a moment later, the very top of the sun eased itself over the horizon.

I let out a breath and smiled to myself before two familiar hands grasped my shoulders, suddenly, but gently. It seemed I was getting used to this tactic of Jet's because I hardly flinched and turned to him, still smiling.

"Ah! Feeling better I see." He rubbed his hands together. "Good. Then since you didn't work yesterday, you can go on and help me prepare breakfast!"

That seemed fair. "Yes, sir. Lead the way." I motioned for him to move forward.

Jet laughed, "Ey, I don't like being called 'sir'. We're informal around here, you know. Jet's the way to address me and I like it fine. Come on, then!"

We went below deck.

It was odd being in a place that seemed so casual about titles and rank, and even traditional duties of gender. I, myself, had never had to bow down to too many people with my high position in the palace. I'd thought it would be fun to have the tables turned, to be the novice, the lowly ranked. However, being seen as an equal might mean that I could truly connect with these people.

I realized, briefly, that I was hardly missing Jevin. Perhaps Jet's larger than life personality was keeping me distracted. I decided to let it, and followed him into the cramped quarters that served as a kitchen.

There was a small, round window flung open to the sea. From here, the horizon went up and down a little more than it had above, and I calmly turned away from the window.

"Right." Jet slapped his chest, then looked at a loss. "Ey, I forgot that we only have one set of meal-ware per sailor." He shrugged. "Ah, you can share with me 'til next port."

Not sure how well that would work, I asked, "What are we making for breakfast?" I'd never cooked a meal in my life. I hoped we weren't making anything too difficult. Though I didn't see how we could be, considering our surroundings.

"Ey, it's easy today. We'll just arrange plates more than cook. It'll be dried seaweed, smoked fish from the market, and sour fruit tea. That'll keep sickness at bay."

This was a meal I frequently gathered for myself. After filling each plate, we distributed them to the sailors beginning their morning duties.

Captain Mercully was already at the ship's helm steering us forward. Jet placed a plate in her hands and she sat onto a small stool holding the wheel of the ship in place with her foot.

Clare was shifting a sail and we waited a moment for him to finish. I got to formally meet the other sailors as well.

There were twelve in all, not including Jet. It would take more time than this to learn all their names, I could tell.

Jet conversed with them ridiculously fast and our introductions were cut off more than half of the time.

A slightly sailor, cleaning bird droppings off the deck, was named Wilhelm. One of his eyes was focused off to the side. He seemed the quickest to laugh. I knew this because Jet kept making terrible jokes to each of the crew members. Clearly, they were used to this and most just rolled their eyes and started into their meals, but Wilhelm snorted a little and bits of his food came flying out as he laughed at Jet's joking.

The other woman sailor was named Sseya. I was still a bit shocked to see the women working right alongside the men. I guess I was right that not all women wanted to stay cooped up inside to sew. These women reminded me of myself, how I should like to be, with hands calloused and arms corded with muscle.

Thinking back to the docks, I realized I hadn't seen any other women sailors. I wondered if there were any female captains besides Mercully. I grinned to myself, surely this had been the right ship to board. These people knew I was a girl and it didn't faze them in the least. They had hardly mentioned it.

I looked over to Jet, talking animatedly to Sseya whose hair was combed straight out from her scalp and rounded about her head. She also wore many pieces of gold jewelry. There was a ring in her nose linking to an ear-piercing and many other piercings forming dotted designs on her face. She seemed good-natured enough but was certainly more reserved than Mercully.

Jet was laughing. I'd thought I would choose a ship to board, but I was glad that Jet had chosen me instead. Though the trip had started off roughly, I was feeling better, and the air whistling through the sails struck up a hunger in me.

When we finished passing out everyone else's meals, Jet and I found a crate in the middle of the ship and sat on it cross-legged, our breakfast on Jet's plate between us.

"So," said Jet between bites, "tell me all the secrets of the great Garden. I've been dying to know each and every one."

I looked at him, catching a piece of fish as it almost slipped from my wide mouth. Did he really expect me to expel the secrets I'd been charged with? Worked my whole life to protect?

Jet started laughing, "I was only kidding you! Ey, I know you can't tell me. I've got a number of secrets of mine own. Just wanted to jest a bit, see?"

I laughed myself, shaking my head, and began eating a piece of dried seaweed. "I thought you only wanted me for my secrets for a moment there, Jet."

Jet sighed, "Ey, it's nice that you know my name already! Now we can be off toward adventure and all!"

The wind brushed by.

"It's good you found me. I do like this ship."

"Even with the force-empty of your stomach yesterday?"

I waved a hand, "I've gone through worse and lived. At least I was sick merely a day."

"When I was sick for those first three weeks," Jet said, shoving food into his mouth, "I was six. Could barely help myself. The crew took care of me well though, Clare more than any other. They're a good group. I've been with them more than ten year now."

16
The Sea's Ribbon

On the third night of our voyage to Klieton, two members of the crew, Fekk and Antan, brought out a game.

They flicked through cards so lightning-fast I couldn't follow.

Besides Jet and myself, there were four others gathered, Clare, Wilhelm, Sen, and Dimny.

Though Fekk wore loose dreadlocks and Antan had his head shaved, their faces were so alike I thought they must be twins.

"What is this game?" I asked Jet.

"Ey," he said, tearing his eyes away from the cards flying from hand to hand, "it's There and Yon'. We play it many nights, though there's none plays so fast as Fekk and Antan. They showed it to our crew in the first place."

Sen let out a large laugh as Antan took half of Fekk's cards.

Jet's head spun back to the action, but he continued, "We'll have you play next, Shay. Got to learn There and Yon' if you're to be one of the crew."

Within seconds, the game had ended, Antan gaining the remaining cards and flipping them smartly under

Fekk's nose.

Fekk good-naturedly knocked them from his twin's hand and the other sailors were discussing whom was to play next.

"It's Shay next, as she's got to learn!" said Jet loudly. The others nodded avidly, "And who's to play her?"

"I've decided it's my turn," said Dimny.

He took the deck and began shuffling it skillfully. I wasn't so sure he was the best to play against in my first match.

"I'm not sure what to do," I said quietly to Jet.

"I'll help you, but don't expect to win first time out, there. Here, these are your cards," he said, picking up the pile Dimny had dealt me.

Dimny was already whisking his cards through his palm, separating them into different piles.

"Look through now," said Jet, "You'll lay the cards one over the other in turns whence you begin. As you saw before, you'd like all to be yours. If you win the pile here, you get the whole of it. Sea cards are laid over flame, flame over earth, earth over air, and air over sea. When you can do no more of this hand, you'll concede the pile to Dimny."

"And," said Antan, sidling up, "whoever wins best two of the first three piles gets half the other's cards. After the fifth, whoever has the most cards takes the lot."

I understood, but I felt my brow furrow to keep track of it.

Clearly this was not Dimny's first game, however. Taking a lot of time to remember which card was to go over the others, I only won one pile and lost all the others.

Jet clapped me on the back, laughing, "You'll get it!"

"My turn next!" said Sen.

I moved out of his way, happy to let someone else play instead, and he took his place across from Dimny.

After a fast game, with much shouting for either side of the match, Sen won, "Heh! Still can't beat me, Dimny!"

Dimny got up onto his knees, leaned across the space between them, and kissed Sen full on the mouth.

I felt my jaw drop in response.

"Wouldn't want to anyway, Sen," said Dimny, gathering the cards now as though nothing had happened.

I felt a finger under my chin as Jet pushed my jaw back up to its place. I looked over to him, his face open in a silent laugh.

Looking around then, I saw no one else was phased, they'd gone back to arguing amongst one another about who was to play Sen next.

Was two men kissing something that was commonly done outside the palace? I'd never seen or heard anything that would suggest that. I'd never even thought of it.

Jet lightly punched me in the shoulder and pointed to the new game that had started for me to keep watching.

Wilhelm beat Sen and I felt my cheeks warm as Sen went to sit close to Dimny. After a few more rounds everyone was growing tired, and we went our separate ways to settle down for the night.

Jet and I went to the prow of the ship to watch as we coursed through the night.

"Didn't expect that, eh?" he said as we sat on a woven crate.

My cheeks felt like fire now. The only time I had even seen anyone kiss was once when I was eleven and walked into the pantry to find two of the kitchen staff at it. "I've never seen two men like that," I said warily.

"Ey, we've had a few couples like them board our ship. It isn't strictly accepted, you must know. Why, we had two women once too who were in love like Sen and Dimny. If they're found out, it seems they have a difficult time finding a place in the world. Mercully doesn't mind though. Seems to me, if they like each other, there's no need for them to be apart."

I was silent for a bit, thinking, then, "In the palace at

Cresstalan, the people we fall in love with are decided for us with marriage readings. Do other places not have that?"

Jet bobbed his head back and forth, "I think they do, but many have done away with it. Especially with sailing life. You need to be in one spot with a set number of people for marriage reading to work, and Readers seem more scarce by the day."

"So, the crew is able to marry whomever they please? Even if they're a man or woman, the same as the other person?"

"Aye, I think it'd work that way," said Jet. "Only, we never stop long in one place and are so busy that romance doesn't cross our minds often."

I nodded, then faded to silence.

Jet and I went to bed after that and I lay thinking far into the night.

Two men or two women could be together in some places of the world.

I uncomfortably turned my inner thoughts to myself. Was that why I'd never wanted to marry anyone? I hadn't known it was an option to be with women.

But as I considered that possibility, I knew it was wrong. I'd never had those thoughts about anyone, be they a man or a woman. No one I could think of had ever made me feel that I wanted to be near them and only them, especially in so intimate a way.

I shifted in my hammock, the sound of snoring filled the cabin where we all slept.

Closing my eyes, I let out a tense breath. I had no idea what I wanted. It wasn't Jevin, nor was it anyone else in the palace.

The only hope I had was that I'd find some answers on this strange adventure I'd set myself on.

17
Klieton

Our first stop was Klieton. The water was a clear aqua-blue as we sailed into the harbor.

I'd heard very little about this particular island, only that Jet wasn't fond of the food and the inhabitants weren't overly friendly.

The second part seemed true enough, as there was no one at the docks when we landed. There was one open air building nearby and no market. The building was more of an empty shack and wind whistled dully through it as we passed.

White hills rose softly behind the building, and further still were sheer cliffs of red rock. I stared, mesmerized. I had never seen rock of that color, it seemed painted.

"Where are all the people?" I asked Jet, whom I was surprised to see turning cartwheels alongside me. He popped up the right way and flashed a grin.

"Uh, uh, uh," he said, wagging a finger in front of my nose until I slapped it away lightly. "Can't give away the best part of Klieton! It's all I've got for you now!" He wiggled his eyebrows at me and ran forward, punching one of the other sailors, a man named Fernt, gently on the arm and talking to him animatedly.

I was unsure how an eerie lack of people could be the best part of a place.

The crew followed Mercully to the tall cliff ahead.

When we neared the base, I gazed up the sheer side rising above me and felt a strange sense of vertigo at its height. I looked back down and followed the crew to a beautifully carved doorway leading into darkness.

There was a guard stationed, but none of the crew was stopped as we went by. He was halfway through a bowl of something that must have been his lunch. Jet made a face as we passed, then smiled back to me.

We entered a firelit city. Dwellings carved straight from the cliff were revealed. Roadways and courtyards settled between the buildings, orange lamps lighting it all. The whole place was empty.

The crew had been laughing a moment ago but hushed abruptly.

Jet fell back to my side. "It's true the docks are always without a crowd, but something's wrong if the city's the same. It's usually rousing with people."

Everything was hushed and still. More than half the oil lamps in this area weren't lit.

"Where do you think the people a—"

A silhouette appeared from the shadows. It seemed to be someone sitting in a chair, and they beckoned to Mercully.

She went forward, commanding the rest of us to stay put with a wave of her hand.

Jet frowned, it seemed he had wanted to go along.

They talked for a moment in hushed tones. The person said something and Mercully brought her hand up to her forehead, kneading her brow.

The other person somehow disappeared into the shadows.

Mercully returned, shoulders slightly hunched. "They don't need our shipment. The whole place has gone into hiding." She shook her head. "There was a fire started on Klieton's shore. It was swiftly put out, but the people retreated right away. They won't see anyone, it seems."

"Stars," said Clare quietly.

She sighed. "We'll have to move on to Morroy Isle. I've been told we can stay on the beach here, but only for the night. They don't want any outsiders near the settlement." Her shoulders back once again, she strode forward. "Let's be off."

The crew was wary as we left. I turned once more to look at the carved, abandoned city.

"C'mon, Shay," said Jet, "Things of this nature have become more common. It's not unexpected."

"Where would they have gone to hide?" I asked. Somehow a whole island of people had been able to disappear.

"If I could say, they wouldn't be hiding well, eh?"

"Ey, you two!" Jet and I turned to find Clare waving us over. He held up a few canvas sacks that were stained with purple blotches. "I was going to go and gather some of the fruits of this island. I know you'll be wanting to as well, Jet. Would you like to come along, Shay?"

I looked to Jet who nodded avidly. "Sure. I'll help."

The three of us broke off from the rest of the group and Jet leapt ahead to lead the way. "The fruits of this island are klie-fruit, they stay ripe only for a few weeks and go for a good price. We'll go about trading some and eat the rest!"

"Aye, they are quite delicious, to be sure," said Clare.

"The crew'll be happy to have them this evening meal," Jet said enthusiastically, turning around and walking backwards so he could talk with us.

I found Clare was quite talkative as well. He told us a story from when he was young as we walked. "And I didn't know exactly how big a tutter fish was at the time, of course. The ship I was serving on was a little smaller than 'The Sea's Ribbon'. Anyway, we were next to a pod of them. I was mesmerized." He raised his hands to the sky, spreading them widely. "Biggest fish I'd ever seen. Thought they couldn't have been real and I called the whole crew over. I thought, perhaps, they had been enchanted. I enjoyed hearing far-fetched tales at the time and thought I was in one. The crew laughed and, of course, now I've seen them many times. Still interesting creatures."

I didn't really understand. I'd rarely seen sea-creatures, and nothing so large as what he was describing.

There was something else that was bothering me, and I decided to ask about it rather than inquire further about tutter fish.

"Why is the ship called 'The Sea's Ribbon'?"

Jet looked like he was about to tell me, his eyes lighting up, but Clare answered first, "Because she makes the sea more beautiful by being on it. Decorates the sea like a ribbon."

I didn't know how to respond to this, thinking of the ship's sickly color.

I simply said, "Ah," and left it there.

Klie-fruit grew on some kind of succulent. Each was an oval the size of my hand and balanced upon long, skinny stalks sprouting from the low plants.

From where we stood, I could smell the rich, sweetly fragrant fruit.

"Hooo," Clare let out a sigh, wiping his face, already red and dripping with sweat. Today was our warmest yet. "I suppose we should get along with it before it gets any more warm."

"Right, Clare. We're on it. C'mon, Shay."

A bird flitted off as we approached the plants, its beak

purple from a half-torn fruit, but the rest were still intact.

The klie-fruit swayed on the stalks, dark purple in color with a waxy skin.

Jet reached out and picked one, twisting speedily to remove it. A bit of the juice came out and dribbled down the stalk.

"Have you had one of these, Shay?"

I'd never seen klie-fruit before this. "I don't believe so."

"Can't say I'm surprised. Don't keep long. They're not to be missed, however, when visitin' Klieton."

He stuck his thumbs into the bottom of the fruit where it'd been removed from its plant. It seemed to split in half quite easily and more juice ran down Jet's hands.

"Put out your palm, there." He put one of the halves forward to me.

Clare plucked his own from the plant and began on it in the same way.

As I took the half, Jet shoved his own into his mouth. His cheeks bulged as he chewed it slowly, somehow still able to smile.

I copied him, putting the piece of fruit wholly into my mouth.

Clare rolled his eyes and simply took a small bite.

It was delicious, the flavor bursting in my mouth. An odd mixture, the skin waxy and the inside quite smooth, it somehow worked wonderfully together. The taste was at once slightly floral and like that of the sweetest renn-berries. There was also something deeper I couldn't place that offset the sweetness.

Jet finished chewing and swallowed. Then licked his thumbs with a smack, getting the remaining juice. "And?" he said, his eyes twinkling.

"Delicious," I said, gulping down the last bite.

"They're good, they are. Here." He took two of the canvas bags from Clare, who was eating the last of his own fruit, and handed one to me.

I saw now the bags were stained with juice from this fruit, they must be only used for gathering it.

"Let's go get them then." Jet turned, picking more klie-fruit in an instant, pulling some stalks together and grabbing three at once. He yelled back to me as he kept working, "Shay, make sure to leave ones that aren't yet purple. Only the ripe ones are what we'll be wanting."

"Alright." I reached across to the middle of one of the broad-leaved plants and twisted a fruit. It broke off easily and I placed it into the canvas bag.

The plants were plentiful, stopping only when the soil got too sandy farther ahead.

Clare had started gathering as well. I was concentrating on getting a fruit from the middle of a particularly large plant, and almost fell face-forward into it, when Clare let out a yelp.

I regained my balance and rushed over to where Clare had been.

"Is it some sort of sink hole?" I heard Jet say and came upon them to find Clare waist-deep in a place where the ground seemed to have fallen away.

"Help me now, you two," said Clare, holding his hands out for us to grab.

Jet and I each took one, pulling with vigor to hoist him from the hole.

More dirt fell away and we were just able to get Clare back up safely.

Standing back, the three of us eyed what was now revealed. On the edge of the grouping of succulents where we'd plucked the fruit was broken ground.

The oblong hole led to a small, barely visible, wall of stacked rocks.

They were large and below ground-level. How could there be a grouping like that here? For what purpose?

None of us said anything until Jet asked, "Clare, is your foot alright?"

I looked down, seeing Clare had his left foot raised gingerly.

"I believe a small rock fell onto it, but I'll be fine."

Jet tilted his head. "I'd say we have enough fruit, and these rocks don't seem to want us bothering them. Shall we head back?"

Clare and I agreed.

Jet started toward the shore, his sack of fruit slung over his shoulder.

We followed, Clare seeming fine walking on his foot.

"Are you sure you're alright?" I asked Clare.

"Ey, no need to worry, let's enjoy resting for the next piece of the day."

18
The Cliff

We lay on the beach for the next few hours, napping through the hottest part of the day.

When Clare woke, he seemed much better, claiming his foot hardly hurt.

Jet had rested a little, but was now moving from person to person, talking animatedly. Finally, he made his way back to my side.

"Shay."

"Hmmm?" I said, lost in watching the waves meet the shore again and again.

"Want to go over now and climb the cliff with me?"

"Climb the cliff?" I'd only seen the giant red cliff earlier, surely that wasn't the one he meant. I hadn't ever climbed more than small rocks.

"I'm not saying we climb the whole of it, of course. There's a spot quite low with a wondrous view of the sun's setting."

It seemed he did mean the red cliff. I looked back, able to see it from here, and shrugged, "I'll try."

"There we are!" said Jet, clapping his hands joyfully. "The red cliffs are only here on Klieton!" He turned to the crew-members lounging nearby, "We're going to climb the cliffs in the case you're searching for us later."

Clare and Wilhelm waved their hands in acknowledgement. Sseya was sleeping nearby and went on snoring lightly.

I brushed the sand from my pants and joined Jet, already on his way.

As we went, he started asking me a stream of questions. "Besides Cresstalan, have you been to the islands of the ring?"

"No. I never had a reason to leave the palace, really." I thought for a moment, "In fact, hardly anyone who lives there strays far. Except, perhaps, the guards."

"Why leave then?" Jet's dark eyes were bright with curiosity.

I hesitated, "You told me you heard what happened at the palace. About who I was...well, whom people thought I was pretending to be."

We picked our feet up higher, stepping through some low bushes.

"Ey, yeah. I thought it was quite remarkable, there."

I smiled softly. "No one else thought that way. Hardly anyone would talk to me after they found out I was a girl."

A small frown appeared on Jet's face.

"It didn't get better for some weeks and soon I decided I wanted to take a break from that life for a while."

"You decided hopping upon a ship was your answer?"

"Just for a short time, but yes." I remembered the fight I'd had before I left, the blood staining Fedrid's teeth. "I truly had to get away. So, I did." Fedrid had been wrong though. "I think I made the right choice coming here."

"Well, ey, we're happy to have you! Seems strange they were so against you."

I shrugged, not knowing what to say. I agreed. I understood a little why people might be mad, at least why Neeren might be, but it still didn't explain everything.

Jet squinted at the sky, "I suppose people get angry when they have to go about changing their minds over something."

"That could be it," I laughed.

He asked countless other questions, mostly of mundane things, such as my favorite food. I said pastries of most sorts, though smoked kenn-fish was a close second. Soon we were back at the cliffs.

Jet looked to the sun nearing the horizon. "We'll have to be quick about it. Sun's nearly below eyes' reach." Jet looked to me. "Mind you, Shay," he grabbed at a handhold in the cliff face, "place your hands and feet where I place my own and you'll have no trouble."

"Alright." I was nervous to climb so soon before the sun would be gone.

I marked where Jet placed his hands as he climbed, then let my eyes travel further up the rock face, feeling slightly light-headed as I beheld the steep face of the cliff. But it was lit boldly by the sun and glowed a warm red-orange. There were many holes, most filled with nesting seabirds and some only with remnants of nests.

Jet was another level up now, his feet in notches as well. He seemed headed for a large hollow, cut into the rock.

"Hurry now, Shay. Not many chunks of light left." He was about halfway to our destination.

Though worried I wouldn't be able to pull myself up as he had, I gripped the first handholds. The rough rock beneath my hands was easy to grasp. As I went, using a few different spots than Jet had chosen, as the reach was easier, I caught up to him before he arrived at the ledge.

I knocked on his boot, calling attention, and his eyes widened as he stretched his neck down and around to see me. "Thought you had no experience climbin' cliffs, Madam Gardener." He seemed about to laugh.

Too proud of my surprise cliff-climbing abilities to worry about being called a Gardener for the first time in too long, I smiled. "I don't, but I do train my arms while sparring with Jev—Jevin. My friend." Remembering how I'd left Jevin without a word, I faltered, hoping he wasn't worried. But I waved the thoughts away. "So, I suppose that helped."

"Impressive!" He looked upwards once again. "We're nearly there so don't fault me for going slower than you might!"

After a few more movements, he hoisted himself onto the rock shelf, throwing his legs over and sitting back. "Your turn!" He peered over the ledge.

Exactly a second later, I was lifting myself up the rock lip as well.

"Well done!"

I sat beside Jet now, awed with our view. The sea wasn't blocked by anything. Though it had been that way on the ship, sitting in the middle of the giant red cliff while watching the orange-painted sea was better. The seabirds were taking a few more rounds of flight before night rose and they squealed with delight, turning circles before us.

"This is beautiful," I said, not wanting to blink for fear of missing a single second of the stunningly lit moment. "How did you find this place?"

"Ah," Jet smirked. "just exploring. The best of it is what I'll show next though. But that's after the sun leaves us."

I laughed. Jet was always hiding little secrets so people could be slightly more delighted with them as they were revealed. Though expected from him, I wished he would tell me things right away instead.

The sun lowered, the birds soared, and soon the fire of it all dipped into the sea, only a brilliant glow lighting the sky.

"Right."

The cliff continued above us, so Jet had to stay hunched over when he stood. He began walking to the back of the cavity we sat in.

About five feet behind us, there was a small door situated, painted the same color as the rock.

Jet pushed on the door and it opened, revealing a black square of darkness leading directly into the heart of the cliff.

19
Disappearing City

Jet brought a finger to his lips and disappeared into the darkness. I watched the short tail of his hair melt away and followed him.

After the first patch of light at the doorway, the black was complete. I felt suspended in the darkness, somehow enfolded in it.

He wasn't talking, so I didn't either. This must be an easier way to get down rather than having to descend the cliff face when the sun's light had gone.

I felt Jet's hand tap my shoulder, urging me to stop, then heard him fumble with something in front of him.

There was a grinding sound and a sliver of light appeared, growing larger as Jet opened what had been another door in front of him.

A dimly lit flight of stairs led downward, an oil lamp halfway down to show the way. Jet continued with silent steps.

I followed just as quietly and heard a sound rising below us. A distant, constant thunder that did not end as thunder should.

Jet must have heard it too. "Shay, would you put the lamp out?"

Without fully thinking, I directed my hand backwards and put it out from a few feet away using the Garden mindset. Too late, I realized it shouldn't be done in front of Jet, who knew nothing of the power of the Garden, but he hadn't seen.

After my eyes adjusted, I saw there was still a faint light illuminating the bottom of the stairs. The carved stone hallway took a sharp turn to the right.

Jet took the last few steps and hesitantly wound his head around the corner, bringing it back a moment later, his finger once again on his lips. He tiptoed forward, and I followed.

The reason I had to be silent was before us. A guard stationed here as there had been outside the main entrance to the city. He sat in a chair in the middle of the carved stone walkway, one lamp lit beside him. He was dead asleep.

Just past the guard was another door. Jet began sneaking towards it. Though the man before us was sound asleep, I was hesitant to walk so close to him. It was clear we didn't have permission to be here.

As Jet was directly in front of the guard, the man jolted upright in his chair, his eyes obviously about to open.

It was one second, the guard about to wake, and Jet looked to me with widened eyes. I had just put out the other lamp, so that perhaps explained my quick action.

Before the guard's eyes might have opened, I extended my hand and, with that same knowing I'd practiced all these years, let the lamp beside the guard go out without a sputter. With that one small movement, we fell into darkness. The flame, Jet, and the guard were gone, though Jet's jaw had dropped slightly as I'd dropped my hand downward.

I didn't dare breathe. The only sound in the blackness was a rasping, "What?" and a groan as the guard must have realized the lamp was out. It sounded like he was rising from his chair and I felt Jet move back into me, getting out of the guard's way.

"Knew I should have brought a tinder stick with me. Knew I should have brought more oil," the guard grumbled. I heard his rough steps upon the rock floor and a slapping sound as if he braced himself against a wall.

Jet reached over as the door opened, filling the hallway with light, and grabbed hold of my hand. I flinched slightly as he touched me, but then held tighter, worried the guard would look back and see us. We backed against the wall as much as possible.

The man didn't turn. We waited a moment for him to clear the area near the door, then exited quickly, Jet let go of my hand and we left the small hallway to walk into a cavernous atrium.

The large space was filled with people.

The hidden people of Klieton, I assumed. I raised my head to look at the ceiling, but it disappeared into darkness beyond large chandeliers which lit the space.

Jet slid into the crowd and we weren't noticed. I did my best to follow.

He leaned back and spoke to me, "Wasn't too sure if they'd be here. Found this place when I explored the cliffs. Always been dark and empty though." Jet met my eyes, and this was the first time I'd seen him hesitant, "How did you go and douse the guard's lamp?"

I didn't think I should tell him of the mindset. "I—it's not really important." I looked warily at all the people surrounding us. "Anyone could do it, I don't think we should talk about it here th—" I blinked as a drop of chilled water splashed onto my nose from somewhere above. I looked up, confused.

"Right," Jet agreed. "Oh, and it did that here before," he

said as I brushed the water from my nose. "Drips an awful lot."

Jet scanned the crowd.

Most were eating dinner from small bowls, many were stretched out on grass mats, resting. There were also people milling about or standing, talking to one another.

Jet walked along the wall, I thought he was looking for something. "I have a friend here abouts in Klieton," he said, "I want to find her. Think it was her speaking earlier to Mercully."

"Ah," I said.

So that'd been Jet's purpose. I was wanting more information as well. Surely a simple fire wouldn't send an entire city into hiding.

We made our way around the great room and Jet's head turned suddenly. "There she is!" He went to the opposite wall, stepping between and around the people in the way of his destination.

I nodded my head in apology to those we disturbed, but no one seemed troubled.

Jet made straight for a girl sitting in a wheeled chair ahead of us. I recognized her as the silhouette I'd seen earlier. She had a bowl of food on her lap and was eating with a small group.

We were close enough that Jet spoke, "Narsha!" to her.

She looked around with surprise as she beheld Jet. Recovering quickly, she motioned for him to go to a spot near the wall, clear of people.

We made for the space. I looked back to see the girl backing out of the gathered circle.

I'd only seen one other person in a wheeled chair. The King of Cresstalan before he had passed away. He'd been injured severely, not even able to push himself around in the gilded seat that bore him.

This girl, however, was in no way hampered. She maneuvered thorough the crowd as easily as Jet and I had.

She used her hands to grab the wheels and roll forward without strain. The chair looked heavy and I thought how very strong she must be.

Finally, we got to the spot she'd designated.

"Jet!" she said, still startled to see him, but lowered her voice, "What are you doing here?"

"We didn't get much information from you, so I wanted to come find out for myself what's happened."

She let out a sigh, "So, of course you used the cliff entrance. I'll have to notify the guards to look after it better."

"That you will. 'Course I'm glad you didn't 'til now so I can get some answers." He cocked his head, grinning. "Do you have any for me?"

The girl smiled for the first time, grudgingly. I thought she was perhaps a few years older than us and she wore a light green dress of delicate material. Her hair was in braids and twisted on either side of her head in a loose style.

"Only things you'll find out soon enough."

The bowl in her lap contained soup and she began eating it, then spoke to us, "We're not exactly sure what is happening, at least as far as I've heard." She swallowed another spoonful of her meal. "It seems there have been minor attacks on multiple islands over the past few days."

"Attacks?" I couldn't help speaking in my surprise.

Narsha looked over to me when I spoke. "Who is this?" she directed at Jet, nodding to me, then scraping her bowl to finish the meal.

"This here is Shay. She's with our crew."

The girl looked up, tracing her eyes over me, taking in my shaved head and male clothing, but said nothing.

Jet turned to me, "And here," he said, gesturing to the girl, "we have Narsha. She oversees shipments when we arrive here."

Narsha nodded.

"What are these attacks about? What is it they've been doing? Who is it?" Jet asked.

Narsha sighed, "Things stolen, fires lit, and ships taken over." She shook her head. "We've only had the small fire, but at least three other islands have dealt with it. We have enough supplies to hold us over for a while and...," she narrowed her eyes at Jet, "we *should* be safe here. We don't know who the attackers are though. That's why we decided to hide."

She glanced around the hall. "You both need to leave. I'm glad to have seen you on this round, Jet, but you can't be here. I don't have more information." She met Jet's eyes, "You and your shipmates should be wary though, watch out for attacking ships. From what I've heard, at least two ships have been struck and looted. No one killed, but who knows what the purpose of all this is. Don't stay in one place for long."

Jet nodded. "We'll keep our eyes wide, Narsha. Thank you."

Narsha pointed to a place in the wall. "The door is just past there. No one is guarding it from this side, but should you run into anyone, simply tell them you forgot something from your home. You know the alternate exit out to the front of the cliff, Jet."

She began to wheel away, not looking back.

"Goodbye, Narsha," said Jet.

She waved back, subtly.

We found the exit and left without issue. The noise of the hall deadened as we shut the door behind us and walked into the dim city. There were a few lamps lighting the narrow street. Buildings rose on either side of us, carefully carved from the rock. The dwellings themselves were dark, windows here and there yawning in shadow. Though we weren't outside, the space around us rose so high we could have been if it was a moonless, starless night.

Our steps were strangely muffled in the cavern as we walked along the rock floor.

I thought on what Narsha told us. Someone had been attacking the islands. I wondered if Cresstalan had been attacked as well. The Great Tree should keep it safe though. Then again, the Tree was supposed to protect the whole of our island ring. That was its purpose.

Twenty years ago, however, someone had been able to attack the Great Tree herself. Was there more that had happened?

Jet startled me from my thoughts, "So. Do you figure you could put out that lamp there from here?" He pointed to a lamp just ahead.

I laughed, "Sorry. I didn't mean to do that out of nowhere, it's kind of an instinct now."

He looked over to me. "It's an instinct for you to go and put flame out by waving a hand?"

"Well, it's a beginning meditation technique," I explained. Meditation was practiced by a few other people in the palace, so I thought I could explain this much.

"Meditation? That's sitting about with nothing in your head, right?"

"It can be, that's another form of it, but it's better if you have a certain mindset. The emptiness of your mind can be very particular. Putting out a candle with only your hand can help to hone that."

"How's that?" he said, stopping.

"It doesn't really matter," I said, still walking and wondering how much of what we did were secret meditation techniques. "Come on, we should leave here as soon as we can."

"Still, it was something to see," Jet said, running to catch up. "And then there's what Narsha was saying about the attacks. Hadn't heard of any of that 'til now."

"Who would do that? We should have asked her which islands had been attacked."

"Hmmm." Jet's brow gathered. "I don't think she was knowing much more about it than she told."

"I suppose it did seem that way."

We reached a wall and Jet skipped forward to a small piece of moonlight, pushing at a place in the rock directly above it. He used that place to slide open a section of wall to reveal a narrow doorway.

"Go on then," he said, nodding me through.

I stepped into the open air and he followed. The door began moving on its own, closing behind us and clicking shut, melding into the wall.

"Now, *that* was something to see," I said, staring wide-eyed at where the door had been.

"Aye! It is indeed! Come on now, best get back to the ship. We have to tell Mercully what Narsha's said." He grinned, teeth flashing brightly in the night.

20
Mourning Isle

Jet and I swept through the night back to the ship accompanied by insects' humming and moonlit clouds.

We found Mercully in the circle of sailors, settled around a large fire on the beach.

"Captain, we've been to talk to Narsha. I think we'd best go about leaving soon as can be." Jet was panting slightly from our hurry.

Mercully had been laughing at something Wilhelm said, but now her mouth straightened. "And this is because?"

"There have been other attacks and ships have been targeted too," I said, trying to help.

"She doesn't think we should stay here longer than we must. May not want the fire burning there either."

Mercully never put something off. One announcement and the fire was doused, the ship made ready, and we were off to our next stop, Morroy Isle, before an hour had passed.

Next morning, we were tucked into the dock at Morroy Isle. Though more people wandered the around here than on Klieton, it wasn't many, and for some reason all of them wore dark colors.

"C'mon, Shay!" Jet called.

I realized the crew was already heading toward the town, Jet carrying a large sack of the fruit we'd gathered the day before.

We plodded along, most of us not having had much sleep as we'd left so late, but soon we came to the town. I, at least, forgot my own exhaustion at the sight before me.

Seven black flags soared atop a dilapidated building where a torrent of people circumnavigated, all going the same way. I heard a gong sound itself in the distance and, as it did, the people turned simultaneously until they faced the opposite direction and began walking that way.

I turned to Jet, "Is it some sort of funeral march?" I asked, noticing these people were also clothed in various shades of black.

"Aye," said Jet with a clipped tone, "but not the kind you may be thinking of and not for recent deaths."

I stared at him, confused, until he explained, "There's been disasters on this island for seven years strong. No deaths, but because of them the population has halved. People are afraid. Food's growin' scarce as well as most things, so they go off. The ones who remain are mournin' their old way of life, see?" He sighed and watched as the people circled the large building. "Some tried going to Cresstalan, but were turned away," he said.

"There's only the palace on Cresstalan. Even the people of the market live there. I don't think there'd be room for many more people." I said this, but realized there was much more island than just the palace. Though, because of the Tree, there needed to be lots of wild space that humans hadn't marred.

Had the Queen tried to help these people? Or the people of Klieton, for that matter...I supposed that wasn't my place to wonder.

Again, though, it returned to the Great Tree. It should be protecting all of us from things like this.

"Jet," said Mercully, "your plan is to trade your fruit for salted fish, right?"

"Aye, Captain, and Shay will come along." He hooked an arm around my neck.

Mercully nodded, "Get a good price, we'll share it for a coming meal. Meet at the main trader's when you've finished."

"Leave it to us here, Captain." He swung to the left of the group and pulled me along into quiet streets. Though there were plenty of people, few spoke.

I'd never tried the salted fish of Morroy Isle, though kenn-fish, also caught here, was delicious.

Jet had gone on and on about how good the fish we were to get was. I supposed when a lot of what you ate was salted, you learned to bypass that to taste the subtle points. Whenever I'd eaten salted fish, I had only tasted salt.

"The fish is packed into a special type of seaweed. It gives such a flavor!"

"Jet," I said, amused, "I know, you've told me twice already." I met eyes with a woman walking past us, hers seemed hollow, her mouth turned down into a thin frown. She looked away quickly, but I was filled with a haunted feeling that seemed to lay over her.

"Ey, but you'll see why I go on about it once you eat it up! Won't want anything else!"

I looked back after the woman, "Jet, how long have the people of the island been this way? All of them look haunted."

His smile waned, and he sighed, "That's the truth of it. Since I can remember, it's been like this."

"It's a strange way to go about things, don't you think?"

"It's the way they want to handle grievance. Can't say why, but it's how they wish it."

I followed Jet into a narrow street; there wasn't room for the two of us to walk comfortably side-by-side.

"We'll trade not far ahead," he said.

I studied Jet while walking behind him, we were about the same height. The silver earrings he wore on the side of each ear glinted dully in the shadows of the street. His hair was tied with a piece of noonyi-fish skin, and his shoulder blades shaped the tunic he wore.

Jet looked back to be sure I was still following him and showed all his teeth as he smiled widely. The two braids on each side of his head were always neat. He must fix them himself.

Ahead of Jet, a man appeared from the shadows, holding a tarnished sword. In a swift motion, he had it pointed directly at Jet's chest.

Jet was about to turn back around. Even before I formed a coherent thought to warn him, I seized Jet by the shoulders and veered him behind me, switching our positions.

I faced the attacker in the eyes and let go of Jet.

My mind emptied, and I narrowed my attention only to the man.

His face was drawn and angry, light eyes wide and shadowed. He may have been shocked by how I'd maneuvered Jet but was quickly coming to his senses.

I knew how to take a sword from an opponent but couldn't be sure of this man's skill-level and didn't want to anger him. I also felt myself wanting to prove that I could solve this situation without violence.

"Give me what's in your purse," he said, jabbing the sword forward, an inch closer to my sternum.

Looking at him, I realized that though his face was contorted in anger, his eyes and features shone with fear.

How could I fix this without hurting the man? What would calm his fear?

I conjured my kindest smile, trying to pack in all the compassion and love I could muster. Love was the opposite of fear, wasn't it?

The man's hand shook as our eyes locked.

"Sir," I said, quiet as possible, "we have no coin on us." I tilted my head the smallest bit to the sack Jet held. "We are going to trade fruit. It's all we have. If you truly need it, you are welcome to it." I bowed to the man, face down. Perhaps respect would counteract how powerless this man seemed to feel.

I heard Jet rustle behind me. One of my hands reached a piece of his clothing and I tugged at it the tiniest bit, hoping to convey to him that he was to stay still. He stopped moving.

"F-fruit?"

I rose up slowly and nodded to the man.

"D-don't want no fruit." He lowered his sword.

"Would you like to come with us and eat a meal then? I'm sure we will after this."

The man backed away quickly, his face confused. He ran.

I felt Jet's hand grasp my shoulder, slower and more comforting than when he usually came up and grabbed me.

"Shay..."

I had been in the Garden mindset, I realized. I turned to Jet, calm. "Jet, I don't think I've told you, but I'm not allowed to use violence unless it's a life-or-death situation."

I wondered if he thought I'd handled the situation right. He might be angry, thinking I'd put us in danger.

It was then I remembered I wouldn't be a Gardener for much longer. Maybe it didn't matter if I used violence. Maybe I hadn't even truly gotten across to the man, but I realized I felt much better in how I'd handled this than when I'd faced Fedrid.

My heart told me that, Garden or no, I would do my best to continue to be non-violent. It wasn't just a rule that had been imposed on me anymore. It was what felt right through my whole being.

Jet laughed, "Shay. You can get rid of danger without lifting one of your fingers. No reason to hurt a man if you can go and do that."

I don't know how I expected Jet to react, but this wasn't it.

His eyes glistened even as we stood in shadow.

He never asked me to be different. I didn't think I could convey how grateful I was to him for that, how rare it was to think that way.

"Alright," I said, simply, and smiled.

∞∞∞

We traded the fruit for 36 pieces of fish wrapped in seaweed. I could smell the fish through the material of the bag we'd been given by the short stall-owner. It had a peculiar, sweet smell that I'd never experienced. It was almost pleasant.

"That'll be a wonderful meal this evening." Jet took a whiff before lowering the sack to his side.

"It smells quite nice," I agreed.

"Well," said Jet, setting off confidently, "let's move on to meet the crew."

We wended our way through the streets toward the center of town, the large building we'd seen earlier.

"What exactly is that building?" It loomed over us grimly and we were caught in the crowd of people moving around it.

"It's the town center where the governor makes his bed."

"And what does he think of the people circling it like this?" If people started doing this around the palace on

Cresstalan, the Queen would probably have the guards put a stop to it.

"Ey, he comes out and joins 'em at times. He's done his best, but what can a governor do to stop the rivers overflowin' or the land fallin'? He's as hopeless as the rest."

We'd been going along with the people around us, but the gong rang-out, and they now faced us.

Most simply looked at the ground, seemingly in deep sorrow.

A boy looked up at me as I went by, his eyes locking with mine. I saw such pain there. I wondered what he'd undergone. What could he have lost to make him look like that?

I felt a hand on my forearm and Jet held my gaze. His eyes were such a contrast, though their laughing light was slightly diminished now.

"Come on now," he said, leading me from the circling crowd to a grey stone building not far off.

I was glad to leave the gathered mass. Walking among them felt like a weight had settled on me, as if I too should mourn.

There were so many goods that come from Morroy Isle, so many coveted fish, including the noonyi-fish whose skin covered my feet. Yet, the people seemed defeated. Thinking back to the man who had tried to rob us, I also wondered who exactly got the money for those goods.

Jet and I entered the building through a curtained doorway. I was surprised to find that it was open to the sky on the inside. We were in a marketplace. No one called out their wares though, the vendors sat quietly and did business when it came to them.

I realized Jet's hand was still on my arm and there was far less bounce to his step. Perhaps the depressed atmosphere of the island was getting to him as well.

I didn't mention him moving his hand. Though I still wasn't used to people touching me in a familiar way, he looked as if he needed to know someone was with him who wasn't in mourning.

We were on the lookout for the crew but didn't have to search long. Mercully swept past us.

"Come along."

The crew rushed after her. I saw that Clare and Neweq carried large piles of noonyi-fish skin.

Jet and I joined them, he finally released my arm, but I realized I'd been needing Jet's support as much as I thought he had been needing mine.

The sorrow here was almost a physical heaviness. I hoped we'd leave soon.

I received my wish immediately as Mercully called back, "We're going to Vernt. Now. There's been a serious attack."

21
Salt

Mercully told us we were going to Vernt, the next island in the ring, to help them as much as we could.

"Their marketplace was burned, as well as a good many homes nearby. We've traded some of our gold for noonyi-skin as it has so many uses." She sighed, "Though I hate to do it, I've decided to give them our whole stock of supplies, save for rations for our own return journey to Cresstalan."

It staggered me how easily Mercully chose to help.

∞∞∞

Dinner that night was the salted fish. Though the day had been quite depressing with the mourning island and news of Vernt's attack, the crew was in decent spirits, even more so when they learned what was for dinner.

The ship was well on its way and, for the first time, the crew all sat down to eat together. Mercully was nearby at the helm, her foot holding the wheel in place as she took a plate from Jet.

He settled himself next to me, and Clare did the same on my other side. The crew formed a circle, beginning to pass plates around. They were empty, but for a piece of fredon-berry gel each.

Jet opened the canvas sack by his side and began pulling out the seaweed-wrapped slabs of fish.

Here, mixed with the sea air on the open ocean, the sweet-smelling seaweed was amplified and the enticing scent curled around me, fresh yet deeply sweet, near honey.

Jet handed the first plate to me and nodded that I should pass it along to Clare beside me. He smiled widely, his large hands cupped to receive the plate.

Clare then passed the plate to Neweq and we continued passing until Jet finally placed fish onto his own plate with a smack of his lips.

As soon as Jet's was set, nearly everyone picked up their piece of fish and took a bite, seaweed and all.

Mine lay on my plate, barely visible in the night air, the fredon-berry gel reflecting the lamplight of the ship.

As I picked up the fish, I noticed the seaweed was nearly dry and its fragrance bloomed around me.

Jet laughed, and I found him smiling, a large bit of fish already swelling his cheek. "You going to write a poem about it or take a tear? Go on, no need to wait." He swallowed and dove back into his own.

I ripped a piece off with my teeth, the air seeming to sing around me as the taste filled my nose and mouth. It was a sweet, woody taste. The flavors of fish and salt were hardly noticeable. The meat of the fish wasn't dry like most salted fish I'd had before. It was moist, and the taste melded wonderfully with the flavor of the seaweed.

I found myself letting out an, "Mmm," closing my eyes.

"Good, ey? Now," said Jet, and I looked over to find him taking a small portion of the fredon-berry gel, "try this." He put the gel onto his next bite of fish and opened his mouth wide to eat them together, sighing in enjoyment as he chewed.

"I thought it was strange at first," said Clare, who must
have seen the face I made at Jet, "but Jet was right. You
must go on and try it."

So, I took a small piece, the gel squishing between my
fingers, and placed it onto my next bite. I sank my teeth
into it to find a wonderful tanginess now added to the
flavors. The texture of the gel wasn't even strange when
mixed with the fish and seaweed. It was amazing.

"Delicious!" I turned to Jet, smiling widely through the
bite still in my mouth.

"Told you," he said, smugly.

I sighed, looking around at the crew. They talked
comfortably with one another, joking or sitting peacefully,
enjoying the delicious food and the comfortable evening.

The sky was not yet black, but a dark, hushed blue.
I felt the smallest raindrop on my wrist and could smell a
faint hint of rain in the air. The lamps on the ship shone
brightly. They were such a wonderful contrast to the
deepening sky that my smile grew wider.

After Clare had taken our plates to clean them and we
were all settling down, there was a noise so far off in the
distance, I thought I might have imagined it. Several other
heads turned in the same direction, however.

It was some sort of deep rumble, but it was a brittle,
hollow sound, without the resonance of thunder. It should
not have been there.

"What was that?" Sseya said, looking out into the inky
blackness.

"Only stars know. Go to the edges of the deck and see if
there's anything about." This was Mercully.

We did as she ordered, but all I could see was the glint
of candlelight on water and stars through roaming clouds.

"Now, what could that have been?" Jet rested his
elbows on the railing of the deck, still gazing out though
there was nothing to see.

"Do you think it could be another attack?"

"May be." Clouds were starting to clear, revealing the pale crescent moon.

We were quiet for a while longer, everyone listening for the sound.

After a while, we gave up, there was no sign of any other disturbance.

"You know though," said Jet, we hadn't moved from our spot, "there have been ramblings, not for a time now, but it used to be thought that the people of Queniil had anger against the islands."

"Queniil?"

"Aye. It's a country that rests not too far from us here. Hardly go about trading with us anymore, prefer to do it all on land." Jet scratched his temple, firelight glinting off his silver earring. "I've heard they have ships, but they're hardly in use."

"You think they're responsible for the attacks?"

"Couldn't say either way. Perhaps they'd be capable of it though."

"Why was there talk of them in the past?"

His dark eyes gleamed, "Well now, for a time they were thought to have led an attack on Cresstalan."

My mouth dropped, "An attack on Cresstalan? I don't remember anything like that. What happened?"

"That's the other part unknown. Think it was before you or I were existing in the world."

Could that be the attack on the Great Tree? I didn't think anyone knew of that though.

"Some of the crew have told me of it," Jet continued. "Twenty years ago the royal guards went questioning everyone in sight. So, some sort of commotion must have gone on, eh?"

It must have been about the Great Tree then. I leaned forward onto my elbows, attempting to hide some of my surprise.

"And...the crew thought it was the people of Queniil?"

"Ey, I don't think there was a firm decision on it, but those people are known to speak poorly of our islands, so they're suspected. They've been quieter about it of late, seems."

"Maybe we can find out more when we get to Vernt tomorrow." It seemed there weren't firm answers to be found now.

"Could be." Jet straightened up. "Eh, there's nothing left to do, but I don't think sleep will come to me yet. Think I'll sit at the prow and keep lookout a while longer."

It was still early in the night. "I'll keep you company."

I followed Jet to the front of the ship where he sat down heavily, letting out a long breath and grinning up at me as I sat beside him.

"Ah, beautiful night." He leaned back onto his folded arms and stared at the now-clear night above.

The stars were brilliant out on the sea. There was nothing to obstruct them when out on the water.

"We have to learn the stars almost first thing when we start on ships," Jet said out of the darkness.

"How can you learn the stars?" There were so many of them. They hadn't meant anything to us on Cresstalan. They were there, but the Tree was our sacred lore, our bringer of seasons, our life's blood.

Now that I thought on it, there had been some nights when members of the crew spoke of the stars in the way I thought of the Tree. It was as though they believed the stars could guide their way.

Jet laughed as though my question were ridiculous and gestured widely at the scattered expanse above. "They create pictures and we make up stories for 'em. At least, I think they're made up, though they've been told too long to know." He sighed, "Lots of royalty in the stars, kings and queens and such. Sometimes I feel they're looking down their noses at me, disapproving. So, for those I don't like, I change 'em to my own stories."

"Like what?"

"Well," he pointed, "see those bright ones, just there? Shaped as an arch?"

"I see them."

"I've been told it's a crown, but see there, it's too stretched to be. More of a doorway, I say. Perhaps to another world."

I leaned back onto my arms, mirroring Jet. I liked the way he viewed the world. I turned to see his profile lined in silver.

"You're right. And doors are so much better than crowns."

He tilted toward me, gazing openly for a moment, then, pulling his lips into a soft smile, "Indeed, they are."

Turning back to the blazing sky, Jet looked as if he'd feast on the starlight.

I laid back, feeling my eyelids getting heavy, and a yawn escaped.

The ship rocked gently as we sailed on into the star-drenched night.

22
Ashes

I lay in my hammock, listening to the breathing of the crew slow into sleep around me. Jet was above me and I could hear his soft snores. There was louder snoring from Sseya and Neweq beginning to swell up as well.

For a time, I lay awake. I was glad to be part of this crew. They acted as if they were a family.

My mind drifted to the attacks. Could they be done by the same people who had cut down the Great Tree twenty years ago? Why had I never even heard of Queniil? Though, in our lessons as children, we mostly learned of Cresstalan and a little of the surrounding islands. It hadn't seemed strange at the time that we didn't learn more.

If it was the same people though, they would have stolen the seeds and might have their own Tree now. They wouldn't need to attack other people if they had the protection of a Tree, would they?

Of course, the law of the Garden forbade planting another Tree. Were the new attacks a result of someone planting their own?

Sometimes I still wondered, however, if the Tree of the Fallen was protecting us as it should. Did any of the rules of the Garden still apply if the original Great Tree had been replaced?

The last thing I remembered, dozing off, was Wilhelm leaving his hammock with a creak to go to the deck, presumably to take the wheel from Mercully.

∞∞∞

When I woke, instead of salt breeze, the heavy smell of smoke was winding its way amongst our hammocks.

None of us mentioned the smell as we began to stir, slipping on boots, and ascending outside. Clearly it was from the attack on Vernt.

On deck, it was such a beautifully clear day with newly blue sky and sea, but then I found what I knew waited.

We were very close to Vernt. On the nearby island, past a black sand beach, were mounds and charred remains of buildings. Tendrils of smoke still rose from the wreckage.

"Goodness," Jet drew up beside me. "Horrible sight."

The rest of the crew gathered as well.

"What a mess. Those poor people," this was Mercully. "Let's drop anchor out in the ocean. Looks as though the docks were destroyed. We'll take the boats to shore." She sighed heavily and broke away from us. "Come on now, let's get to it."

∞∞∞

Not an hour later, we were in two small clay boats with supplies packed around us.

The water was crystalline, the sun reflected as a stinging brightness. It was difficult to appreciate being so close to the water, even when I could see vivid fish swimming beneath us, for ahead was the burned island.

A few people seemed to have spotted the ship in the harbor and began to wander the shore.

We reached our destination before them, quickly gathering the food and other supplies.

I picked up four full bags of food, happy to find I could carry so much.

Jet hauled a large pile of fish skin. "Ey, if you can do that much," he said, nodding to my armload, "I need to start having you help with some of my tasks!"

I laughed, "You'll have to show me, then! For now, I'll start with this."

He playfully bumped my shoulder and we followed the crew up a path toward the blackened buildings.

Six people of the island came to meet us, looking longingly at the supplies we carried.

Mercully decided we should sit with them and find out exactly what had happened on the island.

We lowered our burdens and brought out small pieces of fish and seaweed for the people to eat while they talked.

They devoured the food gratefully and, between bites, they told us of a mysterious ship sighted a few nights before. It had presumably set fire to the docks after everyone had gone to sleep. The flames spread quickly with the brittle vegetation, there having been a recent drought. A storehouse of supplies had also been lost. Vernt would be grateful we'd come, we were told.

After finishing the food, we thanked the people, then followed Mercully as she rose. "We'll go to the town center and ask the best way to distribute our goods."

The people around us looked slightly disappointed and stuck close as we made our way. A gathered parade soon filed behind us when we reached the town center, eager to get supplies.

An older man who looked exhausted and seemed to be a town official, came over and asked what we were doing.

Mercully explained that we wanted to help, and a system was worked out to distribute supplies. The ones we had were gone within minutes and, after two more trips back out to the ship, we gathered the remainder of what we could offer.

The town official thanked us profusely, tears limning his eyes in relief.

There were already so many people in need that, the town official was sorry to say, we couldn't stay anywhere on the island.

Mercully brushed it off, only apologetic we didn't have more supplies.

∞∞∞

"Our next stop will be Fainia." Mercully had gathered us around as she paced thoughtfully, "We'll gather the leaves to sell on Cresstalan, trade them for supplies, then return to Vernt to distribute those supplies."

"The leaves she means are those to make the waterproofed coating of ships." Jet whispered this in my ear, I leaned closer to hear him better. "The people of Fainia would go and do it before, but they abandoned their island just this year."

I leaned back in surprise, but Jet nodded for me to keep listening to Mercully.

"We'll go," Mercully said. "We've done it before. The leaves will garner a high price and we'll return as quickly as we can."

"Yes, Captain," everyone intoned, and, our plan set, we sailed for Fainia.

23
Fainia

The Sea's Ribbon cut through the water smooth as wind through grass.

Now that we were on our way to Fainia, I couldn't help but think of the Fainian Peal-Digger that graced Jevin's sword; and of Jevin himself. I had felt so very alone when I left him and Cresstalan. Here, among the waves and the ship's crew, my life at the palace seemed another life entirely.

I missed Jevin though. He was my friend, and though what we were going through was difficult, I should have at least let him know I was leaving. He'd stood up to my father for me, after all. I would tell him I was sorry when I got back, perhaps try to share why I'd been upset.

Out of all the islands in the ring with Cresstalan, Fainia was the one I most wanted to see. I didn't actually believe in the Fainian Peal-Digger...though, if I should happen to come across it, I was sure I'd be able to laugh in its face and receive some luck.

As I watched waves tumble from the ship, Jet came up behind me, handing me a cup full of something. He held one that was identical.

"Juice from the klie-fruits. I went about saving some pieces. After a few days, you must turn them to liquid or have 'em spoil beyond repair."

I nodded, smiling, and drank deeply only to gasp and nearly spit it from my mouth. Court upbringing, however, gave me the gut instinct to swallow politely instead, still sputtering.

A rasping laugh burst from Jet. He downed his own cup and stood grinning.

I glanced back at the cup warily, "The fruit tasted nothing like this! Has it gone bad?"

Jet swiped the cup from me and finished it off. I gladly let him have it, my lip curling at the taste still lingering on my tongue.

"Ey, no. They just get like that when turned to juice. As to why, I've no idea. Must be good for you though as it tastes so bad."

That was faulty logic in my opinion, but I simply turned back to the sea.

Jet leaned against the railing alongside me and playfully bumped my shoulder with his.

I scowled at him, "You might have warned me about the taste."

His smile split even wider, maniacal, "Might have, but I wanted to see that face you made." He twisted his own into a gruesome expression.

"I doubt I looked that badly."

He shrugged and laughed, "Was bad enough though."

We quieted as the first faint line of land appeared on the horizon. There was Fainia.

We began circling the island when we got close. It was all dense foliage dripping from tall rocks. That was what we could see, anyway.

"We're going 'round the back," Jet explained. "The plants we're needing will be found there, though the abandoned dwellings are at the front."

I marveled at colorful birds sitting in and flying amongst the island's plant life.

A narrow gorge halved the isle, I saw when we reached the back. This seemed to be our destination.

The crew was called back to their duties to make sure the ship was under control. We entered the gorge, the ship becoming steeped in the cool shadows of the waterway. It seemed to run straight through the middle of Fainia.

Leaves hung from the steep rock walls of the canyon, hanging in tangles, it looked as if we sailed through a green dream. Vines crossed the width of the passage overhead, the top two-times taller than the ship.

No longer did I have to wonder why 'The Sea's Ribbon' was painted in its sour green. While looking over the side of the ship, I saw the light reflecting off the surrounding plants blended perfectly with the paint color.

I went over to Jet. He was standing in place, keeping an eye on a few ropes as they pulled slightly.

"The ship is hidden perfectly in this place. Is that why it's painted green?"

He seemed pleased. "Ey, that's it. We weren't welcome here when there was still people livin' on the island. Made it difficult to get the coating needed for the ship, so we found a way to get the leaves ourselves. 'Course we didn't let them dry as they should, and it came out the color it is." He laughed. "Helped further trips, didn't it? Never once got caught."

"Why wasn't 'The Sea's Ribbon' welcome?"

The green wooden beads around Jet's neck jostled as he shook his head. "As to that, we never found out. Tried to get through the docks a few times but were always sent away. This was just in the short months before the people had gone, mind you."

"Why did the people of the island leave?"

"Don't know. Didn't associate much before. One voyage they were here, the next vanished. No sign of struggle or anything bad going on," he said, seeing my face teetering near fear, "simply packed up and left for somewhere else to live."

I knitted my brows, "Jet, how can there be so many terrible things happening on all of the islands? It seems each one is a mess."

"You're right about that," he said, adjusting a rope, his long arms reaching as high as they'd go. "Something rotten in the air so's they're falling apart in one way or another. Seems worse as time goes on."

⚬⚬⚬

On a small, secluded beach, we settled the ship.

My toes curled into the black Fainian sand as we ate lunch. After finishing, Mercully and the rest of the crew were going to scout out where the leaves grew thickest.

Mercully pulled me to the side after we ate. "Shay, there are some points of this island that we like to keep secret, though you're a part of the crew, you won't always be with us, and we'd prefer as few people as possible knew of them, is it alright if you stay behind for a while?"

"Of course, Captain."

Mercully patted my shoulder once, "Excellent."

This was all the better for me. I was left alone for the first time in a week, and I didn't mind one bit.

Jet looked a little sad as he walked away with the crew.

I'd known that sea life was a bit rougher. It meant being less well-fed, a lot smellier and, in my case for the first day, a lot sicker. I hadn't had time to think of that before I'd left the palace. Though I didn't regret coming in the least, I was keen to enjoy being alone on this foreign beach.

There was a path near the water and I followed it, leaving my shoes to enjoy the sand between my toes.

A stone archway crossed part of the waterway, broken off halfway and hanging suspended.

There was another beach here, wider and longer. The plants and rock walls sat back a bit.

Here, it was peaceful. Empty. The small waves rolled in lines with white bubbles. Black grains of sand swallowed the sunlight unlike the white sands of Cresstalan that shone intensely in it. There were bushes on the rocks behind me, what looked like the start of a small jungle, and a few birds called, joining the soft sounds of the day.

I became transfixed by the waves but looked up as I realized the birds had stopped their singing. Looking back to the bushes behind me, nothing seemed amiss. The black sand sparkled here and there.

Out of the still sands leapt a creature. It seemed to have sprung from the dense beach itself.

The creature sat, unmoving, but tense. It clearly saw me.

Taller than the rocks behind it, sinuously long, what I could see of it was colored a fiery-gold. It gaped at me with a sharp, dark mouth.

I'd seen that creature, though then it had been cast in silver, surging toward me. The Fainian Peal-Digger.

The animal wound its way to me, fast as a flashing glint of reflected light. Perhaps it was nonsense, but if I wanted the luck spoken of in legends, I had to laugh right now. Any luck I could get would be welcome.

Yet, I found myself frozen. For a moment we stared straight into each other's eyes, the Peal-Digger's vividly gold. I could not move, could not breathe.

Then it bellowed happily, contracting itself down, and leaped clean over my head.

I watched as the Fainian Peal-Digger glided over me, somehow detached from myself. I followed the progress of its jump, its belly a shimmering pearly white beneath the cloudless blue sky. I felt a spray of sand behind me as it no doubt leapt back into the sand.

Then it was gone.

The birds resumed their cries a moment later.

My chance for luck was lost.

24
Ruins

The Peal-Digger was real. Whether it gave luck or not, I wouldn't be able to tell, but I'd seen it. Though I hadn't been able to laugh at it, I wasn't frightened. Just immobile with perhaps awe or disbelief.

Sprinting back to the smaller beach, I was excited to tell Jet when he returned, but the crew was still gone.

My body vibrated. I needed to calm down. Deciding to do what I'd not done, in fact, what I hadn't needed to do since boarding 'The Sea's Ribbon'. I sat down, crossed my legs, slowed my breathing, and meditated. The sound of the waves lulled me back into a relaxed state, though a smile still curved my mouth.

Feeling a hand shake my shoulder, I roused myself, taking a deep, settled breath, and found Jet staring at me.

"What's that you're doing there?" he asked, sitting down beside me.

"Meditating," I said simply, still in a state where I didn't wish to talk.

"Ey, no candles?"

I smiled, "Most of the time I don't use them. I just wanted to calm my mind."

"And why did you need to go about calming your mind?" he tilted his head.

At that, my face split into a grin so wide it immediately made my cheeks sore. "I've just seen the Fainian Peal-Digger!"

He clearly hadn't expected that to be my answer and actually seemed to be speechless, his eyes wide.

"It was down there," I pointed to the path. "I could hardly believe it. I still hardly believe it."

"I've been coming here for a good chunk of time, and never saw a hair of it! That's amazing!"

"I'll show you where it was. Do you want to see?"

I'd already jumped up and taken Jet's hand to help him rise as well.

He leapt up spryly, laughing, "Aye! Why're you askin'?"

ᐤᐤᐤ

Though we searched the area where I'd seen the Peal-Digger thoroughly, there was no trace of it, to Jet's great disappointment.

Even the places where it seemed to have sprung straight from the sand were without disturbance.

As we went back, I consoled Jet, "Don't worry. If I saw it the first time here, I'm sure you'll see it soon. At least you know where it could be now."

He turned to me. "Were you able to go and laugh at it?"

At this I felt my face fall a little. "No. I was frozen to the spot."

"What was it lookin' like?"

"It had a really long body. Its underbelly was a shimmering off-white color and its eyes were gold. The inside of its mouth was black with sharp, white teeth. The rest of it was a color somewhere between orange and gold." I gazed, unseeingly. "It seemed like a really happy creature.

It wasn't afraid of me and came right up. When it leapt away, it made this joyous sound. Maybe it was excited to see a human on the island." I shrugged, "Something had cheered it up."

"How did you go about seeing its underbelly?" Jet asked, he hadn't looked away from me this entire time.

"It leapt over me, straight into the sand, I think. I was too shocked to see how it went away, All I could do was look up and see its stomach."

"I never imagined it to be real." Jet sat back.

"I'd hoped it was, but I don't think I ever truly let myself believe that it could be." I dropped down beside him.

The voices of the crew were in ear-shot a moment before they came back to the beach.

They gathered around us, already discussing plans for getting the leaves.

"Ey, listen up!" Jet interrupted. "Shay's seen the Fainian Peal-Digger!"

Everyone stopped their talking to look to me.

"Did you really?" asked Clare.

"I'm sure it was. It came right up and leapt over me before it went away. It was amazing." Fekk and Antan's mouths start to move in what I assumed was the same question. "I wasn't able to laugh at it though."

"I thought I saw it once," said Neweq softly, then looked up to me, "was it sort of gold in color?"

"Yes, it was!" My heart leapt.

"You never told us of that." Jet said to Neweq, disappointed.

"I wasn't sure if it was," he replied, abashed. "I caught, but a brief glimpse and thought it may have even been a trick of the light."

"It's true, it seemed unbelievably fast," I said.

"Well, you've had quite the luck in seeing it, alone," said Mercully. "As you might have guessed, none of us has ever seen it, apart from Neweq here, it seems."

"It's pretty unbelievable," this was Sseya, "but don't we have to hurry to gather the leaves?"

"Yes," said Mercully, looking at the sun. It was falling into late afternoon. "Jet, you and Shay go and gather roots by the ruins. Neweq, Clare. You two go get a couple sacks of the berries by the stream, and the rest of us will gather all the leaves we can manage. Meet back at the ship at dusk."

After grabbing baskets and sacks to carry all the different items, we went our separate ways. I followed Jet.

Realizing what Mercully had said, I asked, "There are ruins here on Fainia?"

"Ey, yes. Not too much to see of them, but they're there. In fact, most of the islands have a bit of a ruin or two upon them if you search a bit."

I stopped, "Most of the islands have ruins?"

"Sure." He turned to look at me. "Buildings can't go around lasting forever, can they? So, we go and build new ones."

It had seemed like an unsettling coincidence since Cresstalan had ruins, but I supposed Jet was right.

We arrived where we were to gather the roots and I did my best to not stare at the ruins too long. It was silly, I told myself, eyes grazing the weathered stone. They had no significance.

Though, there was more to these ruins than Cresstalan's. A low wall outlining what might have once been a round building, and a few pillars and small platforms, some upright, some toppled, within.

Pulling at the first root I saw, I tried to ignore how the color of the stone the ruins were made from was the same as the ruins on Cresstalan.

Soon though, Jet's constant conversation and the task at hand took my attention.

One particularly large root needed the strength of both Jet and I to get it out of the ground and, when we did, we laughed at how it was as long as one of our calves.

Nearly hitting my head on a slab fallen outside of the ruin circle brought me back to them. I drew in a sharp breath when, in front of me, there were symbols carved into the rock. Some I didn't know. Others...matched the ones I painted onto my face every two weeks.

I was stunned. All that was known of the symbols we put on our faces was that they represented different parts of nature and would help us connect with the Garden more fully.

Yet, here were those symbols in this ancient, broken place with stone worn and cracked, bleached and decayed in the sun, wind, and rain.

How were they here, clear across the islands from Cresstalan?

I remembered Jet was there. I wanted dearly to tell someone what I'd just discovered, but this would definitely count as a Garden secret. I needed to discuss this with my father or Jevin when I returned.

∞∞∞

With two full baskets of roots, Jet and I returned to the ship.

Needing light to see our way out the other end of the gorge, Mercully announced we would stay the night, sleeping on the beach.

Because Vernt needed our help as soon as possible, we'd cut through the middle of the island ring. I didn't understand why this garnered disgruntled groans from the crew until Jet explained it to me the next morning.

We'd gone off to the side, awaiting the sunrise, and didn't want to disturb the crew's slumber.

"The reason this isn't often done, see," explained Jet, "is a barrier in the middle of the sea."

"A barrier?" I asked, raking my hands though the gritty beach sand.

"Mmm, of sorts. Spires that rise straight from the sea." His black eyes glinted as he turned to me, though the rest of him was barely visible in the grey light. "Have you truly not heard? Thought you had all the secrets of the nation at your fingertips."

I shook my head, "I know the secrets of the Garden. I've never heard of these spires though."

Jet laid back onto the beach, letting out a sigh. "I was hoping for some answers to this from you. No one else has 'em. The rest of the crew fears even speaking of the spires, at times."

"They fear them?" I laid back as well. "I wonder why? I'll look forward to seeing them."

Jet laughed up at the sky, "As you should."

We heard some stirrings and Jet hopped up. "Come along, let's get ourselves back to the crew and be off."

I started to raise myself up, lifting my arms, then felt Jet's hand grasp mine, calloused, warm, pulling me up to him, to his smile, flashing bright in the morning light.

"Thanks." His hand held mine for a moment more, then we both let go.

CCOO

The sea was calm and the sky clear, but the crew was anxious. Hardly joking, hardly even speaking. Jet tried to make a joke at breakfast, but Mercully gave him a glare that drove him back to his dried seaweed.

"It will take us four days to cross the central sea, as you all well know," Mercully began. "We'll sail just to the north of the spire line. There's no faster way."

The crew nodded, save for Pace who raised a hand warily. The Captain nodded for him to speak.

"The last time we sailed past the spires we—"

Mercully cut him off, "*This* time, is what I am concerned with." She brushed her hands off, finished with her meal, and rose to her feet, boots shining in the morning light. "Many ships make the passage, no issues in sight. That is what we're doing. Eat your breakfast and let's be off."

My last piece of fish stuck in my throat as it went down. Was this route truly so dangerous? I thought of Vernt. They needed help, supplies, things that we could get easiest at Cresstalan. And soon.

The crew finished eating hurriedly and began their tasks.

Running from sailor to sailor, helping a little with whatever they needed, I did my best to stay in the flow of the jobs done to embark.

As I worked though, I thought of going back to Cresstalan; to the Great Tree. Though I was sad to have been away so long, I would have to get used to it. Soon I wouldn't be able to enter the Garden. Jevin would be matched before long and I would not be needed as a Keeper of the Garden.

Still, I worried over the Tree of the Fallen. Was it truly doing its job?

I tugged a rope, helping Clare to raise a sail, but I barely felt the coarse material on my palms. If only the other islands had trees of their own to protect them.

The rope was pulled back through and out of my hands, the slack tied off.

Why didn't the other islands have their own trees? It was a written rule that there should be no more, but why had that rule been put into place?

I walked to the edge of the ship and looked out over the deep-blue stretching out before me, wind shifting over my bare head. We knew it was possible to grow more trees, my father had done so with the Tree of the Fallen.

Perhaps the Tree of the Fallen wasn't big enough yet, or powerful enough, to protect the islands as it should though. Maybe it needed help.

We didn't know the full potential of the new Tree. What if we tried to give the other islands their own—

I yelped as Jet came up from behind me and grasped my shoulders simply saying, "We're off!" He let out a small laugh. "Haven't gotten you like that in a while, have I? Thought you're used to my ways of saying hello!"

I rubbed my face, laughing a little. "You caught me deep in my thoughts."

He leaned against the edge of the ship. "Oh? And what were you thinking so heavily of, eh?"

I sighed, "Can't tell you yet, but I may have an idea to help the islands in need."

"Do you now?" He quirked his head to the side. "Well, not sure why you can't tell...but if it's to help and do what's needed, I wish you the best with any secret rescue plans."

I grinned, "Thank you."

Jet raised his eyes to look straight into mine, "Here's hoping it works, whatever it may be. Supplies can only do so much, seems there's something deeper at work."

"I don't know if what I have in mind is possible, but if this won't work, I'll try to think of something else."

He nodded and began to turn away.

I grabbed his shoulder and turned him back, "Jet." I lowered my hand back to my side. "I can't say much now. I'm not sure what the future holds for me, but I might need a new place to be. New things to do...I...," I hesitated, but continued to press forward, "...would it be possible for me to stay on 'The Sea's Ribbon' at some point? If I need to?"

He grasped both of my hands and looked at me seriously, "You're already one of the crew, Shay. Anything you might be needing, any time you might be needing it, long as we're able, it's yours."

My eyes stung, and I could hardly speak.

I had never, never in my life been so readily accepted, asked for so little and been given so much.

I tightened my grip on Jet's hands for the briefest moment. "Thank you."

He didn't look away, but nodded and shrugged as if it were nothing.

"Come along now. We have to prepare some of the things we've gathered from Fainia to sell." He dipped his head.

I smiled and took my hands back. "Lead on."

25
Sea Spires

The first two days of our return journey were uneventful, the only item-of-note being I finally won a game of There and Yon'.

When the day we were to reach the spires dawned, however, the sails themselves seemed strained, though the wind lay low, and the crew was tense and quiet.

"We'll be reaching the spires around mid-day," said Jet, as he and I worked to fold extra blankets.

"And no one has any idea what they are? Are they some sort of natural phenomenon?"

Jet shook his head, "No one knows it for sure, but I'm in doubt of that. They're stuck in rows too straight to be of a natural way and go too deep for anyone to know the sure end of 'em."

"They're in straight lines?" I picked up the pile of blankets and we took them back below deck, passing Clare on the way down. His smile seemed strained.

"They are, indeed," Jet said, continuing our conversation while placing the blankets on their shelf.

"What do you think they are?"

"Haven't an idea. I've thought on it time again, but

there's not a way to be sure. I've only seen them twice myself." He looked off to each of his sides, before whispering, "We were attacked when we last passed by. Not sure of it being pirates, but someone may be guarding or searching or looking out over the spires, not letting some others get too near. Pace was so ware of them for that reason, the others as well. The attack then was three years past, so it may be a foundless fear. We'll be alright, I'm thinking, but we'll be on wary lookout."

"So that's why everyone is afraid of going back. But why would there be people around the spires? Is there anything else out there?"

"Ey, no," Jet shook his head. "Far as we can see, just the spires made of stone. It was dangerous for quite a time to go near them. Haven't heard of attacks near 'em for a long time now though."

∞∞∞

Just after we'd eaten lunch, Jet pointed out the spires from a distance.

Light-colored pillars of rock, not more than a hand-span in diameter rose from the water, reaching to different heights. Many looked as if they'd been broken off. None were more than seven feet above the water. Other than that, they were alike and in perfect rows, each one about two feet away from the one beside it.

There was no one else around and no land in sight. The eight rows of spires went on far into the distance. We couldn't see the end of them.

I rushed to the side of the boat to view them better, but as we drew close, all I could see was that they were covered in barnacles. Other than this, they were just skinny, stone pillars sticking out of the water.

Leaning over the boat though, I saw one, broken quite low, had a hole in it. The hole was dark and perfectly round. It must go down further. But why?

Most of the crew ignored them and went on working.

Jet stood beside me. "Strange, ey?"

"Very," I said, still staring as the spires fled past. "How old do you think they might be?"

"Perhaps ancient. Never met one person who's known the world without them. Those willing to talk, that is."

I hung my hand over the deck, feeling the breeze trail past my fingers.

"What could they be? I wonder if my father would know." I'd have to ask him when I returned home.

"Can't see how they'd go with the Garden but askin' can't hurt."

While doing chores throughout the day, I looked out to the spires, but saw no change, no detail of interest, and went back to work each time. It was an intriguing mystery, but I didn't see how I could figure it out by watching them. Eventually, I just worked and let them be.

∞∞∞

Evening fell, and the darkness was nearly complete with no moon in the sky, though the stars were brilliant.

The tasks of the day complete, we lazed about the deck. Mercully had the wheel, but looked exceedingly relaxed, once again using her foot to hold our course and stretching her arms behind her.

Neweq had brought out his yuf, a 30-stringed instrument I'd only seen played one other time by a traveling musician at the palace.

I was entranced as his fingers flew over the strings, the flurry of sharp notes backed by softly sighing waves.

Those of the crew that hadn't been sitting with us made way over to bask in the music. Mercully stayed where she was, but the foot that wasn't holding the wheel was tapping along to the rhythmic tune.

Jet and I had been sitting beside each other, a game of There and Yon' between us, but we lost interest when the music started.

With a sizable audience sitting at rapt attention, Neweq stoked the song higher, notes flowing effortlessly from the yuf, swirling about us.

Sseya hopped to her feet, to my surprise, and began dancing. Her feet moved faster than I could follow in a complicated piece of footwork.

Fekk and Antan rose and began to dance as well, their style quite acrobatic, and Sen and Dimny joined, taking the chance to dance happily with each other.

The music swelled, and I leapt up. I hadn't danced since I was small, but I started moving freely, letting the music take me where it would. A lot of my swordplay moves, steps I knew well, mixed into the rhythm.

The twelve of us then began to dance together as we went on, holding hands and spinning in a great circle. Or, as much of a circle as we could make while on the ship. Jet was on my right side and Venn on my left. We laughed heartily, spinning.

That's when the cannonball struck the ship's prow. The silence was abrupt. We stilled faster than I would have thought possible, our joy fleeing into the darkness.

Orange flame glowed from lamps on a ship just on the other side of the barrier of pillars.

"They're back!" screamed Pace, backing away.

Their ship was pointed the opposite of ours but was anchored to its spot.

"Calm down, Pace!" bellowed Mercully. "Everyone adjust the sails to catch all the wind we can, and let's be on our way."

I stayed out of the way, behind Mercully, the surest way of helping when I still didn't quite know what I was doing.

My mind leapt to the razor hidden away in my bag, but I quickly discarded the thought of finding a weapon. That wouldn't be any help unless our attackers somehow boarded us, if at all.

The men on the other boat were shadows swarming angrily. They looked to be preparing to load the cannon again.

Luckily, the crew was fast, and we were quickly gliding away from the other ship, leaving it behind. Shouts followed us, but we were soon out of range of their voices and cannons.

Clare came up to us at the wheel. "It appears they have taken over these waters again, Captain."

Mercully's face was sullen. She didn't reply.

More of the crew began to make their way over, but the Captain finally barked, "They may yet follow us."

Everyone halted, staying put at Mercully's warning.

26
Divided Continent

Jet was at the rear of the ship, watching to see if we were followed. I went to him, passing the rest of the crew on the way.

They were talking to each other in low voices, only pretending to work, they'd all done what they could for the moment.

"Seems their fears weren't unfounded," I said, coming to rest next to Jet.

"I'd say not." We both started as a small shot of sparks fired out of the night. The other ship seemed to have shot a cannonball, perhaps in warning, as we were far out of range.

"Who are they?"

Footsteps came from behind me and I was surprised to see Sseya beside us. "No one is sure," she said, answering my question, "but I think it's the same people trying to disrupt the islands."

"And who and why would they be, Sseya?" asked Jet.

Her gold jewelry glinted in the low light as she rested her chin on her hands, leaning on the railing of the ship. "The country I came from was not of these islands. And there we mingled more with people from all areas of the world."

Jet and I both stayed perfectly silent and still. Sseya hardly ever spoke.

"There are legends of this place. Ones that led me to jump on a ship and seek out this ring of islands." She looked at us each in turn, searching our faces. "Since I have been here I have heard no more of these tales. Have either of you ever heard stories of what this place once was? Before it was islands? Before they were separated?"

Separated? What did she mean by that? I shook my head and Jet looked at me, seeing if I'd heard of this, he seemed as confused as I was. He turned back to her, shaking his head as well.

She sighed, "No. No one here has heard of this and, as these spires aren't spoken of, I'm always afraid to bring up the tale. I think it is important now though. With all that is going on, we must know truth and speak of it. At least to discuss what might be true and what might lead to an answer."

Jet and I stayed still, hoping to hear more, but Sseya was silent as well.

"What are the legends, Sseya?" I asked softly.

The wind brushed itself against our faces, the faintest tinkling coming from the gold chain going from Sseya's nose to her ear. We all turned to keep our eyes on where we knew the other ship to be.

"The main legend I have heard," she said, then looked around. No one else was near us, "I only tell you two because you were so curious about the pillars. You don't seem to fear them as the others do."

We nodded.

"A man came through our village when I was very young and when he was very old. I knew of your island ring, though I had never been here. He said that this place was cursed." She clenched the clay railing before her. "I don't know if you know this, but these islands are generally avoided by the rest of the world. You are self-sufficient and so do not know all that you do not have. But the world is a great place with so many different lands, foods, animals, and things that you are without here. Yet, no one seems to leave, just as few come here."

Another small glow went off in the far distance, the ship warning us away again.

Sseya continued, "The curse is said to have been put on this place long ago. When these islands were bonded together. When they formed a continent."

"All one land?" Jet spoke, incredulous.

I placed my hand on his, trying to silence him to hear more of the story, though I was biting back my own questions.

"Yes. At least, this is what I was told. Some say the continent broke apart, some say it sunk in whole and is lost below the sea, and many think the story cannot be true at all."

She looked to the spires at our side, the white, skinny stone ghostly in the darkness. "But these pillars speak otherwise to me. They could be remnants of some structure lost beneath the waves. The islands could have been mountains on the continent. I do not know, but it seems an explanation. I don't know if the part about this land being cursed is true, but it seems likely as anything with the events that have arisen."

With these attacks, tragedies, and the loss of the Great Tree. When had this madness started on the other islands? Was it only after the Great Tree was lost? Could the Tree have been protecting us from whatever this curse was?

Sseya continued and I hung on her words, "As no one is sure if this story is true, no one has any idea what happened to the people of the lost continent. Perhaps they were lost to the sea, but I think it unlikely that, if there were indeed people living there, they could have all been lost. I think these that are terrorizing the islands now were enemies of the people of the continent and are trying to take out whatever remains of its people. I think the pillars must guard some great treasure and that is why they don't want anyone near them."

Jet spoke into the night, "Treasures of a continent lost to the sea, ey? Could explain some things. What should we go about doing, then? Allow them to retrieve this treasure? Or do they want to go and drive us from the islands? Fainia may be their doing."

Sseya tilted her head. "Perhaps. I don't know if there's anything to be done at all. I simply wanted to give you what may be another piece of the puzzle." She turned to me, "Especially you, Shay. I don't know what secrets you keep, but I know you must know some. You are a Keeper of the Great Tree. If this information can help you at all...," she sighed and shook her head, "maybe it's all fairy tales, but better to have it than not."

A sunken continent? It seemed a stretch, but why not? There was surprisingly little written about our people and the islands we inhabited. Our greatest record known was the one of the Great Tree and how to care for the Garden, which gave more reason for its importance.

Sseya said no more and walked away. Jet and I looked to each other.

"Well, that's an interesting piece to have, if it goes about fitting."

I nodded, looking off into the distance.

The night passed without further incident. Mercully led the ship away from the pillars.

We were still on course, but far enough so we wouldn't warrant further incidents and there was no sign of anyone following us.

Sseya's story seemed more plausible by the moment as I thought of what might lie beneath those waves amongst the stone pillars.

27
Goodbye

I enjoyed the last day and a half I had with the crew.
I played and won three games of There and Yon', fished
with Jet, and enjoyed the view of endless water and sky.
But below all this and behind all those moments, I knew I'd
be home soon.

Though I was somewhat worried about my troubles
there and how I would be addressed when I returned,
I wanted to tell my father what I'd seen. He should know
the stories I had heard and the idea that was taking root in
my heart.

When we docked at Cresstalan and it was time to part
ways, I shook hands with Mercully and got shoulder and
back pats from most of the crew.

Then, of course, I had to say goodbye to Jet.

The crew would trade for supplies and be off to help
Vernt. They scattered ways as soon as they said goodbye.

It was just Jet and I left.

"Why don't we eat lunch together once more before
you go?" he said, wrapping an arm around my shoulders,

and pulling me in the direction of the food stalls before
I could protest.

Not that I would have.

I grinned over at him as we walked. I would miss him.
How easily he had become my friend. How willing he was
to give a smile. How included and welcomed I'd felt from
the first moment he'd startled me.

I gazed at his eyes, looking forward and glinting in the
bright mid-morning sun. And his hair, smoothed down
with two braids woven tightly on either side of his head,
the ends tied in a bunch on the back. The string of green,
wooden beads he always wore around his neck. And his
carefree, loose clothing. I didn't want to forget him. Not
one small detail.

Jet had made me happier than anyone had in years.
I was sad to be parting ways.

"How about we go findin' something besides fish or
seaweed?" he said, turning to me.

"I'd say it's about time," I laughed.

"Right you are. Fruit and wild lizard steak, then?" he
said, pointing to two stalls ahead of us. One sizzled with
sides of fresh meat, the other had people lining up to
gleaming leen-melons, the fruit rosy with ripeness.

"Perfect," I said, extricating myself from Jet's arm and
making my way over to the meat stall.

Half a silver coin later, we had our meal. I insisted on
paying as Jet had been so good to me these past two weeks.

We tucked into our meals, the leen-melons were
succulent and so was the meat. I enjoyed that food more
than any I'd had in a while.

The company was some of the best as well. Between
bites, Jet and I quietly discussed what the new information
we had might mean. I still didn't let him in on my plan, as
I wasn't sure I'd be able to carry it through.

We had plenty to discuss though with deep mysteries of
a sunken continent, what treasure its enemies may be

hunting, and what they and our next steps might be.

Our plates were empty far too quickly and before I wanted it to be, it was time to say goodbye to Jet.

He reached over and hugged me tightly and I hugged him back, reveling in the comfort.

Then he drew back, still grasping my shoulders. "I hope you'll come back any time you may be needing anything. Or just drop in to say hello." He lowered his hands, playing with them, moving ceaselessly. His earrings glinted as he shifted.

"Of course. And thank you," I said, smiling widely.

Before I could blink, I felt Jet's lips on my cheek. Just as swiftly, he was walking away, waving a hand back without looking and calling, "Do come back, Shay."

I brushed my cheek with my hand, unsure of what to think, but smiling nonetheless. Then I turned and made my way home.

28
Help

Three steps away from leaving Jet and I already felt I'd perhaps entered a different world.

Behind me was the feeling of family, of friendship, of new discovery, and maybe of belonging. Ahead was me going backwards. Back to uncertainty, of people not being able to accept me, and of a stolen future.

No. I shook myself. I couldn't think that way. Nothing was certain, and it had been nearly two weeks I'd been gone. There could have been changes.

I shifted my pack on my shoulder and entered the palace in the way I'd left. My window was closed, but unlatched, and I landed heavily back in my room.

It was a startled meeting. Jevin was wearing his green robe, symbols painted on his face, standing near my desk.

My heart lurched at the sight.

"Shay?!" He looked shocked. "But...where were you? I've been...I was just getting my sword back from your room...I thought..."

I held up a hand, stilling his words, and pulled the window closed behind me. "Do you have a bit of time? I see you're headed to the Garden."

He turned in that direction, seeming hesitant, "I don't actually have to go until tomorrow, though I was hoping..." He turned back, looking me in the eyes, "People have been asking after you."

"I'm sure they have. If you have time, I need to talk to you." I gestured for him to sit in my chair and slumped onto my bed, sighing slightly at the softness. "I'll tell you where I've been and there are a couple things I need to discuss with you."

I knew what I wanted right now, and I had a way that I might get it, but I needed Jevin.

My room seemed foreign somehow. Though I'd only been gone this short amount of days, it felt empty. Abandoned.

I threw my pack off to the side.

"So?" Jevin said, clearly curious.

I quirked a smile, "So. I hopped a ship and have been traveling around the island ring for the past two weeks."

Whatever Jevin had thought I'd been doing, it clearly hadn't been this, his eyes widened. "A ship? What, you just went down to the docks and hopped a ship? How? Why?"

I took a deep breath. I'd left after hearing Jevin and my father speak, had gotten my feelings hurt all on my own when I probably should have spoken to them, at least Jevin.

"Jevin, I heard you and my father before I left. Two weeks ago. I know he wants to pass the Garden knowledge directly on to you. How I'm—," my throat caught, and I cleared it before emotion could build behind it. "How I'm not needed anymore."

"Shay...I—"

"It's fine. Really." I looked him in the eye, wanting to get this across, "I should have figured it out for myself. My father could have trained you from the beginning. I'm not needed." I smoothed the blankets of my bed. "I admit though, I felt as if the seagrass had been pulled from under me. I didn't know what to do. So, I left. No one at the palace wanted me around, I wasn't needed to help with the Garden, so I decided to go off on my own and try to figure things out."

"And did you?"

"I'm not sure."

"I still think that you can stay on as a Gardener. I won't be ready to take over for a long time." Jevin's eyes were wide, it seemed he truly wanted me to be with him in the Garden.

"We can talk about it later. There's something I found out while I was away, Jevin. The other islands are in trouble. Some are being attacked, some just falling apart from the inside. There's talk of a curse, though I'm unsure how much of that may be true."

I looked around, the door was locked, the window closed, most of the palace would still be down at lunch at this hour, still I talked low. "I don't think the Tree of the Fallen is protecting the islands as she should. I don't think she's strong enough on her own. Not yet and not for a long while yet, perhaps."

Jevin was silent, his brow pinched. "You don't think she's working as The Great Tree should?"

"I think she's protecting Cresstalan, things seem alright here, but she's also supposed to protect the rest of the islands." My heart started racing as I began the next part, "I had an idea. It's the only one I could think of, but I don't know if it's possible. If it is, I'm not sure my father or the Queen or...anyone would ever agree to it."

"Go on." His attention was rapt.

I spoke slowly, "Wouldn't it make sense that having more than one Great Tree would protect us more?"

Jevin's eyes wavered, "I—I'm not sure."

"I know it says not to, but we don't know why that is and haven't we already started growing a new Tree? What if we planted another Tree, another Garden? What if we planted it on Fainia? Hardly anyone inhabits it now. It's been abandoned and it's directly across the island ring from us."

Jevin said nothing.

"Of course, I came up with this idea by myself. Perhaps it won't work, but I don't see what harm it can do. You haven't seen what I have, Jevin. It's heartbreaking the way things are on the other islands. The ship I was on is quickly stocking up on supplies and going straight back to Vernt to keep people from starving. It made me ask myself what I could do. This is what I decided on." I was silent for a minute. "What do you think?"

Jevin looked out the window behind me, seeming to turn the idea over. "I have heard a few rumors of the troubles on the other islands. I'm not sure if it would help to create another Tree. Goodness," he shook his head wearily, "another Garden altogether. If anyone found out, I don't think it would be favorably looked upon. But, as the Tree of the Fallen is all we have now, things are different. We don't know what she is capable of; if the same rules even apply."

He understood.

"Exactly. I know it's against the texts to plant more trees, but I think that's already been done with the Tree of the Fallen."

"Perhaps. Though your father may be against it."

"That's why I wanted to talk with you. I hoped you might be able to help me convince my father. Then we'd have three people in trying to persuade the Royal Family. I don't know, maybe it's crazy, but I feel I must do something. This feels like the right answer."

"Shay, I don't know if I'm entirely with you, but I don't mind helping bring it to your father and hearing what he has to say."

I'd hoped Jevin would agree whole-heartedly, but I suppose that was simply asking too much.

"Why don't you get into your Garden attire? We'll go there now."

Now seemed just as good as later. And the islands couldn't wait.

"Alright."

"I'll be in my room. Come by when you're ready and we'll go to the Garden together." I nodded once again.

Before he left, he turned back to me and said, "I'm glad to have you back. I missed you."

"I missed you too." I had, though he seemed more earnest than I felt.

When he'd gone, I lay on my bed and closed my eyes, just for a moment. It would be nice to have a comfortable mattress to sleep on tonight, but first I had to go through the uncomfortable task ahead.

I changed; from tunic to robe, from bare face to painted, from sea-faring adventurer to solemn Gardener. Then I retrieved Jevin from his room and we were off to the Garden.

We didn't speak much and, as we padded down the dirt walkway, I saw something glinting near the rock where we would place our shoes.

My heart dropped as the object came into focus. Jevin's sword. It'd been hidden in my room. How had it gotten here?

I stared wide-eyed at Jevin and my expression was reflected on his face. "Oh, no. How could he have found this?"

Jevin was hesitant, "But it will be alright, won't it? You barely used it since I gave it to you."

"I don't know. I'm not supposed to be in possession of a weapon at all. He left it here knowing I'd be at the Garden within the next few days. I don't think this is going to go well."

"Let's go in and see. No use putting it off."

He was right. We removed our shoes and moved on to the Garden.

The tall hedges folded us in their soft green leaves and fresh, bright essence.

My father was trimming a bush and he stood and turned immediately to look at us, then at me, his face stern. "Shaylite, I must speak with you."

I gritted my teeth and walked forward.

My father rose up from his work. It felt as if he towered above me. "Care to explain the sword that was found hidden in your closet?"

"I—Master, I—"

"It was mine, Master." Jevin came forward to stand by me.

The Master Gardener swept his gaze to Jevin, "You, Jevin, are not allowed to own weaponry either. Why would your sword be with Shaylite?"

"Fath—Master, you know I practice swordplay for exercise. I had been using a sword from the palace armory, but—" Here, I stumbled over my words. I was still ashamed of what had happened with the Derrif. "But I—"

"They wouldn't allow her to use those weapons anymore when they found out she was a woman." Jevin spoke earnestly, "I told her to use my sword instead. Only for practice, of course. She kept it with her."

My father was silent. Then he let a long breath out through his nose and flexed his fingers. "Be that as it may, you are not allowed to possess a weapon, even if you only use it for practice."

I bowed my head. "I'm sorry, Master. I was wrong. I simply wanted to train, but I knew that I wasn't to have a blade."

"Shaylite, you have taken the oath of non-violence. I wasn't aware you still trained in combat so regularly. You shall not train with a blade anymore. If you must continue to exercise, I suppose you can do that. Learning to fight

further however, particularly with weaponry, is not
something you should be doing."

What I wanted to say was, *even if I'm not to be a
Gardener anymore, Father?* Instead though, I simply nodded.

"Jevin, I am aware that you have not taken the official
oath as a Gardener, still though, I think it would be wise for
you to cease your training as well. Both of you, leave the
sword where it is and I will keep it safely from now on."

I looked to Jevin. That was his sword. He'd had it as
long as I'd known him, even when he had been too small to
wield it. His face revealed little of that though, if he did
have an attachment to it, he didn't show it. He nodded as
well.

"Shaylite," my father continued, "you are not needed in
the Garden today. Come back in three days when it is your
allotted time once more. I have more to discuss only with
Jevin."

I bowed, disappointed in myself for even thinking of
keeping the sword in my room. I knew it had been wrong
from the beginning and still I'd gone forward with it.

ᕙᕗ

It was only after I'd returned to my room I remembered
my purpose in going to the Garden; asking to plant another
Tree.

I knew though, it would have been unwise to ask with
my father so angry.

202

29
Matched

What I was to do for three days, I didn't know. I only wanted to get my father's permission to leave and start a new Garden, but it was better to let him settle from finding Jevin's sword.

The next day however, I was not in want of something to fill my time, for it was the day of Neeren's Matching Ceremony.

I'd only remembered it was her birth-day when everyone was called to the throne room to witness.

It was late morning and it seemed only Jevin and my father were excused from attending Neeren's ceremony. I supposed the Queen wanted to have Jevin learning of the Garden as often as he could.

A steady flow of people carried me to the throne room, so much so that I went unnoticed. I was worried of meeting Fedrid after I'd hurt him, but I thought I should see whom Neeren was matched with. As long as she wasn't set as a Wild Soul, as I had been, I thought she'd quickly get over any pain I caused her.

Peeking between the line of shoulders before me, I saw the Court Reader's table set before Neeren's throne.

After a few minutes, everyone had been gathered and Neeren, urged forward by her mother, went forward to the Court Reader.

The Queen rose to address the room, "Today is the day that Neeren, Princess of Cresstalan, will be matched with her future husband."

Neeren bowed to the Court Reader who beckoned her to his side of the table, gesturing for her to kneel.

She shifted her skirts and did so.

Just as my ceremony had been, the Court Reader placed a hand on her forehead and moved the other over the sticks, eyes closed.

Finally, his hand stopped and picked up a stick. Neeren returned to her throne to await the result.

"Neeren, Princess of Cresstalan has been matched. She is matched with...Jevin. The Apprentice Gardener."

It was my own, small, "No," that woke me from my stupor, but talking rose up around me and no one else heard.

Never before had the Royal Family and the Keepers of the Garden been part of the same family. Jevin and Neeren? What would it mean if they had a child? Though, it wouldn't inherit the throne, so perhaps it would be okay.

I looked around me, the crowd was beginning to leave now that the official match had been announced. I went with them.

And Jevin wasn't here. He didn't know he'd been matched with Neeren.

He wouldn't be done with his Garden work for most of the day and I wasn't allowed to go in to see him.

The Queen would let him know he'd been matched. I saw through the crowd that the thrones were empty. The Royal Family must have gone to Jevin already.

That evening, Jevin found me, he knocked on my door and flopped onto my bed, upset. "I assume you heard?"

"I was at the ceremony," I said, shutting the door behind him.

"My matching wasn't supposed to be for another year."

"You know it's possible to be matched before your turn." I didn't know how to feel about Jevin being matched with Neeren. Since she'd already been talking to him about me, he was probably the best option. Jevin had been a Royal Aide for so long that he knew the family well. He knew Neeren.

"It's too soon. The Queen is already talking of the wedding when we've just been matched, and I have so much to do with the Garden. Too soon...and why Neeren?" His jaw was clenched.

"You don't want it to be Neeren?"

Jevin looked at me, grey eyes sad. "No. I don't mind Neeren as a person, but I didn't want to matched with her. I—," he hesitated, seeming like he wanted to say something, but couldn't. "I wanted something else."

"What?"

He shook his head, "Perhaps it doesn't matter, I can't go against the decision now." Standing abruptly, "I have to go change from the Garden. I'll see you there in a couple days."

Folding my arms, I stayed where I was near the door. I wasn't mad with Jevin, but I was annoyed. He was getting the best things the palace had to offer, yet he seemed unhappy. What did he want?

"Are you alright?"

He met my eyes once more. They seemed to contain too much for him to say. "I'm not sure."

He sidled past me, out the door.

30
Rejection

I didn't know when 'The Sea's Ribbon' would return, but I had to ask my father for permission to plant the new Tree soon. With Jevin being matched, I was now even more useless.

It was the morning after the matching.

The more I thought about it though, the more forbidden planting a new Tree seemed. Was there any chance my plan would work?

But then, there was something inside me, something perhaps in my heart and in my very bones. A resounding, "YES." This was the way to help. I had to gather up my courage and ask. And then do. And then see where I was.

Eating breakfast, I thoughtlessly moved teelhen beans around my plate with a spoon. I was going to the Garden today.

Believing in my own plan was the first step. I would ask my father, he would say yes, and I would have a new purpose. I scooped up the last of my food in one mouthful and went to ready myself for the task ahead.

My father's shoes were already on the carved stone near the band of bright light. Jevin's sat beside them.

I don't know why, but my heart seemed to suspend its beating for a moment. It had been only my shoes beside my father's for so many years. I'd been the sole Apprentice for so long. And now, suddenly, I was not.

With each thing taken from me, though I understood, I felt an immense sadness. A sense of loss for these things that were never supposed to change.

But here I was. No matter what I wanted, things were different.

I wasn't the same either.

If I got what I asked for, I'd be leaving to start anew, leaving behind this life.

For some reason it was too much for me to bear. I felt a knot of emotion tangle in the center of my chest.

Stopping those thoughts, I removed my shoes, took a deep breath, savoring that sweet smell of soil, and entered the Garden.

Inside, the Master Gardener was explaining the various blooming times of the plants to Jevin. Jevin stood, taking notes, brow furrowed in concentration...at least I was leaving the Garden in good hands.

I bowed to them both. Jevin returned my bow.

"Shaylite," said my father, stiff.

"Master." I hesitated for the slightest moment, then plunged forward in my request, "There's something I must ask of you. Something of dire importance."

His brow wrinkled, only slightly, but he didn't turn me away just yet.

Jevin met my eyes solemnly. "I'll continue sketching the blooms and taking care of the plants, Master."

I started to say that Jevin didn't have to go. I'd thought he could be there when I brought up the plan, some support, but before I could get a sound out, my father sent Jevin on his way.

Jevin nodded to me as he went. At least he knew what I was to do and was nearby.

"Come," said my father, turning to me, "we will speak in the main alcove."

I followed him to the room that held the Garden Handbook.

It was too silent today. The great book of the Garden rested quietly, and the ornate table and chairs nearby seemed emptier than ever before. Gold lamps that ringed the quiet, dry room seemed made of glowing glass, for they hardly fluttered as living flame should.

The Master Gardener took up a seat at one side of the square table, and I took the one opposite. I did my best to look at him fully and not run my fingers over the shaped metal of the table.

"What is it you wanted to speak about, Shaylite?" asked my father, his head tilting ever so slightly.

I cleared my throat, "I wish to speak to you of what I've seen lately and to make a request." In my lap I clenched my fists, gathering strength. "The two weeks before I last entered the Garden, I was not at the palace as usual, Master."

"Oh?" Nothing shifted about him.

"Yes," I continued. "Because of various circumstances...I decided I wanted to explore the islands around us more. I found passage upon a ship and went on a voyage for those two weeks."

This did seem to have surprised him. His eyes widened, and his lips parted, but he said nothing.

"While on this voyage, Master, I discovered things I never thought to see. Some were wonderful, but the most apparent were poverty, desertion, hopelessness, hunger, hate, violence, and fear." I gulped.

"Master, the people of the islands are suffering. There's something amiss. I don't know what it is, but—," I stopped here, I didn't want it to sound like I thought it was his fault. "The Tree. The Great Tree is supposed to protect them from these things, is she not? She should stop things like this from happening and keep peace and prosperity among the islands. Fath—Master, I don't think the Tree of the Fallen is strong enough to protect the islands yet. I'm not sure she will be for a while."

He was silent for what felt like several minutes, his face unreadable.

Then he said, "If that is so, though I've heard none of it, what do you suggest we do?"

How had he heard none of it? But then, he hardly talked to anyone.

"I have seen it with my own eyes, Master. I'm sure if you ask the Queen she'll tell you. She must have heard."

He said nothing.

I continued with the most controversial part, "I am suggesting—I am suggesting we plant another Tree."

Anger. It flared in his eyes, lighting them on fire, though he stayed still.

I attempted to make my case, "I know it is not done. I know it should not be, but perhaps if we had two—"

"Out." His voice was so low, I thought perhaps he'd not spoken after all. When I didn't move though, he said it again, "Get out."

"Master I—" I stayed in my place, not expecting a strong reaction like this.

"I will see you for your turn in the Garden in another two weeks," he said, anger fading, but for the tenseness in his body, "and we will not speak of this again. Ever." He rose, leaving me at the table. "Come in full array. Jevin will take the oath of the Garden then."

I rose, unthinking, and went to leave the Garden. Jevin caught my eye on the way out, but I looked away and left.

Hardly seeing where I was going as I walked the hall, my breath beginning to run ragged, my father's face swam before my vision again, filled with anger. At me. I tried not to remember the last time this had happened.

As my hands began shaking, I knew I had to calm down. Though my room was closer, it'd be loud in the middle of the day as it was in the youth wing. The tower. The spare room where Jevin and I had practiced, not so long ago.

I got there quickly, scarcely paying attention. The room was dim when I entered, but I left the torches unlit.

Surrounded by unused sheets, clay candle-holders, and spider webs, I took a breath. Attempting to slow my racing heart, I crossed my legs and closed my eyes.

The volume of the world turned down. Not only muffled by the bedding around me, but sound stopped by my own mind. That is, except for my breath which immediately went from an anxious flurry to a slow, steady depth. Relief flooded my muscles and I was almost surprised how quickly my mind clicked into that soft, deep place of non-thinking.

I allowed myself to stay like that. Disconnecting, calming, letting my body become itself again.

∞∞∞

When I finally opened my eyes, orange light softly lit the room. Sunset.

I took one more deep breath and suddenly knew what to do.

Exactly what I was going to do before. I'd just have to do it without permission.

Though my father wouldn't help me, I wished he could have explained to me why he was so vehemently against the idea.

And Jevin was to take his oath. I was surprised, but
I found I wasn't upset about this. I had come to terms with
the fact that he would be a Master Gardener.

Now I had a plan to become a Master Gardener as well,
and to maybe help the world while I was at it.

Jevin was still my best friend and, perhaps, he might
help me to carry out my plan anyway.

I went down to dinner, but Jevin wasn't there so I went
to his room.

A drying cloth was held to his face when he answered
the door, his Garden paint still not fully removed. He
looked glad to see me. "Shay. Come in, I just have to finish
up here."

He went immediately back to the washbasin, lifting
soap-flakes to scrub his face.

I pulled the chair from under his pristine desk and sat
myself down.

"I wanted to ask you about today. Why did you leave so
quickly?" he said, his voice muffled as he dried his face.
"Let me just change out of this robe."

Going into his closet and out of sight, he came back a
moment later in a worn tunic and sank onto his low bed to
face me.

His face was wide open with curiosity, "Did you ask
your father? Did you tell him about your idea for the
second tree?"

I let out a long breath, "Yes...and for a moment
I thought he would physically throw me from the Garden.
He was truly angry. He said we should never speak of it
again." I decided not to mention Jevin's oath-taking unless
he brought it up himself.

"What?" He rubbed his chin, "Is it truly that
forbidden?"

I shrugged, "It can't be any more forbidden than
replacing the original Tree," I said, my voice low, "but
I

can count him out of the plan and, I assume, anyone else in the palace."

He stilled, "You're still going to go forward?"

I stared directly into his eyes, "Jevin, the people are in need. I believe this is the best way to help them. I have to do something." I paused, then continued, "Will you still help me?"

"I—," his eyes shifted away, "I'm not sure what I can do."

Afraid of anyone overhearing, I lowered my voice to a near-whisper, "I don't believe my father will allow me into the Garden before my next turn in two weeks, but I don't want to wait that long. The seeds, Jevin." He stared at me, startled, but I continued, "I believe my father will burn them somewhere in the next few days. Has he shown how you must burn them?"

He shook his head.

"He may offer this time around, but if not, you must persuade him. And you have to steal some seeds, just a few, to make sure it works."

He was quiet. I knew it was asking a lot. Perhaps it was too much. If Jevin would help, it would make things much easier.

Somehow though, I would find a way to make this work. I knew I was desperate, knew it wasn't entirely the fate of the islands that drove me. It was me trying to continue to have a reason for being. I needed Jevi—

"I'll do it." Jevin's face was set. "I'll do it, Shay."

I'd never seen him so serious.

"You will?"

He gave one sharp nod.

"Thank you." I was surprised he agreed so readily. "Are you sure? What if it doesn't work? What if you get caught?"

He shrugged, "I won't. And if it doesn't work, at least

we tried." He was staring so intently.

I felt my heart start to beat faster and yet, was overcome with a huge sense of relief.

"Right?" He gave me a soft smile.

I let out a breath, and returned the grin, though a smaller one than his. "Right. Alright."

"I think your plan is simple. I think I can do it." He looked over, out the window, "Your father has mentioned the burning of the seeds and how I'll have to learn it. I think he may teach me this time anyway."

Jevin was going to do this for me, so I decided to support him in return, "My father also said you'll take the Garden oath officially in two weeks."

"He did?" Jevin looked like he was trying to contain some of his happiness. "He mentioned that it might be soon, but I had heard nothing certain."

"That's what he told me," I said. "Congratulations. You've been working really hard and I'm sure that if my father thinks you're ready, then you are."

Jevin stood up and came over to sit down on his desk so he was close to me. "Shay...I know...," he turned away for a moment, his throat bobbed, "I know that it cannot be easy for you to be handing off the Garden to me." He met my eyes again and they were wide and pleading, "I'm doing my best, but I know every step forward I take to become a Gardener pushes you further out of the way."

I almost leaped up when he set his hand down onto mine, grasping it, but did my best to continue looking at him. He was engaged to the Princess now, even if we were friends, he couldn't act so familiar.

All of this was difficult.

"I don't know if planting a new Tree is the solution to whatever problems you've seen with the islands, but I'll help you. At least you'll still be a Gardener this way and when I'm the Master Gardener, perhaps we can officially recognize the one you're to plant."

Maybe he was only doing it because he felt guilty and sorry for me, but it was certainly a nice thought.

It'd grown almost completely dark in Jevin's room and he still hadn't let go of my hand. I didn't grab his back in return.

As I felt Jevin's hand and the arms attached to it move ever so slightly towards me, I drew my mine back and stood. "Thank you, Jevin," I said kindly.

He looked slightly disappointed for a moment.
I thought I knew why.

I left him as he started going around the room, lighting the lamps.

"I'll meet you in the morning for breakfast, Jevin. See you then."

He agreed, seeming cheered with that.

Back in my room, I sat at the desk and thought...only for a few moments. Did Jevin see me in a romantic way? I thought, for a second there, he'd been leaning forward to kiss me in the darkness.

It was a terrible idea for us to do anything like that. Jevin was officially matched.

Though, I realized, even if he was doing all he could within the circumstances, I was still incredibly hurt by him being the new Apprentice. I was coming to accept that fact, but I couldn't connect with him quite as I had before. I would still be his friend, but even that was a little bit difficult.

As for romantic things...a vision of Jet, smile wide, rose in my mind.

I gently smiled to myself as I put out the lamps of my room.

31
Taken

It was the day of the seed burning, and my father had told Jevin he'd show him how to do the task. The plan was in place.

I was restless the whole morning. Jevin and I ate in the dining hall. We spoke little. There wasn't much of the idea that was difficult. Any issues would most likely come in the moment, and Jevin would have to deal with them on his own.

I wished I could go to the Garden with him, perhaps be a distraction...or something, but the look in my father's eyes when I'd spoken to him came back to me. He wouldn't want me there.

"Perhaps I should try to go along with you," I had suggested to Jevin the day before.

"Shay, I can do it, don't worry. It might make your father more suspicious."

So, I ate breakfast with Jevin, trying to be normal to encourage and calm him.

Except...he was calm. Jevin was acting the same as ever and, now that I was thinking about it, every time we'd gone over the subject of his mission in the past couple days, he had seemed fine and not at all as nervous as he'd seemed the first night I brought it forward to him.

I lowered my voice so it was almost inaudible and, while scooping up another bite of the renn-berry gel on my plate, I asked, "Are you sure you're fine with all of this?"

Jevin also lowered his voice and looked down at his food, relaxed. "Yes."

He didn't say anymore, so I didn't ask anymore.

We went back to talking at a regular volume about regular things, but I was hardly paying attention. I wasn't the one who was going to steal seeds today, yet I was more nervous than Jevin. Would this plan work? Was it alright that I was asking Jevin for help?

It would have to be.

∞∞∞

We finished eating and went back to our rooms, Jevin to his to change and prepare for the Garden.

I tried to sit down and read an instructional book on fighting without blades, but I couldn't concentrate and ended up simply pacing my room and staring out the window until a knock sounded.

Jevin had gotten ready quite quickly; I opened the heavy door.

My relief faded as I saw it was not Jevin, but Fedrid.

"I heard you were around again." His eyes were a cold, icy blue and his nose seemed slightly swollen. It must not have fully healed from when I'd hit it.

"The Queen would like a word with you."

I contemplated asking to wait a while, for Jevin, but with Fedrid's expression growing more furious by the second, that wouldn't do me any favors.

Jevin would have to go to the Garden and get the seeds on his own. I was worried for him, but he'd seemed fine.

"Lead the way," I said, dipping my chin to Fedrid.

His eyes narrowed suspiciously.

Perhaps he'd expected me to protest or to run, but I knew what I had done to him was wrong and I was willing to face the Queen for it. I would tell her my side.

A small part of myself, the one that rebelled against me when I decided against violence, wished that his nose had completely broken. I took a deep breath and quieted that part, following Fedrid.

Our steps seemed to echo more than usual and both of us were silent. He looked back to me a few times to check I was still following.

I wondered if the Queen would inform my father as she'd done the last time I'd used violence on Fedrid. Would I be kicked out of the Garden sooner than planned?

The guards on either side opened the intricate, clay doors to the throne room. Fedrid went first with his chest puffed out and I came second, humbled, and slightly ashamed of myself.

Even though Fedrid had been wrong, I'd lost control. I had gone against the orders of the Garden and committed an act of violence. I could've broken free and run away, probably without hurting anyone, but I hadn't. I'd let my anger and fear get hold of me and had given in.

The Queen sat on the middle throne. Neeren was at her left side, only looking at Fedrid.

Fedrid sat on his own throne.

"Shaylite..." said the Queen.

I bowed, "Your majesty."

"I would appreciate if you would inform me what happened a few weeks ago and how the Crown Prince's nose and face were harmed so brutally." Her eyes simmered.

"It was me, your majesty. The Prince and some of his friends ambushed me and wouldn't let me go. I believe they were going to harm me. Though I shouldn't have, I

defended myself to get away." I saw no alternative, but to
own up to what I'd done.

Fedrid leaned forward in his throne and glared, "We
were trying to make her behave the way she should."

"The way she should?" asked the Queen, looking over
to him.

"Just look at her," said Fedrid. "She's a woman, yet here
she is with her head shaved, wearing leggings, and using
swords. I was trying to get her to act the way she is
supposed to."

"And you, Shaylite, you don't believe you should act
properly?"

"I—I've always been this way. I was to be a Gardener
and all Gardeners wear the same thing. I thought perhaps it
was fine I dressed like this." I wasn't sure what to say.

"Yet, you aren't going to end up being the Gardener
you were to be. Therefore, shouldn't you perhaps stop
feeling like you can be exempt from certain expectations?"

My stomach seemed to disappear. She was right. I had
the plan to be a Gardener somewhere else, but now that
plan wasn't approved by my father.

My father. "Perhaps I should think on that. Your
majesty—," I hesitated. "Does my father know about this?"

"We have decided that this can be solved without
making an issue of it. Therefore, we are telling as few
people as possible. You are old enough to know that you've
done wrong and that you should receive a punishment."

I thought it strange that my father wasn't told of this at
all, and the Queen seemed un-swayed by my words.

If I truly wasn't to be a Gardener though, did it even
matter that I'd used violence? It was forbidden for Keepers
of the Garden, but not for regular citizens...except if you
used it on a member of the Royal Family, I supposed. That
wouldn't be looked upon favorably. I still had no excuses
for what I'd done.

The Queen didn't seem to care Fedrid had attacked me. She agreed that I should act like a lady. Perhaps she thought Fedrid had been right to force me into it.

No one was on my side. The Princess had her arms crossed and, in all appearances, seemed to agree that I should dress like a girl. She may have been humiliated that she'd ever liked me in the first place, considering I was also a girl.

I thought briefly of the relationships Jet had told me of between two girls, I doubted anything like that would ever be accepted on Cresstalan.

What could I do, but take whatever punishment the Queen had in mind?

"I'm sorry I attacked the Prince." Perhaps an apology would ease whatever harsh feelings were against me.

"Too late for that," spat the Prince.

"Indeed, Shaylite," said the Queen. "You have acted inappropriately and will receive a punishment."

I nodded, not able to think of anything to say to defend myself.

"I have decided. Because you are no longer going to be a full Gardener and, therefore, will not be wearing your Gardener's robes for much longer, you must wear proper attire for a lady. Dresses; not robes or tunics. You mustn't shave your head either. Grow your hair out."

I listened in confusion. Could this really be the punishment? Could they force me to dress in a way I didn't want to? Force me not to cut my hair?

"You must have a new occupation as you won't be a Keeper of the Garden for much longer. I will think on that. It will be hard to place you, as you don't have many skills. Perhaps we can allow you to water the upper gardens. Fedrid seems to be healing quickly and I am pleased that you apologized to him, so further punishment shouldn't be needed." She raised a finger, "Ah, but you will also be forbidden from using the training grounds." Her hands clasped precisely. "If I find you rebelling against any of these rules, you will be called back to speak with me and your punishment will be more severe."

I was at a loss. Everything was going to be taken away from me. The Garden, my combat training, in a way, my identity.

If I tried to fight her on this, to defend myself based on Fedrid and his friends' behavior, she'd give me a worse sentence.

If I didn't have another plan, I would have.

There was now a lot more riding on Jevin being able to get those seeds. If he did, I could leave, and no one would know where I went. I could attempt to save the world by growing a new Garden and live my life how I wished.

I bowed deeply to the Queen.

"Very good. I'm glad this was settled easily. I will have some dresses made for you, same as your Garden robes were, and have them to you in a few days. In the meantime, do not shave your hair or set foot on the training grounds. Is that clear?"

"Ye—" My throat had caught, but I cleared it and went on, "Yes, your majesty."

"Very well." With a smooth wave of her hand, she said, "you are dismissed then, Shaylite."

I bowed. And turned. And left. Not knowing where else to go, I went back to my room. It was past mid-morning now. Jevin would be in the Garden.

I didn't know how to feel. Had I been in the wrong? I'd defied the rule of non-violence. I was partially wrong, but I could have gotten away, hurting no one, and kept living my life the way I had been.

But, no. I couldn't have. I would have been miserable. Fedrid would have kept hunting me down, perhaps in worse ways, and eventually I would probably have had to live with these punishments anyway, just because it was how a girl was supposed to behave. Whether all of this would turn the way of good or bad was yet to be seen.

I'd do my best to avoid the punishment altogether and help the people of the islands who were in need.

The sea-grass filling my mattress crinkled as I lay down and sighed out a breath. The sun was bright outside my window and lit up the room brilliantly. I looked around and my eyes landed on the gardening handbook.

There was a lot of information in that, but would it be enough to start a new Garden? Even my father hadn't had to do that. In fact, I thought for a moment, I had no idea who had grown the Garden in the first place. I assumed it was one of my ancestors, but that hadn't been part of the Garden training.

I knew how to germinate and grow different plants. I knew most care techniques, but my garden on Fainia wouldn't be as sheltered as the true Garden was, would it be alright? All I could do was try my best and hope that it worked out.

I'd bring my own handbook, at least. That would have to be enough.

32
Abandoned

Jet and the crew would hopefully be back in a few days.

What happened next depended on Jevin, but he wouldn't be back from the Garden until sundown, seeds or not.

What should I do for the moment? How could I work toward my goals? I couldn't train. I couldn't be in the Garden, couldn't do a lot of things. I didn't want to stay in my room.

The ruins. I remembered how the stone of Fainia's ruins had been so close to our own, though the ones on Fainia had symbols carved into them.

Never having thoroughly searched Cresstalan's ruins, I wondered if there were symbols hidden here as well.

Perhaps none of it was important, but it was something to do. I went out into the sweltering day.

The foliage along the path to the ruins was withering. Rains of summer would come soon, but we had a while to wait yet. The plants didn't seem to be enjoying the long dry-spell.

They looked even more parched than most summers.

A humming wind wound its way around the carved rock when I reached my destination.

The white stone was surely the same as the Fainian ruins, the texture and color seemed exact.

It struck me that the rock near the Garden entrance, the one we always placed our shoes onto, was also made of the same stone. Was that rock from these ruins? How had it gotten to the Garden?

I started looking among the broken bits. Many of the rocks were piled on top of each other. Running my fingers along the rough stone, it seemed almost as if it'd been scraped or chipped away at. It could be from initially carving the stone; it seemed deliberate.

For a few hours, I examined every piece of the ruins, finding nothing but the strange scraping.

It was as I wedged myself between two stones that formed a small angle, sweat dripping from my brow and neck, that I saw them. Though faint, I could tell they were symbols. I inched myself closer, my breath coming back to my face against the stone. They were symbols of the Garden. The crescent, the wave-form, three wavy lines.

I stared at them for a few minutes, looking for signs of other markings, but the heat and muscle aches forced me to push myself from the space.

Out in the open air, I didn't know what to think. Somehow both ruins were connected.

I looked out to the horizon, where blue met blue in the sea and sky.

Sseya had said our island ring had once been one continent. Though some sea-faring people could have gone island to island and built the now-ruined buildings, Sseya's story sounded more likely.

Did that mean there was truly treasure lying at the bottom of the sea spires?

Though I searched thoroughly for more symbols amongst the stone, I found none.

The rock in the earthen walkway must have been moved from the ruins here to the entrance of the Garden. It was such a small piece and there was no other stone like it anywhere around the palace or Garden. Why had it been taken there? Was it just someone's passing fancy or had there been a reason?

I let out a breath, realizing there was no way to answer these questions.

The sun lowered itself in the sky. Jevin would soon be finished in the Garden.

This mystery was interesting and certainly distracting, but that's all it was to me. A distraction. I was just trying to waste time.

What I wanted most right now was to know how Jevin had done. Had he gotten the seeds? Was he alright?

Jet might be back within the next few days. My heart sped slightly, but I couldn't yet let myself believe that Jevin had gotten the seeds and I'd be able to live the new life I planned.

Returning to the palace, I tried not to think too hard, tried not to hope too hard, tried not to think about any of it. Just appreciating the soil beneath my shoes, the low plants brushing the sides of my legs, the soft breeze blowing over my face, and the sunlight as it shifted the shadows of the day into the shadows of evening.

I went back to my room. Exactly where I'd been this morning, lying on my bed and trapped in that awful waiting. I couldn't do anything else, so I found myself closing my eyes and attempting to meditate.

∞∞∞

Jerking into a sitting position, my eyes opening, it was now mostly dark. There was a knock on the door.

"Just a minute," I said, hoarse, rubbing my face to return to consciousness. I hurried to the bathroom lamp with a tinder stick and lit the other lamps in my room, basking it in an orange glow.

Shaking the tinder stick until the flame was extinguished, I opened the door.

It was Jevin this time and he looked both ways down the hallway before entering my room. I closed the door quietly behind him.

Before I could speak, he reached into the pocket of his tunic. He'd already changed out of his Garden garb.

Extending his hand to me, I saw three things I'd not dared hope for. Seeds.

"You did it?" I whispered.

The seeds sat in his palm and he nodded solemnly. He took hold of my hand and turned it so my own palm was facing upwards, carefully transferring them from his hand to mine. They were soft, round, smooth, and I tried not to hold them too tightly as I lowered my fist back to my side.

I let out a long breath, not sure what to say. Jevin didn't say anything either and we simply stood. I was flooded with thoughts. I knew I could try to help a lot of people now. I was so thankful to Jevin and unsure how to express it. He'd risked everything to get these for me, had agreed quite readily to help, and now I had the seeds.

"Thank you," I managed to get out.

Jevin dropped onto my bed. He laid back fully and closed his eyes. "That was more stressful than I thought it would be, but doing it was quite easy. Your father explained to me how to burn the seeds and went on with other duties, taking some was simple. I burned the rest. I don't think he suspected anything." He opened his eyes and looked to me, I'd sat at my desk. "I think you're safe to go and to start a new Garden."

"Thank you," I said again.

"What did you do today? Where were you this morning? I came by, but you were gone," he asked, closing his eyes once again.

I decided to tell him exactly what'd happened, though his casual tone suggested he'd be surprised by the seriousness of it.

"Fedrid came to my room this morning."

Jevin sat up and looked at me worriedly.

Since I wouldn't have to bear the punishment I'd been set by the Queen, I tried to play it off as if what happened was fine as I explained it to Jevin, "I don't know if you heard, but he and his friends ambushed me before I left and I sort of...lost my control...I think I may have broken Fedrid's nose."

"What? You were the one who did that?"

"Anyway," I continued, still ashamed of this and wanting to move on, "the Queen called me to the throne room. I received my punishment. I'm to be forced to get a regular occupation at the palace, since I can't be Gardener anymore. I have to wear dresses as a lady should and I have to grow out my hair."

"You what?" Jevin winced. "Can they really force you to do that?"

"The Queen said she would punish me harshly if I didn't follow what she ordered." I drew up a corner of my mouth and held up the hand containing the seeds. "But none of that should matter, thanks to you. I have the seeds now. I can start a new Garden and...and never come back."

"Shay..." Jevin's face sagged, he looked hurt. He looked as if he hadn't thought I was going to leave for good.

I lowered my head. "I have to leave. There's nothing else for me here, Jevin. The Queen said perhaps, with my skills, I could help the upper gardeners here for my occupation, but because I was a woman, the most I would be allowed to do is water the plants. That's not enough for me." I raised my head once more, hoping Jevin understood. "I've decided I'm going to leave and I can't come back. That way I can start at least one new Garden. Hopefully that will help the problems and I can live however I want."

Jevin looked down at his hands now, I knew he was upset. "I—I didn't think you would have to leave forever. And—," he lifted his face to me, "why didn't you tell me Fedrid tried to attack you?"

"It's fine...it's all fine now." I turned away from Jevin's gaze.

"Shay. If you had to break the vow of non-violence, it must have been malicious. It must have been warranted."

My eyes strained to hold back angry tears. I hated what had happened and I hated how I'd reacted to it. I spoke harshly, "Neither of us was right, Jevin. He and his friends were out of line, but I went overboard when I escaped. I don't know what would have happened if I was to still be Gardener. Perhaps I would have lost my position anyway. Now I have a new purpose."

Jevin rose and folded me in his arms.

My eyes went wide, body tense.

"Jev—"

His chest rumbled against me as he spoke, "Don't go. You can't leave me. Shay—I...," he nearly whispered, "I think I love you."

I pushed him away. Harder than I meant to, for he stumbled backward a few steps.

I didn't regret it.

"Jevin." I felt my face contort. "You are matched with Neeren. You can't have me too."

He circled his arms around himself now, clutching. "I didn't want that. It wasn't supposed to be her!"

"What do you mean, supposed to?" I rubbed my face. "It's fate, Jevin. We can't change it!"

He opened his mouth, but no sound came out. A tear fell from one eye, though he smiled brokenly. "I thought I could."

I looked straight into Jevin's eyes once more. "If my fate had been different, I wouldn't have had to invent a new life! This isn't what I want, but it's what is real. I'm going to grow this new garden and do what I must to keep going!"

Jevin's face shifted. It had been more vulnerable than I'd ever seen it, but now a pallor came over him. His eyes seemed to sink into his face, drawing away from me. "And you're just going to leave me here?"

My brain seemed unable to comprehend what he was saying. "Jevin..."

"I wanted to be a Gardener, but I thought I'd be with you while I did it."

"Jevin, you heard my father. I can't be a Gardener, you're matched with Neeren who hates me now, and I'm not even allowed to come near the training grounds. What do you need me for?" I felt anger filling me.

Jevin was my best friend. I would miss him, but he didn't need me to be here anymore.

"I thought maybe you were different than these other people. I thought we were something more...," Jevin laughed then, "...but I was wrong." He turned to me, preparing to leave. "Well, you have the seeds. Go and start a new garden and live your new life and do whatever you want to do. All the better," he said it as if throwing the words away.

He walked out the door, shutting it harshly as he left.

What had he meant by that? Jevin was engaged, he would be the Master Gardener and learn the greatest secrets of the kingdom. I knew we were best friends, but I also knew he would have plenty of things to help him get over any sorrow he felt in losing me.

How could he love me? He didn't even know me anymore. We'd been growing so far apart lately.

I sighed and leaned back in my chair. "Should I go apologize?" I asked into the shadowed room. Perhaps I shouldn't.

Though I hated to leave things like this with Jevin, I had to go. Maybe this would make it easier.

I looked at the seeds in my hand, tears blurring my vision, then turned toward Jevin's room.

"I'm sorry," I whispered.

33
Gone

Before dawn the next morning, I awoke and listened to my room around me.

The faint sounds from the water in the washroom, the soft brush of wind outside my window, the slight sound as I shifted my weight on the mattress below. I opened my eyes and found a dim bit of light illuminating the room. The softest light before dawn.

I looked around me. At the clay door across from me, the time-watcher on the book shelf, the books that filled the shelf, my desk and chair, the wardrobe off to the side and the closet to the other, and then the crack of the washroom door slightly open so I could see the looking glass.

I found I didn't want to linger over it all.

In the middle of the night, I'd decided. Now that I had the seeds, I would go down to the docks and wait for 'The Sea's Ribbon' to return.

This life had given me what it could, and now I wanted to do something new. Rising, I gazed out the window. Sparse clouds were scattered, lit brilliantly with the sun that was soon to rise. Bright pinks and oranges smeared the sky and increased in brightness as I watched with a wide smile on my face.

I thought of the crew and of Jet. They were out helping the people of Vernt. I was ready to join them. Jet had said the crew might need more supplies soon. I hoped it would work out perfectly for them to be here any day. Just maybe, they would agree to drop me on Fainia and I could begin my new life.

Finding I hardly wanted to bring anything with me, I packed a couple pairs of sturdy clothes, my gardening handbook, face-paint, razor, all the money I had, and a hat and cloak. Thinking briefly of the precious items I'd stored at the back of my closet when I'd left before...I decided to leave them be. I took the three seeds I'd placed into my desk drawer and pushed them into a small, noonyi-skin pouch I hung from my neck and tucked beneath my tunic.

There was only one loose-end left, and I wasn't sure how to tie it off. My father.

I couldn't tell him the true reason for leaving. Though he hardly saw me, though we barely talked, he was my father. And I was the only family he had left, even if we didn't act like family.

Hoisting my knapsack onto my back, I went to my father's room, a place I hadn't been in years.

Hearing stirring inside, I knocked, and his large voice said, "What is it?" He opened the door, already wearing his gardening robe, but his face wasn't yet painted.

His eyes widened, "Shaylite?"

"Good morning, Father. I need to talk to you."

He huffed out a short breath. "If this is what you were talking of the other day—"

"It's not."

He didn't look convinced.

"Though, if you changed your mind about that, I'd be grateful. What I wanted to do was say goodbye."

"Goodbye?"

"May I come in, father?"

He didn't move for a moment, but then stepped to the side and gestured for me to enter.

We entered a sitting room containing two comfortable chairs and I took one, the chair letting out a hiss as air seeped from the cushion. My father lit lamps around the room and sat as well.

"Father, I heard you and Jevin talking, and I know that I will no longer be able to be a Keeper of the Garden."

All he did was nod, though I thought I saw the slightest haze of disappointment cross his eyes.

I continued, "I don't know if you realize, but growing up, everyone thought I was a boy. I didn't know any better to correct them. After a while I didn't want to because it would have meant some large changes to my life." My fingers grazed my leggings. "I was shunned here at the castle for a time when they learned of it."

I wanted him to know why I was leaving and braced myself. "Prince Fedrid and some of the boys ambushed me one day and said they wanted to make me act more like a girl. They ganged up to try and make me wear a dress, at least. They were being extremely forceful, and I think they were going to try to hurt me. When that happened I—," I let out a breath. "Father, I broke the vow of non-violence."

Wincing, I continued, "I believe I broke Prince Fedrid's nose. I lost control and was more vicious than intended. Not knowing what else to do, I left on a ship. I knew I'd done wrong, but they had as well, and I wanted to get away and clear my head. The crew of the ship thought I did well and told me I could join them, should I wish. The captain is even a woman."

My father's fingers were pressed into his brow and his eyes were closed wearily. I'd disappointed him again.

I continued, "I came back here not knowing what I intended to do. I thought if there was a new Garden for me to work on I could continue what I'd been doing. Since you disapproved, I was going to do all the other things I always had instead, but the Queen sent for me and set me a punishment for hurting Fedrid. She says I can't train at all. I must live as a girl, grow out my hair, and wear dresses. She said she'd find me a position in the palace watering the plants of the upper gardens, as women aren't permitted to do more than that." I tried to convey how all this felt. It was such an intense build-up of emotion when I explained it at once.

My father stared at me intensely, frowning. His face had a look of remorse I'd never seen him wear.

I decided to continue. I would defy my father and the history of the Garden, and go plant another one, but I wanted him to know that I was going away.

"I don't want to live that way, father. I wouldn't feel like myself. With that small responsibility when the true Garden is just beneath my feet, I couldn't be happy. I hope you can see that. So, I'm going to join the ship's crew. It's called 'The Sea's Ribbon'. I feel I can make myself useful there. I wanted to let you know." I was unsure what else to say. "Are you alright with that?"

My father looked out the window, silent. Then he spoke, "Perhaps I have not lived precisely the way I should have, nor brought you up in the right way. It seems many things have happened that could have been prevented by me." He sighed, but it sounded more irritated than anything. "There is nothing for it now, however. I see that you cannot remain here. So, go. Jump onto a ship and become a sailor, I suppose. You have my blessing, though that counts for little. I wish you luck and fair winds." He looked back to me, meeting my eyes briefly, his the same green as mine, and nodded.

Standing then, he gestured for me to follow. "I will give you one thing that should help."

He opened a drawer in the large desk along the side of the wall, grabbed a silken bag from the drawer, and handed it to me.

The weight and muted clink gave it away. Coins. Gold, from the sound of it. He released a breath and led me to the door, letting me out to the hallway. The only bit of affection he showed was one more nod and a squeeze on my shoulder.

Then his door was shut, and I was on my own.

I put the bag of coins into my knapsack with my other possessions. I suppose they would come in useful. I hadn't been expecting my father to stop me, but I'd hoped for something more.

There was nothing for it. He was always like that.

It was time to go down to the docks.

I walked along, not really thinking. I felt partially in shock. I had left behind everything I'd known. For good this time.

I noticed the day was still dim as I walked, though the sun should have fully risen by now. A layer of clouds coated the sky and the air felt heavy. Perhaps it would rain at last.

34
Jet

Before it seemed possible, I was at the dock. I'd hardly been aware of walking. The whine of my stomach reminded me to eat.

There was a stall nearby selling steaming biscuits filled with what looked like spiel-fruit jelly and pieces of another fruit I hadn't seen before, but was golden, and looked delicious. I paid one copper coin for the food and sat to eat on a bench nearby, it had a view of the ocean.

I looked out to the vast expanse of water. The sea was a muted green with the clouds overhead, somber.

I found I wasn't sad, but empty. Perhaps relieved, perhaps lost. I just stared forward at the clouds and water and took a bite of the steaming, sweet biscuit in my hand. It was flavored perfectly, and I relished the warm food. At least for this small pleasure, I could be thankful.

That's when I felt it and nearly cried from the sheer relief of the hand on my shoulder. The quick grab of, and as I turned, yes...it was Jet. Grinning as widely as ever.

"You sharing any of that?" he asked, stretching out a palm for my breakfast.

I laughed, which sounded more like a cough through the

biscuit, and a few crumbs flew forward onto Jet.

He sighed and brushed them off. "Ey, not quite what I meant."

I tried to swallow the large bite in my mouth, but instead tore what was left of the biscuit in half and handed one to him.

"There you are." He smiled and sat down next to me, taking the food.

I finally gulped and said, "When did you get back? I wasn't expecting 'The Sea's Ribbon' for a few days."

Jet nodded and swallowed. "Our supplies were snapped up when we went back to Vernt. Last we were here, we got a high price for all the coating leaves we brought along. Went right back and gathered four times as much. Now we're here. We'll trade them again and go back to Vernt. They're getting back on their feet, to be sure, but it'll take longer than anyone can guess. We've enough money and supplies left over for ourselves and it's not much work for us to go about helping." He popped the last of the biscuit into his mouth and smiled contentedly.

I just stared at him for a moment. "I've never known anyone to help others as much as all of you do on 'The Sea's Ribbon'."

"Well," Jet licked his thumb, eating a bit of jam from it, "most of us aboard know what it is to be the one who needs help and doesn't get any. I was left abandoned when I was still a small child." He bobbed his head. "To be clear, I don't remember this myself, but it seems I snuck my way onto 'The Sea's Ribbon' and they were kind enough to keep me. They found me on Ransett." A fly landed on Jet's shoulder and he brushed it away gently. "There are hot springs abouts there where water comes from the ground in tall jets. Clare suggested they call me Jet and that's what I've been since. They all took turns caring for me."

I'd finished my food and brushed my hands off. "I thought Jet was an interesting name." I thought for a moment, "Does the rest of the crew have similar situations?"

"Aye, most do. Couldn't find places where they were happy or wanted, so's they found their way to 'The Sea's Ribbon'. Word that Mercully would take you on with little experience was around, and our crew has grown little by little. Not all stay, but they enjoy sailing along with us."

"She's really amazing."

"Ey, that's too true. Well," he said, turning to me, "that's enough of that talk for now. I'm glad to have found you. Got here yesterday and I wanted to stay one more day to see if you'd be wanting to come along. We're off now. Got all our trade done yesterday!"

"Do you think you'll land at Fainia again soon?"

"Vernt to Fainia to Cresstalan will surely be our duty for the time. Plenty of ships see to the other islands, this is where we're needed."

"Jet," I said, thinking of the seeds nestled near my chest.

"You're needing to go to Fainia, are you, Shay?"

I nodded, "There's something I have to do there. It's to do with the plan I have. The I told you about."

"One that'll help with the islands?"

"Yes. I—" I had thought a bit about this. It would be best to tell him. I'd need help.

It was still early, and the only people around were the stall-owners of the market. They were busy setting things out for the day and were a way off.

"Jet, I think I'm going to need your help with this plan. Is there any chance you can be away from the ship for a little while?"

"On Fainia, is it? And what shall I be helping with?"

My voice came out as low as it could possibly go while still allowing Jet to hear what I had to say, "I can't tell you absolutely everything, but...I'm going to grow a new garden...and I'll need someone to assist me."

He said nothing. His mouth tensed, and his eyes went wide.

"What do you think? Will you do it?" I asked.

"You...want me to help with a new Garden there? With..." His voice went even further down into a whisper, "with there bein' a new tree?"

I nodded earnestly. If he said no, I wouldn't know what to do. Though I liked the rest of the crew, Jet was the person I trusted the most and whom I thought would be able to help me. I wanted him with me.

"We would be staying on Fainia, then?"

"We'd have to watch over the garden constantly. In its infancy a garden...a tree...is extremely delicate. The smallest mistake or neglect, and it will die."

He looked at me, his dark eyes holding my own seriously. "You think you'll be able to go and grow a new garden, do you?"

I let out a long breath, "If I'm being completely honest, I don't know. But I think I can. We'll also keep different varieties of plants around the tree to help it succeed in growing. I believe I can do it."

"I'll admit," Jet said, now looking out over the ocean, a breeze fluttering past us, "starting another garden sounds far beyond something grand. Something no one else alive has done, I'd believe. For a time, at least, I should be able to stay. Help you start the garden, there. The crew won't do without me forever, but helpin' you start up, showin' you whereabouts the food of the island may be, I can help with it." He whirled his head to me suddenly, his jaw slack, "If it's a garden you're starting though, you'll be there always, won't you?"

I nodded. "Which is why I'll need your help. And—" I had to tell him if he was going to get into all of this. "I...I don't have permission to grow the garden." I stared down at my hands, now clasping each other tensely. "I set out to get permission and to get the seeds from my father, the Master

Gardener, but I was unable to convince him of the importance of it. I had to steal the seeds and I'm going to do it without permission, whether I have help or not."

Jet didn't speak right away, but then said, "Your thoughts are that another tree will go about protectin' the islands?"

I dipped my head in acknowledgement. I wouldn't tell Jet about the Tree of the Fallen, at least not yet. "The Great Tree doesn't seem to be protecting them. I tried to think of a way I could help, something big I could do. This is what I decided on and I'm the only one capable of it. I've been relieved from my duties as a Keeper of the Garden...because...well, it doesn't matter right now." I still felt pain around any thoughts of Jevin. "So I'm free to do what I please. I've trained as a Gardener all my life and perhaps that knowledge can be useful."

"It's as good a plan as any. Are you sure you want to go about with it though? Seems you could get in mighty trouble if you're found out."

"I'm hoping we'll just have to keep it secret until the tree is old enough to make a difference."

"And how long should that be?"

"I don't know," I said, shyly. "I know it's a lot to ask, Jet, but I think it will work."

He stood up and stretched his arms over his head. "Well, you know I'm always up for a bit of adventure, especially if there's danger involved. If it succeeds, seems we'll be thanked more than I can imagine. Let's go on with it, then. I'll think on a story to go tellin' Mercully as to why we'll be staying there. We'll start on it all soon as can be."

I smiled, a weight lifting off my shoulders. I'd been wondering if Jet would think to keep it a secret from the crew as well. It seemed I'd nothing to worry over.

"Alright, well then you are officially my new partner in starting this Garden."

Jet laughed, "Let the fun begin, eh?"

I winced. "Not all of it...not most of it. It's going to take a lot of work."

"Ey, a lot of the best things take the most work. We can do it well, I know. Let's get back to the ship." He jerked his head toward the docks and waited for me to stand and then go to his side before setting off.

The sun had broken through the clouds and our shadows led the way to 'The Sea's Ribbon'.

35
Closer

Life on 'The Sea's Ribbon' was easy to fall back into. If the worst should happen and none of the seeds I'd taken lived to form a new tree, I thought I could actually do the plan I'd told my father.

My mind never left the seeds though. They were so precious, I constantly felt at my sternum to see if they were still there.

I truly loved being a Gardener and wanted this new garden to succeed. Though I liked the crew immensely, I didn't want to join them fully.

It would be good to have Jet for a time. He'd be able to learn the basics of being a Keeper of the Garden and had the right temperament and enthusiasm I believed was needed to help plants grow.

Though I felt silly in thinking it, I felt that he'd helped me grow since I had met him. Perhaps that could translate to the plants.

Tempers were slightly shorter aboard the ship, however. Tension lay over everything as it hadn't before.

I asked Jet about it.

"There has, indeed, been some stepping lightly needed,"

he said. "It's just fear. We've been going as fast as we can between the islands and that has meant taking the route through the middle twice more now, 'bout to be thrice. There's been no other ships, thank stars. Going to be fine, but nothing is as planned. That'll set anyone off on a bit of a worry chase."

"You've still been going past the pillars? Even though the ship was nearly attacked last time?"

"Last time for you, but as I've said, that was two times ago. Mercully wants to help the people of Vernt as fast as we can and I'm of the mind to be agreeing."

Though it worried me slightly as well, Jet was right.

"Did you ask Mercully about helping me on Fainia?"

"I let her know it all the first night. We're good to go on and do it. We'll be going to Vernt first, then straight off to Fainia. She'll go about telling the rest of the crew herself."

"Thank you!" I smiled.

"Ey, I'm glad to have a new adventure in sights." He elbowed my arm.

❧❧❧

Things went smoothly as we passed the strange spires. I thought I could just see them in the near distance, for we didn't venture too closely. I wondered if there was truly some mystery about them.

I didn't think on it long and concentrated on the seeds and task at hand.

Every morning I made it a habit to meditate, striving to be as prepared as possible.

The first day was difficult.

"You alright there, Shay?" this was Clare.

"Yes," I said, breaking open my eyes and doing my best to smile into the bright sunlight. "I'm meditating. It's a practice Gardeners do. I plan to do it each morning."

"Ah, alright, then. Seems strange, but as long as you know what you are about."

There were a few more questions like this from Wilhelm, Dimny, and Sen, but soon everyone seemed to know I was going to sit with my eyes closed for a while each morning.

Maybe it was that my odd behavior distracted them, but everyone seemed more at ease after I started meditating once more.

If I was being honest though, I was hoping for more. I thought I may have some sort of epiphany over how exactly to plant the Garden, but nothing came.

At least I felt calmer.

The people of Vernt knew what to expect now.

The day we landed, there was one other ship in the harbor that dropped supplies. We went to the governor at the town center, carrying all the provisions we were able. Two more trips were needed, even with a few of Vernt's people helping, before we were finished.

A small bit of commerce and normality was working its way back and we were invited to stay the night at a close-by inn. A hot meal was offered as well; all free of charge.

One other ship had helped as well and was staying at the inn. Still, we had two rooms assigned to our crew. Much of the inn was filled with people whose homes had been destroyed in the fire.

Though people seemed polite and willing to help each other, there were a few small scuffles I witnessed break out over distribution of supplies. There was a lot of work still to be done on Vernt.

I worried we shouldn't use the rooms of the inn or eat the meal prepared, but Mercully said they'd tried to turn these generosities away last time and the governor had insisted to the point they couldn't refuse. He'd wanted to pay them back for their kindness in some small way.

We ate a hearty fish stew for dinner and laid ourselves out around the two small rooms; seven people to each.

Mercully stood and spoke to us all, "I'm glad to have a crew such as you that is willing to help those in need." She folded her arms. "Stars know, we've all been in need. As I've said, I don't know how long we'll be at this task, but we'll keep on it long as we're needed. Though, it seems we'll be missing two of our crew members for a time." She gestured to Jet and I who were sitting next to each other. "Shay has work on Fainia and will be staying there for a while. Jet will join, as he knows the island, though he won't be there long as her." She smiled to us, "Jet hasn't told me the specifics, Shay, but I wish you both luck."

Many of the members looked surprised, but did not comment, Clare just grinned. I assumed Jet had already told him the basic plan.

I looked gladly over to Jet who winked, he hadn't even made up a story for Mercully, just left out the important details.

Settling down for the night, legs and arms stretching comfortably, I realized with a laugh that we had more room here than on the ship.

☙∞❧

Waking to stirrings around me, I found the crew eager to get going. After a fast breakfast and a quick goodbye to the ever-thankful governor, we went to Fainia.

Everyone was much livelier now that we'd crossed the dangers lurking in the middle of the island ring and, though they asked what Jet and I would be doing on Fainia, I simply told them it was Garden business. Most shrugged and nodded, but Sseya had a significant look in her eyes, as if she knew what we were working towards.

∞∞

After arriving once more on the small, Fainian Beach, we spent a day harvesting leaves with the crew.

Jet and I then enjoyed our last night on 'The Sea's Ribbon'. It was one of those musical nights again. Instruments were brought out and we all danced together long into the night.

Though I had fun, there was one moment that stood out from the rest.

When the music slowed and most of the crew was dozing, Neweq slowly strummed his yuf. The instrument hummed a slow tune that swelled and retreated like the sea, and I somehow found myself in Jet's arms.

We hadn't danced together, just the two of us, before. It had always included other members of the crew. I hadn't noticed it was only us for a number of minutes.

We were simply swaying to the slow tune, both sleepy. I felt so relaxed though, until I realized what was happening, and looked around for the others.

"What is it?" asked Jet.

Embarrassed to say anything, and not wanting Jet to think I didn't want to dance with him, I simply said, "Looks as if everyone's almost asleep."

He smiled, looking around, "That it does."

We continued to move unhurriedly under the stars.

Soon the notes of the yuf slowed and stopped; it seemed Neweq had succumbed to sleep as well.

Jet and I didn't look over to him. I simply stared at the reflection of the lamps in Jet's eyes and, somehow, beyond that. And he did the same to me. I felt it; as if a cord connected us and had tensed. We said nothing.

When the song that seemed to have been playing in both our heads finally ended at the same time, we released each other. I felt Jet's fingers slide from between my own, but my fingers felt his still.

We continued to exist in the other's eyes.

When we finally looked away, I still felt like I was holding him.

The next morning, we didn't linger in goodbyes. The crew would be back, most likely, in a little over a week.

'The Sea's Ribbon' left through the narrow, stone channel. I watched Clare wave once more from the deck, his long hair billowing behind him, then turned back to Jet.

36
Fainian

"What's the kind of land we should be lookin' out for?" asked Jet, taking a large step around a rock.

"A place that has some shelter and other lush plants, so we know the soil is good." I hopped over an overgrown bush. A lot of the soil on the island was quite sandy. Hopefully we'd be able to find a good place.

"Good soil." Jet panted slightly as we walked up a hill. "Shelter. Seems to me the place you're looking for is back among the ruins."

The ruins...the soil there had been quite dark. There were several overhanging pieces of stone that would shade and protect the plants nicely, and...there'd been symbols of the Garden there.

"I think that could work. Unless you think you know of a better spot?"

"Ey, there's a few that would do just as well as far as growing plants goes, but the ruins are tucked away. A Garden there could be looked over without other eyes prying in, should they come."

That was important as well. "Perfect."

"Well," said Jet, "we're going the wrong way if that's where we're to be headed, turn about."

I laughed, and we started back down the hill we'd just climbed.

∞∞∞

Both of us were breathing heavily now. It was a hot day and the air felt thick and close. I noticed steady beads of sweat making their way down Jet's neck as he walked in front of me. He turned back to grin and I felt my heart lunge somehow. I just smiled back.

My fingers traced the small lumps that were the seeds.

I still didn't know if I was doing the right thing. It seemed to go against much of what I'd learned in my years as a Gardener. But somehow, this felt right. Not keeping the power of the Tree for ourselves, but sharing it with so many others who needed protecting, for that was the Garden's purpose.

Perhaps the power of these seeds wouldn't be felt for years, but it was all I could do for now and, damn it all, I'd do it. I had started it in the wrong way, but I hoped to finish it better.

Sunlight sifted down to us. Though there was little chance there was a soul on this island besides Jet and I, we were silent as we picked our way through the jungle greenery. Perhaps Jet realized this too, for he began to hum a cheery tune as we walked.

He must have gotten a second wind. I panted heavily as he hummed.

Jet checked back again, his face spattered with sun and shadows. "We're nearly there, Shay!"

I noticed a thinning of the plants around us and a clearing ahead.

"If there's anywhere on the island best to hold a treasure like the seeds there, it's here."

I followed him forward to the sunlit space. There were the ruins. After thoroughly exploring the ones on Cresstalan, I saw now how strangely similar these ones were.

The low stone walls, chalk white, circled an open area, not unlike the true Garden itself. There was soil in the center of it all, rich and dark, though a little dry and filled with random plants. It was nothing we couldn't fix.

"There's a stream not far as well. Can't be much better than this. Maybe we can pay the Peal-Digger to guard it."

I let out a bursting laugh, "It is quite perfect."

There was a large platform of stone under an overhanging rock hung with vines. Jet and I sat down here to catch our breath, drink water, and cool down. We'd brought food with us and ate, hardly talking after our long walk.

I knew I could make this place into a garden, perhaps it wouldn't be perfect, but I thought it would work well enough.

If there was a ritual for planting a tree though, it was not known to me and had most likely been lost long ago. As there was never supposed to be another besides The Great Tree, it would have been silly to record one.

I hoped the face-paint I'd brought, what little ritual I'd learned, and my sincere desire that this tree would grow strong, would be enough.

The greater part of the ritual planting ceremony, I would improvise. There were smaller ones for some of the other, more important, plants. I knew three of the simple ones and perhaps I could make everything work.

Since this was to be the new sacred space that held a garden, I wanted to start treating it that way as soon as I could. I got the small clay pot of paint out of my bag and screwed off the lid, cradling it in my palm. The earthy scent rose to my nose and I already felt more confident, my mind clicking into the mindset.

"Jet," I turned to him, realizing I'd need help with this part, "before we begin, I need to paint my face." I saw no reason to delay beginning work on the Garden and held up the pot to show the slick, teal paint inside. Reaching into my pack once more, I brought out a small looking glass. "Can you hold this up for me so I can apply the paint?"

He skipped over and took the mirror from my hand. "'Course." He smiled and kneeled, holding it in front of my face.

I dipped my fingers into the paint pot, the oily, familiar texture flooding me with memories of the real Garden. The first day I'd gone there. The first day Jevin had gone there. My father. The Tree.

I took a breath and let them all go. This was a new beginning and I would make this new garden flourish.

Dragging my fingers along my face, I applied the symbols. My eyes slid up to Jet after a minute. I laughed as he stuck out his tongue at me. I stuck mine back and finished painting.

"Okay, all done," I said, taking the looking glass back. "Thank you."

"Not a problem," he said, a smile lighting his face. "So that's what you wear going into the Garden?" he asked.

"All the Gardeners have to," I said. "Actually..." A thought struck me. There was a lot of work to be done and I wanted to get to planting as soon as possible. I did trust Jet, and after a mere moment's hesitation, I was decided, "Would you be willing to help me remove the unneeded plants?"

"S'pose I could," he said, eyeing the paint pot. "Do I get paint upon my face as well?"

I considered. He was the closest thing I had to an Apprentice. This was also to be a new and different garden, I decided it would have new and different rules.

Jet was a good person. He seemed like someone who wouldn't hurt anyone. That was the most important part of being a Gardener. With a little bit of training, he might be able to connect with the plants, he was already so good at connecting with people.

The paint was made from special soil and plant-fibers to help us meld easily with the Garden, it would be better for Jet to wear the paint than not if he was going to help.

"I think you should," I said. "Come over here. I'll put it on for you."

He hurried to sit down and faced me, cross-legged, jutting his nose forward and closing his eyes so I could apply the paint.

I laughed softly at his eagerness and his willingness to jump into whatever was in front of him.

Still staring at Jet and gathering paint on my fingers, I hesitated a moment. His cheekbones were almost shining in the bright, afternoon light, lips quirked into a small smile.

Focus. I shook my head.

I began applying the symbols to his face, starting with a crescent beside his eye.

He winced slightly. "Cold."

"Sorry. Stay still."

"Mm," he said, ceasing his movement.

Though perhaps it shouldn't have been, it was strangely intimate to be touching his face like this. I lingered over it, smiling at the small twitches of his eyebrows or lips.

"Okay, finished."

He met my eyes. For the shortest moment, there was a look in them that was more serious than I'd ever seen.

He turned to look for the mirror. "Where's the looking glass? Let's see it."

I handed it to him.

"Oh!" he said, turning side to side to see the extent of the designs.

"Good?"

"Very. Now I'm lookin' like you. But with hair, ey?"

He smiled widely.

"I suppose," I said, laughing. "It was a little difficult to do it on another person. It felt backwards."

"Looks right good to me," he said, handing back the glass. I took hold of it, pulling it away, but he held on for a moment longer. "It felt nice..."

My face filled with heat, what did he expect me to say to that? I just looked away, placing the looking glass into my bag. "Good...I guess." I laughed nervously and stood up. "Let's get to work, then."

CGCOO

For the rest of the day we removed plants that wouldn't be needed. I showed Jet how to transplant the larger ones outside the garden circle. It would be good to have their extra protection around the area.

The work we had to do today didn't feel like the Garden work I was used to. Instead of caring for plants, we were primarily ripping them from the soil. The larger ones that flourished, we replanted. Still, it felt opposite of what I'd always done.

And then there was Jet. Instead of the usual solemnity and silence that accompanied work in the Garden, it was a constant stream of light conversation and jokes. I almost snorted laughing when he pulled two weeds from the ground and held them above his head as if they were long ears.

CGCOO

At the end of it, when the sun was near going down, we stopped for the day. It was still warm and both Jet and I were finally speaking little, worn out from working in the soil.

I felt really good. I knew I was doing something with true purpose. Finally.

"We'll go on back to the dwellings of the island," said Jet, cleaning his hands in the clear stream near the ruins. The water cascaded past his hands and a cloud of dirt was removed, spreading into the slowly flowing water. "Not too far. We'll be picking one to stay in before the night's in full."

We finished washing and started our trek.

"No one's been here for so long, going on. Might be a bit of cleaning to do, but we'll have a roof at the least."

The houses of the island weren't that far, but it was a strange, winding way that took us to them. How Jet had found it in the first place, I wouldn't have been able to guess and was too tired to ask.

Descending a small hill, there were the houses laid out.

They were all very small, but quite beautiful, shining softly in the last dregs of sun. They seemed made of the same stone as the palace on Cresstalan.

Now and then we heard animal noises. The sound of the ocean, though a little way off from where we were, still added an ambience to the air. Rustling leaves shifted smoothly around us as well. Apart from our footsteps though, these were the only sounds. When Jet and I spoke to each other, not often now, it felt as though our voices were immediately absorbed by the air.

Amongst the buildings, we looked to find one to stay for the night.

Windows were broken, the paths between the buildings worn and overgrown as we tried to navigate them. I looked into a house across from us as we passed, its door opened wide, slightly hanging off of the hinge. Small, reflective eyes stared from the darkness inside the house, still, but accompanied by small squeaks.

"There's one that's ahead lookin' as if it might work," said Jet, his voice pulling me away from the staring eyes.

"Don't think it's got broken windows or doors."

The house was undamaged. We entered, finding dust covering chairs and rising from the seagrass rugs on the floor. This was all barely made visible by slanting moonlight coming in from dirt-covered windows.

There was a small bedroom at the back of the house with a large bed lying on the floor. It was as dingy with dust as the rest of the place. When Jet and I pulled off the top cover to see if we could sleep on it, we found holes and a couple miniscule shrieks came from them.

We backed out of the room and shut the door.

"Could be one of them small lizards," Jet offered. "We've had trouble with them scurrying onto 'The Sea's Ribbon', eat through clothes and blankets."

Jet and I decided to use our own blankets and sleep on the grass rugs of the first room in the house.

First, we shook out the dust, releasing clouds into the moonlight. We then brought everything inside, used a rolled blanket each as a pillow, and another to cover up.

Before sleeping, we pulled some of the food we'd brought along from my pack and ate. We would probably have to gather more food the next day, but for now, the dried fish and fruit that we had was enough and would likely last another few days.

Sleep came easily.

37
Blooms

Waking, I found Jet sleepily staring at me. The room was beginning to light up.

"Ah, I was just trying to think if I could get away fallin' back to sleep." His voice was scratchy, and his hair mussed.

"Though I'd like to," I said, "we should probably get started since we're both up. There's a lot to do today." My voice was also rasping.

Jet let out a groan but sat up and pulled my pack over to him, it had been lying near the foot of his blanket. "Then I'll be needing breakfast."

"Agreed." I said, yawning.

I took the piece of dried fish that Jet handed me and started to gnaw on it, still not fully awake.

Dust swirled slowly in the sun beaming through the windows.

I looked to Jet, eating his own breakfast. He pulled another piece of fruit from the pack. His eyes were still fluttering closed.

"Is there somewhere I can go and get water nearby, Jet?" I yawned again, wider this time, my jaw cracking slightly. "I brought some tea. If we build a fire, we can brew some."

"Mmm?" He looked over at me, hair from his side-braids sticking out strangely. "Ah, there's a stream nearby. You should be able to hear it without much trouble."

I nodded and pushed myself up to my feet, finding the kitchen. In it there was a slightly worn, but still apparently watertight basket. I grabbed it.

Passing Jet on the way out, who seemed to have fallen asleep again with a piece of dried fish hanging from his mouth, I left and directed myself to the sound of flowing water.

The stream was close, just past a few houses. They looked even more derelict in the light of day. The water was clear, and I saw a fish dart away as I drew near.

After filling the basket with water and bringing it back to the kitchen, Jet snoring as I passed him, I saw a small fire-pit in its middle and an oil reservoir to fuel a flame. There was oil in it remarkably, and I started the fire to boil water.

When I went out to wake Jet again, I found he was already up and much more alert. He'd brought the small bag of tea out from the pack. He handed it to me and I brought the tea to the fire, found cups, and threw a few fragrant pieces in one for each of us.

Jet took his gratefully and started sipping. I grabbed a handful more of food and sat to finish my own breakfast.

The tea was delicious, heat invigorating me, and I started to feel awake.

Before long, we were up and moving, back to the ruins.

Clouds hung low. It looked like there might be rain later. The wind was picking up, blowing us about as we walked. If it did rain, it would be good for the new Garden, but it would be best to plant everything before it started.

This Garden would be more exposed to the elements, but I'd learned a little about tending the upper gardens.

Perhaps that would help.

I found myself immensely pleased upon seeing the results of our work from the day before.

The soil was visible with the weeds and un-wanted plants removed from the area. We'd used large leaves to bring water and moisten it, and it looked nearly as nourishing as it should.

Looking to the sky again, I found a few more clouds, but it was still quite clear. Jet's hands were at his hips and he smiled even more widely than I had a moment before.

"Ey, look at that! We got quite a way yesterday!"

There were still some weeds around the edge of the ruins, but it was almost completely clear where we needed it to be.

"You did a great job yesterday, thank you for the help."

He waved my compliment away, "It was quite fun. What are we doing today?"

I was glad he was ready to move forward. "If you'll pull the rest of the weeds at the edges, I'll start replanting inside the Garden where they need to be. We'll also try to find a few particular plants that will help keep the tree alive."

Jet nodded eagerly, and I saw him get ready to step over the low, ruined wall to go into the Garden.

I grabbed his shoulder, "Wait."

He looked behind to me, eyes questioning widely.

I realized he still had some of the remains of paint from the day before. I must have been too tired yesterday to notice.

"We forgot to wash the paint off last night. Let's go do it now."

Jet let out a quick sigh, "Ey, it's easy to forget about all these rules." He nodded, "Let's go along then."

At the stream, we quickly washed our faces. The water was cold, and I splashed it up quickly to avoid numbing my face. We sat down on rocks nearby to reapply the paint.

Jet kept making faces at me as I did his, making me laugh.

"Hold still," I told him after he'd done this a few times. "It looks as if there may be rain coming in later today. I don't know how much work we can get done, but I'd like to plant the tree before the rain comes. We have to go as quickly as we can," I said, smiling despite myself.

He stilled, and I finished his paint and then my own as he held the looking glass.

Back to the ruins, Jet pulled the weeds in what I thought was an incredibly short amount of time, and helped me to finish unearthing and re-planting the shrubs needed for the Garden.

Having walked among the artistic patterns of the Garden for so many years, and seeing it from above, I remembered it well and marked where to place each bush. I'd never learned the meaning of the specific shape and whether or not it was truly important, but I thought I should make this garden as true to the original as I could.

We finished the tasks within two hours; amazingly fast. Jet was made for gardening. We took a short break and ate.

"Now," I said, brushing food from my hands as I stood up, "there are a few plants that we have to find before we can plant the tree." Jet stood as well, nodding. "Do you know the plants of this island at all?"

"Can't say I don't," Jet smiled and winked, "we mostly go about looking at the plants of Fainia as that's what we must collect. We've looked for many places that the coating leaves go to grow, so I've seen lots of other plants that prove interesting."

I felt a bit of tension release from my shoulders.

"Okay." I looked Jet in the eyes, wanting him to remember the plants I was about to tell him, "There are three plants that we must have before we can even consider planting the tree. They keep away certain insects and add different nutrients to soil that the tree will need."

I continued, "The first is called 'Light's Shadow'. It has dark green, round leaves and deep purple flowers that open in wide, circular shapes."

"Ey, I've seen those not far from where we go and dock. We'll have 'em right quickly."

I clapped my hands together, "Great! Okay, the next one is called 'Sight Lost', as it kills certain insects and can kill humans if they ingest the leaves." Jet gulped at this. "It has yellow flowers that never truly open, but look like spikes. The leaves are light-green and skinny."

Jet thought for a moment, "Can't be sure I've seen them. Know where they may be though."

I looked up to the sky once again, wondering of our time. "Okay, since you know where the first ones are, let's start on our way."

I grabbed the pack and Jet sidled up beside me.

"The third one has red flowers that look a little bit like seashells. They have two petals that look like a mouth, in fact, its name is 'Glory's Lips'. The leaves are yellow and grow from just below the flower in a ring."

Jet was thinking hard, "Ey, they sound like something I may have been seein' before there, Shay, but I can't for the life of me think where. They're on Fainia, I know."

"Well, that's encouraging," I said, undaunted. "We'll find the first ones and go from there."

Jet brought me back to the ravine. 'Light's Shadow' grew plentifully amongst waving grasses nearby.

Luck was on our side, for we found three small gatherings of 'Glory's Lips' on the way. We pulled them carefully out of the ground, taking care not to tear the roots, and set them gently into my pack. I had emptied it for this purpose.

Now ready to gather 'Light's Shadow', Jet and I made our way carefully through the grass. We needed to gather eight of the plants.

Clouds were filling the sky swiftly. It wouldn't be long before the rain came, perhaps I'd have to let go of the idea that we could plant the tree today.

I freed the last of the plant's roots I was working on and shook the remaining soil loose. It was the final one I had to gather, so I went over to Jet to see how many he had.

He was concentrating hard on removing one from the soil and there were three others laid out beside him. This must be his last.

I watched as he worked, face wide with enjoyment and concentration, his broad hands carefully brushing away soil and freeing the roots of the healthy plant he'd chosen.

He finally got the last of the roots out of the ground without ripping them, and held the plant up saying, "Ha!"

I chuckled at that, he looked over and grinned widely.

"Not doing too badly, am I?" he said, proudly.

"You have the makings of a great Gardener, Jet." He did. I would be hard-pressed to find a better person than him.

He stood up carefully and brushed loose dirt from the roots of the plant. Then he slowly gathered the remaining ones he'd uprooted and placed them into the pack.

It wasn't going to close this time, but I didn't know what else to do. I could only hope the plants wouldn't get too smashed on the way to the garden.

I hoisted the pack back onto my shoulders. "Do you have any ideas about where we should look for the last plant?" I asked Jet, "'Sight Lost?'"

"Well," he said, bending down to pick a long piece of grass. He placed it between his teeth to chew seriously.

I tried not to laugh.

He didn't seem to notice, looking off into the distance. "I do remember seeing some plants with yellow flowers not too far from the ocean. I say we go about checking there."

"That sounds like a good idea," I said, almost laughing again.

"What?" the piece of grass fell a bit, tilting down as he looked at me blankly.

At that, I did burst out laughing. I shook my head, not sure what to say, "Just you. Come on, let's go." I pressed Jet's shoulder, urging him forward to the beach, though he still looked confused.

As I followed him through tall grass and under the shelter of rocks, I realized that most every time I'd been looking at him lately, I had smiled. He was always completely himself and I found myself admiring that. Admiring him.

Was I? I watched him.

My height, with broad shoulders and a wiry frame. His clothes a bit loose, comfortable. A soft, tan tunic with a faded dark green shirt over it that fell to his waist. An ocean-blue cord that served as a belt tied around his middle in a complicated knot he must have learned from some sailor. Brown leggings that covered strong legs. Hardened cloth boots with some sort of sturdy sole. The silver earrings near the top of each ear, looping around, glinting whenever Jet turned his head.

His black hair, I realized, I'd never seen down, but if it was, it would probably come to his shoulders or a bit above.

His face usually held a smile that was full. Full of teeth, filling his face, and full of an unrestrained joy that reached to his eyes. Those were black and overflowing with feeling and laughter, twinkling more than not. He had a long nose that turned up just barely at the end and full lips.

I realized after a moment that, after thinking about his lips, my mind had gone temporarily blank. I barely caught myself after tripping over a small stone on the ground.

"You alright?" Jet turned around, having heard my small scramble.

I smiled painfully, embarrassed. What was I doing? Jet...I..."I'm fine," I said, casually.

He nodded, smiling brightly.

That's when I felt it. A feeling as though my heart almost dropped from my body, as if time had temporarily forgotten that it was supposed to keep moving.

It was over in what must have been a quick moment when Jet turned back to continue our way.

I knew it then. I liked Jet. I liked him more than anyone else.

I didn't know what to do with that, so I kept following him.

38
Torrent

Soon we were at the place where Jet said he'd seen the yellow flowers. I did my best to keep my mind on what he was saying, shoving the realization I'd just come to aside. This was important. We had to get these tasks done as quickly as possible.

"Mmmm," said Jet, bent over and looking amongst the grass, plants, and stones on the ground for yellow flowers.

There was nothing here that was blooming, I saw, but this wasn't the time of year for 'Sight Lost' to be in flower. I seized the chance to distract myself and began to look around as well.

I tried to ignore a small, swelling feeling inside myself that came every time Jet circled near to me as we searched. Then I caught sight of the skinny, green leaves I was looking for just past a large rock. I let out a noise of excitement and ran over.

The plant was stunted, but it was 'Sight Lost'. However, it was the only one there.

I took my time unearthing it as Jet stood over me. I pulled it from the ground and held it carefully in my hand, then took out a small cloth and wrapped it loosely. It wasn't good for this plant to be too close to the others, or for humans to touch for long. The cloth would protect me.

Jet and I had searched this area quite thoroughly now. This seemed to be the only one of its kind.

"Do you remember having seen any more plants or flowers that could have looked like this?" I asked Jet anxiously, now thinking of what this would mean for the new garden.

"I'm sorry, Shay, but I truly don't."

I let out a sigh. We were supposed to have eight of this plant for its formation in the garden.

I was still worried that my father would figure out what I was doing or that someone would happen to stumble upon Jet and I here on the island. I wanted the tree planted as soon as possible so it could be strong, should it ever be found. Would it be alright to plant it if I only had one?

I opened the cloth and looked at it once again. It was such a small plant too. The ones we had in the garden had grown into bushes that almost came up to my mid-thigh. This plant was as tall as my ankle and had only four stalks. I thought for a moment about separating the stalks and planting them as separate plants, but looking at the plant, I wasn't sure it would be able to survive that.

The clouds were gathered now, and the rain would surely come soon, perhaps before we got back.

"Then let's get back to the garden as fast as we can without shaking the plants. It shouldn't take long to plant them. We'll do what we can before the rain."

Jet nodded, and we hurried back.

A drop of water fell onto my nose as we reached the garden. I pulled the plants from the pack and lay them out under a short, overhanging piece of ruin to protect them.

I'd already plotted out the pattern that they would be settled into. Jet started on the process of planting the flowers where I'd marked.

I set 'Sight Lost' first in a point closest to where the tree would be. At least it would be able to protect it quite well there.

Leaving 'Sight Lost', I hoped it would be okay in the rain. I started on 'Glory's Lips' as fast as I'd ever planted anything.

Rivulets of water started streaming down my face and neck and I tried to ignore them, but I finished sooner than I could have expected.

Jet still had one plant to finish besides the one he was currently placing, so I ran over and placed the last one.

Afterwards, I picked a large leaf from a short plant nearby and placed its concave form over 'Sight Lost' to form a shelter. The rain ran off the leaf and melted into the surrounding soil.

I looked over to see Jet finished and nodded that we should go.

We left the Garden, the rain coming down in what would soon be torrents. Jet's face-paint was nearly washed off already, mine would be the same.

We turned to each other and laughed as we ran.

We would have to plant the tree tomorrow, I supposed. There was at least a bit of a ritual I wanted to perform, and I didn't want to do it in the rain.

On our way, Jet said he knew where roots grew that we'd be able to eat. We stopped to gather some, filling my pack with as many as we could. It would be good to eat something different. I was getting tired of dried fruit and fish. Perhaps if we got the tree planted tomorrow, we could go catch fish to eat fresh.

With the rain though, it would do no good to be outside any longer.

When we returned to our dwelling, we were both drenched and immediately went to change.

As I peeled the wet clothes away from myself in the back room, I heard thunder outside. A small squeak came from the mattress in response.

I came out to find Jet starting a fire in the pit in the kitchen. He was seated next to it, stoking small flames.

His hair was loose, lying flat and straight to just above his shoulder as I'd guessed. I felt a lump form in my throat.

"Thought more tea was warranted after that soak, eh?" he said.

I sat down next to him, clearing my throat, "That would be nice."

"We'll fry roots as well." He reached behind him to pull some out of the pack. "I could do with a meal that has some heat to it."

I nodded.

My hands were vibrating. I was a bit chilled from the rain, but it was a summer rain, so it hadn't exactly been cold.

Jet stoked the fire to a decent size and I held my hands forward to heat them up and let out a sigh. I saw Jet's own hands reach forward to get warm as well.

He grinned widely at me as I looked over to him. "That'll be much better," he said.

I felt my mind go blank again for the slightest second but realized it and nodded back to Jet.

We sat for a moment, listening to the rain, and I felt my face getting hot.

I rose, "I'll see if I can find a pan for the roots." After minimal searching through the shelves along the walls of the kitchen, I found a hardened clay skillet.

Jet got the tea out again and put water over the fire so that we'd soon have it to drink. I washed the roots and sliced them with a knife I found, but realized I had no idea what to do next. I'd simply seen how roots were cut when I ate them.

Luckily, Jet stretched out a hand for the pan holding the roots. "Give it here. We make these often when we stay on this island. Most times we go about stabbing them onto the end of sharpened sticks to roast. We can do that for breakfast, perhaps."

My mouth watered at the thought of roasted roots. I was looking forward to the warm food.

He placed the pan over the fire and let it sit there for a few minutes until steam started to rise and hiss from the vegetables. The water for the tea also seemed to be hot enough, so I let Jet finish cooking the roots and took the water from the fire, preparing the tea, handing a cup to Jet a few moments later.

I almost drew my hand away when one of his fingers brushed mine.

He was focused on the roots and set the cup down beside him. "These here are almost done." He took the pan from the fire. "Are there plates for us?"

I'd pulled a couple out when I found them a minute ago, so I held one to him. Jet let half the roots fall onto the plate. I held out the other one and he put the rest there.

After getting more dried fish and a little fruit, we both sat down at the fire to eat our food voraciously, starting with the hot vegetables.

The food seemed to bring me back to my senses.

We grinned wildly at each other as we ate. Though there was no seasoning for them, Jet had cooked the roots well and they tasted quite good.

When we finished, it was still raining. I didn't think the sun had quite gone down, but it was difficult to tell for there were so many clouds.

My eyelids started to droop, I was exhausted.

Jet had leaned back onto his arms and was lounging before the fire. I smiled. We had just found this house yesterday. It was dirty and musty, but he was as relaxed as if we were back on the ship, gathered in a circle with the crew.

"Are we going to go about planting the tree tomorrow?" he asked. It looked like he might be tired as well, for his eyes were half-closed and he looked content as he spoke.

"We will if it's not raining or, at least not raining too harshly," I said. "I say we try to go as early as possible. You can come with me, but tomorrow I'll do the work myself. As I'm the only one who was trained to be a Gardener, I don't want to risk anything when planting the tree. There's a certain mindset you must be in, but it won't take too long."

"Sounds good," said Jet, yawning now. "I'm interested to see you plant it. How that all will work." Jet shook himself and opened his eyes again, looking over to me and smiling sleepily.

"I don't know about you," I said, "but I'm ready for bed."

"Mmm. Let's go and do that," he agreed.

We settled into our blankets, the rain still falling hard overhead.

Jet seemed to fall asleep right away.

39
Ritual

It was dark outside and inside was pitch black. The thunder had stopped so only the sound of pounding rain broke through the night.

My heart beat fast. I knew Jet wasn't far from me, though his breathing was masked by the rain. I needed to sleep and be prepared if I was to plant the tree tomorrow. My mind couldn't be so uneasy.

I laid flat on my back and started doing my meditative breathing to calm myself. It seemed to work. I felt calm seep into me, and soon fell to sleep.

∞

Before the sun had risen, it was silent. It seemed the rain had stopped.

I listened to see if Jet was still sleeping and heard a light snore coming from his direction.

Because I wanted to get started as soon as possible, I decided to meditate now. I'd need to be in an optimal state of mind for the tasks ahead.

I touched the noonyi-skin pouch at my neck. In case anything went wrong, I didn't think I should have all the seeds together. Carefully taking out two, I wrapped one in the blanket I was using as a pillow. Then, getting up as silently as I could, I placed the other in a half-cracked cup on a shelf in the kitchen.

Cinching the pouch closed over the final seed, the one that would become the new tree, I went out the door and into the dark morning.

There was a faint grey glow in the distance and the stars were still vibrant above. The moon was gone so it was hard to see the path I walked, but I felt my way forward and made out the shapes of the houses nearby.

I knew there was a nice place with lots of plants and a rock to sit on next to the stream. I made my way there by what little memory I had from the day before.

The ground squelched slightly as I walked. Drippings of water surrounded me. It was a nice temperature out. Definitely not cold. It had never gotten cold on Cresstalan, even at night, in the summer.

Small rustlings sounded, perhaps birds or other small creatures, but they left quickly, and I was soon at the rock I'd been aiming for.

I sat down, crossing my legs and letting out a long breath, then I brought in a fresh lungful of the moist, dirt and plant-scented air.

All was renewed after the rain and I drank it in.

With the peacefulness of the world around me, I easily clicked into the mindset for the Garden and let myself sink into meditation.

My breath eased in and out and I began to picture myself in the true Garden.

I walked up to the Tree of the Fallen, she was standing tall and her leaves were bright and glowing in afternoon sun. I placed my hands onto her trunk and closed my eyes, connecting with her. I pictured the water she drew up to her very top branches, her roots reaching into the rich soil, and her arms stretching up as high as could go.

Sometimes when I meditated I liked to speak to the Tree, at least in a way. It really was communicating without words. I didn't know for sure if I was understood, but somehow, I felt I was.

I tried to convey to the Tree what I was doing. How I was going to take one of her seeds and plant and grow a new tree. I tried to express how very important it would be and how I would do my best to take care of this tree. I also tried to tell her I was sorry that I had to leave and wouldn't be around her anymore.

I felt it, clear as anything. A swelling sense of joy and approval, tinged with a bitter-sweetness, but it was all there inside the Tree of the Fallen. I knew I'd gotten permission to continue in my pursuit. I started to say thank you, but then a yell tore me from my trance.

I looked around, worried, the sun was nearly up now. The sky was fiery with the sunrise, clouds lined in orange and pink streaks.

"Shay?!" It was Jet.

"Over here, Jet!" I called back and pushed myself off the rock to go back towards his voice.

As I got closer, I heard hurried footsteps headed to me. We met, both of us glowing in the pinkish light that was filling the air.

"What is it?" I asked.

Jet's eyes had been slightly wide when he was walking up to me and I saw he wasn't wearing any shoes.

"I...Just didn't know where you were."

I was slightly surprised at this but supposed I should have told him the night before that I might be going early to meditate.

"Sorry, Jet." I hadn't meant to worry him. We were the only two on the island. We had to look after each other.

"I just went to do a meditation before the garden this morning. I didn't want to wake you."

He ran a hand through his hair, "Ah. I admit I was a bit worried, couldn't think where you'd gotten off to." He looked at me and smiled warily.

"Sorry," I said again. "I should have thought."

"Well now you know, I suppose," he said this slowly and I don't think either of us were listening to our words anymore.

Again, time froze as he looked at me...though...from the look in his eyes, I thought, perhaps, he felt it as well this time. The breeze rustled his loose hair slightly.

I was the one who broke the moment, "We should eat breakfast and go to the garden."

He seemed to shake himself at my words and put on a relaxed smile. "Right you are."

We ate, got ready, and were back to what was becoming a garden, not long after the sun had risen.

"If you can hold the looking glass," I said, swinging the pack off my back, "I'll put on my face-paint for the day. I'm not sure I'll need your help today, so I won't put on your paint."

Jet nodded and took the glass as I handed it to him. I set down the pack and pulled out the paint jar, opening it and relishing the lively smell.

I purposely didn't look at Jet while I was putting it on. I found myself more and more nervous around him and felt bad I'd worried him earlier.

When I finished, I thanked him and walked to the garden area.

I sat on a piece of the low wall surrounding the garden and took off my shoes, placing them outside the circle. I then turned around and took a deep breath, clicking into the mindset and pressing a hand to the small pouch of seeds I still wore.

Letting my feet down from the wall, I stepped into the moist soil and squeezed my toes in it. How wonderful that feeling was.

Walking forward to the middle of the garden, I removed the leaf from 'Sight Lost' I'd placed the day before. It looked as if it'd been protected well. I threw the extra leaf from the garden.

Then I knelt in the center of everything, where the tree would be planted. I pushed my fingers into the soil and began to dig a shallow hole for the seed.

When it was the correct depth, I placed my hands on either side of the hole and closed my eyes.

Using the mindset, I pictured all the plants surrounding me being connected to this area. I communicated to them that they needed to protect what was to be planted here. Wind breathed against my bare head.

I opened the small pouch and reached in two fingers to grasp the seed inside.

Holding it in my palm, I pictured life flowing in. From the air, from the soil, from the surrounding plants, and from me.

"Grow strong. You are a Great Tree," I whispered to it. Then I released it into the hole.

I'd dabbed a bit of the face-paint onto my palm to use now and, coating my thumb in it, I used that to draw a circle around the inside of the hole.

When there was a full circle, I carefully filled it in with soil and pressed down gently.

I didn't know if the series of movements I was about to do would be correct for this task but did my best to know with all my heart that it would work. If I had that sense of knowing, I thought it would be possible.

Sweeping the air back and forth with my hands, I pleaded with it to be gentle with the new tree when it sprouted. Then I pointed my hands up to the sky and down to the earth, asking them to nourish the new tree and help it grow strong and true. I then circled around the tree with slow, careful steps, telling it again to grow strong and to protect our lands along with the Tree of the Fallen. I did my best to impart its task to it.

I felt it. I was sure I felt a consciousness spring to life then that simply hadn't been there before. I knew it was her. It was the new Tree. Young and unknowing.

Lowering my hands, I bowed to her, then backed away. I felt in my heart that my task was done for now.

Jet and I had filled a watertight basket for what I was to do next.

I went back to the wall and he handed it to me. I didn't even have to ask. I smiled widely, then turned back to the Tree and brought it to her.

I cupped my hand and filled it with water, then let the liquid stream through my fingers onto the Tree, gently. I turned my hand over then, spread it wide, and poured water over it. I was bonding myself with the Tree so I could take care of her. It was something I'd done with the Tree of the Fallen when I took the Garden oath.

Then I let a small stream of water fall from the basket, using it to draw the symbols painted on my face. The crescent, the floating leaf, three wavy lines, the wave-form, the flower's petal, the soil specks, the splayed root, and the open circle. The water sketched them onto the soil over the new Tree.

I thought I felt the consciousness of the Tree reach out to the rest of the plants in the Garden and to me as well.

Whispering, I said part of the Garden Oath, "Never shall I hurt another living soul, for we are always protectors, you and I."

I nodded, satisfied with the job I'd done.

Exiting the Garden slowly, I was finished.

Jet looked at me with a sense of awe.

"Ey, that was quite something. I didn't know what you would be doing. In all honesty, I'm still not sure exactly what you were doing, but it looked like it should do something."

I laughed, "I hope so. I think it will work." I had another thought now, "Jet."

"Yes?"

"Do you still want to help me in the Garden?"

"Of course. As long as I can, that is."

"I want you to try something, then." I brought out a tinder stick and a candle.

I sat on the ground and he did the same.

"This is the exercise where you put out the candle. It's for the Garden and I'd like you to try it. To put it out, you simply have to lower your hand, but what is most important is having the correct mindset. Not forceful, just allowing the candle to go out. You'll find that when it goes out, if you're truly relaxed and in a neutral place with your mind, for that split second, it will be nearly completely blank and a sense of knowing and trust will fill you."

I couldn't read Jet's expression after I said this, but he looked at me seriously and nodded.

I activated the tinder stick and lit the candle.

Demonstrating what Jet was to do, I put it out quickly. It made no sound and simply extinguished.

Jet looked from me to the candle, wide-eyed. "I can do that as well?"

"I think you can, Jet."

He shrugged and smiled, "If you think I can, Shay, I must be able."

At his words I tried to ignore the pulsing of my heart.

I lit the candle again.

Jet let out a few long breaths and stared at the candle. Then, he lifted his hand to his forehead. There was a small, calm smile on his face. He let his hand fall...and there it was. The candle went out.

His eyes went up to mine, they overflowed with joy, and he laughed heartily, "I do see what you mean. That was something else, then."

I wanted to be surprised and shocked, but I simply smiled wide. Somehow, I'd known that Jet would be able to do this easily. He was an extraordinary person. Always relaxed, always connecting to people.

"I knew you'd be able to," the words leapt from me.

"As I said," he didn't look away from me, "if you think I can do it, I must be able."

"Do you want to help me water the other plants of the Garden?" Now I knew I could trust him to enter the Garden and help me, even with the Tree in it.

He nodded.

"Okay, let's put some face-paint on you."

"Aye."

∞∞∞

This was the third time I was putting the paint onto Jet's face.

Things seemed changed now. In this very small instance something was there or, maybe, it was just that what had always been there was suddenly stronger.

This time, when Jet closed his eyes and pushed his face forward for me to apply the paint, I couldn't help but look at his lips. I wanted to...

I started painting the symbols onto his face, first the crescent, then the leaf structure onto his cheek, then the lines that brought my fingers far too close to his mouth.

My mind went blank again, but this time it was a comforting blankness and I stopped applying the paint without realizing, my finger motionless beside Jet's lips.

Vaguely, I realized that Jet had opened his eyes. He reached up and took hold of my wrist, pulling my hand down, then folded his fingers into mine. He leaned forward, only a little more...we were so close already...and our lips met.

We kissed. So softly. So warmly. I felt us both relax into each other.

He released the hand he was holding and brought both hands up to my neck, cradling my head. My own found their way around him and up to his shoulders. I dimly realized that my fingers still had paint on them, but I didn't stop. Especially when our speed picked up and our kissing became more frantic, my need to be close to him gaining power over all else.

I realized what I was doing then. I separated my mouth from his, not only my lips, but my whole face throbbing.

"I'm...I" I saw the lines my fingers had drawn on Jet's tunic with the paint. The paint that had been near his lips was smeared and I tasted it in my mouth. I brought my hand up.

Before I could say anything more, Jet got up, grabbed my hand, and helped me to stand.

"Let's go catch some fish." He laced our fingers together and I felt my heart thunder.

We started walking to the beach.

Neither of us said anything, but we held hands and I couldn't stop thinking of his fingers touching mine.

When I finally looked to Jet's face, I saw he seemed a bit nervous as well. He could only look to my eyes the slightest bit as he saw me staring, but they were twinkling with a sort of unrestrained joy.

This made me smile once again.

"What is it?" He asked when I smiled.

I shook my head. "I...I really wanted that to happen."

His smile opened wider than I'd ever seen it. "Shall we take a break and sit a while?"

40
Lost People

Vines cascaded down standing rocks, making the area quite cool. I sat down close to Jet when leaves rustled beside us and the last thing I expected to hear came out. A human voice.

"And I say we could lure the Peal-Digger out from the tunnel." A line of people broke through the greenery to our side.

Because we were sitting, they passed us. It was so unexpected that Jet and I didn't react, but to squeeze each other's hands tighter.

Then, one word expounded from my mouth without thought, "Heyda!"

She wore a dress of rusted orange and her hair was free of a maid's cap, but here she was, Heyda, walking with strangers.

She turned to me and froze.

A tall man next to her gripped her shoulder and the other five people stood staring.

"Apprentice?" Heyda's fists clenched. "What are you doing here?" Her head darted to each side and then her eyes blazed. "You can't take me back. Where are the guards?"

I was unable to string the words together. Why was she here? How could this have happened? I'd last seen her dragged forcibly from the throne room.

She spotted Jet and her eyes flicked down to our clasped hands. "Who is that?"

"I'm Jet," he said, then nudged my shoulder, rousing me. "Shay?"

"Why are you here, Apprentice?" asked Heyda again.

Now I wasn't sure how to answer. I couldn't tell her it was to plant a new Tree, but how else was I to explain my presence here?

"I'm here because they wouldn't let me be an Apprentice anymore."

I thought her face looked slightly smug at this, then her eyes widened angrily. "So to get back in the palace's good graces you found where I'd gone after I escaped?"

I shook my head dumbly, "I had no idea you'd escaped. I don't even know what they took you for in the first place."

"Heyda." This was a woman near her, but Heyda waved her off.

"I am an enemy of your people, Apprentice. That is why they took me. And if you truly did not bring guards here, then my people can strike against you alone."

Jet released my hand preparing to stand, but I placed my hand on his leg, willing him to still.

"I am of no importance to them anymore, Heyda. I'm in trouble with the palace as well. That's why I came here. There was no one on this island, at least that was what I'd heard. And...what do you mean you're an enemy of my people? Aren't *your* people my people?"

Those surrounding Heyda seemed to bear down on Jet and me now, but I had to know what was happening. There was no need for any of us to attack each other.

If Heyda truly was an enemy of Cresstalan, I wasn't far from one as well. I'd stolen the seeds of the Great Tree and planted a new one, I had broken the Crown Prince's nose, and I was on the run from the Queen's punishment. What had Heyda done that was worse than this?

Heyda laughed, "We are not of the same people." She seemed to think for a moment, "Why are you of no importance, Apprentice? Have you abandoned your father? Your Garden?"

Jet placed his hand on mine, but I didn't look to him.

"I broke the Prince's nose and was set a punishment by the Queen. I didn't want to comply with her terms, so ran away. Jevin is the Apprentice now. I'm no longer wanted in the Garden either."

This didn't make sense though. "Why are you here? Do your people live here? How did you escape?"

"Does that mean you are against Cresstalan now?" asked Heyda, her eyes narrowing. "I did nothing but convey information to my people. We live here temporarily, and they rescued me."

"Heyda, I've been traveling the islands. I know things are bad. Have your people been suffering as they have?"

A man spat at me now, "All your islands deserve to die. They were never yours to begin with."

Heyda continued, "You really want to help, Apprentice? We could use you, but you should know the true problem. It's all of you. All those who populate the island ring. You are scavengers."

"You said that before," I said, surprised, "what does that mean?"

"It means," said a man, the metal rings he wore on multiple fingers clanking as he opened and closed his hands, "that our continent was taken by the sea and it destroyed our people, our buildings. We fled because we thought we were in danger and your people took our land for themselves while our backs were turned, while our people were trying to recover from the devastation. The islands now suffer because we make them suffer. We will drive you all away and take back what is rightfully ours."

I looked briefly to Jet, his eyes shone with sorrow.

That was what happened to the people of the sunken continent. We had our answer now and it was that we didn't belong here.

Yet, how far were Heyda's people willing to go? They were hurting people and driving them from their lands.

"Why the sea spires though, ey? Why must you attack ships that stray near?" asked Jet.

"There's a way to the palace nearby," said Heyda. "The tunnels that now lie beneath the sea permit access, but only in certain places. Many have collapsed, yet it worked so my friends could rescue me."

"There are tunnels beneath the sea?"

"Of course, all our people's buildings and homes sunk to the floor of the sea, but they are still there. Our culture was stolen by you." Several eyes shifted behind Heyda. "They Great Tree? Ha. There should be eight; and their temples, ravaged by your people, were once connected by grand tunnels so the priests could go between them in secret. What you call Gardening is a sham. It is play at what our people achieved through centuries of work. And you tore it down and tried to claim it as your own."

Another woman behind Heyda added, "We cut down the last Tree to save it from you, but the seeds would not take root in Queniil. Our Gardeners were killed when the sea rose. This is why we must take the Garden and the palace of Cresstalan from you. We will claim what is ours once more."

Ringing filled my ears. Queniil? And, if what they said was true, everything I'd known was a lie. It made sense if it was the truth, but where did that leave me? Should our people truly be driven out? Where would we go? Where had we originally come from?

It seemed I'd also, somehow, planted a Tree where one may have been long ago. In one of the ruined temples that used to house Trees. Eight Trees.

Why did the Handbook say there should only be one Tree? But it only said that at the end of the book. Had it been added later? By my own people?

Heyda had been working to destroy the Royal Family at least, that was why she had been taken. But what had she done to be found out? What was the extent of the destruction she'd wrought?

Perhaps I would have asked, tried to get more answers, but a boy entered the clearing, slightly younger than I was.

"There are ships in the harbor. Someone has come. Cresstalan ships, by the looks."

Heyda's eyes were molten, "Here you are distracting us. You liar. You led them straight to us."

"I didn't know. Heyda..." But the group of people and Heyda herself were disappearing once again through the bushes.

She looked back once, and her eyes said that if I followed, I would die.

If there were ships here from Cresstalan, were they here for me? No. No one knew I was here. They would be if I was found, however.

I grasped Jet's hand once more and pulled him up to me. "We have to hide." I couldn't lead them to the Garden, so we couldn't go back, and the houses would be too obvious. "Jet, where can we hide? We can't let them find us."

Jet's brow knitted as he thought. I looked to my left at a pathway leading into dense plant life and turned back to Jet who, in one second, had a dark sack pulled over his head and started to yell.

Before I fully understood what had happened, black fabric obscured my own vision.

41
Captured

I heard Jet shouting and struggling. I wanted to help him, but there were too many hands holding me still. Struggling, I attempted some unarmed techniques, but couldn't make headway with any of them. It simply forced my captors to have someone place a hand over my mouth as well, and yell, "Shut it!"

"Shay! Sh—" That voice was Jet's, and someone must have placed a hand over his mouth too, it stopped so abruptly.

I still made angry noises, though I couldn't shout, my hands and legs were being bound up. I kept trying to fight whomever was doing this but could do nothing. There must have been at least six people holding me. But why? Where would they take us? Were these Heyda's people? Or had those ships truly been from Cresstalan?

They were already dragging me somewhere. I heard another struggle and small noises from Jet. Hopefully he was at least coming along with me. I didn't know how I would be able to rescue him if we were split up, so this was the slightest relief.

I was hoisted up with a number of grunts and unable to do anything.

After a while of being carried, writhing ceaselessly, I heard one of the people holding me, a man, yell, "We found them! Call off the search. We're leaving within the hour!"

Someone yelled back, "But there were others. They've disappeared!"

"No matter," said the one next to me. "These two should have all the information we need."

Jet and I continued our wordless protests.

I was clumsily brought aboard what must have been a small boat. I heard the water of the beach and felt a slight swaying under me as I was laid down and held still.

It seemed Jet was put into a different boat was nearby, for I heard muffled sounds coming from him and an "Ey!" that escaped when they must have released his mouth for a moment.

The boat ride seemed much longer than it should have and much more precarious, as I couldn't see. I could feel each dip in the ocean.

We were brought onto what I assumed was a ship. The sound of rigging being adjusted and feet traveling over clay seemed to confirm it.

Without a word, I was taken somewhere dark. It smelled slightly of rot or mold. I was set down and released. I tried to leap up, even still being tied, but a door was slammed before I could do anything. Someone, somehow, still reached my head and tore the sack from it.

"There you are." The person in front of me grinned wickedly, revealing his sharp teeth.

My blood seemed to slow. It was the palace guard. The one I'd beaten in combat mere weeks ago, and there were almost ten guards along with him.

"Who are you and what do you mean by capturing us?!" Jet's voice came from the other side of a carved stone grid.

We were both in locked cells.

The guards merely huffed, said nothing, and ascended back up some stairs. The one whom I'd fought looked back to me for a split second with a face that said he'd beaten me this time. I couldn't disagree.

"OYYYY!" Jet screamed after them.

I knew what was happening. At least I thought I did, "Jet. I'm sorry. It's my fault." My voice was faint.

He'd been shouting through the stone grid that was in front of him and now he looked over to me and fell silent.

"What? And are you okay, there?"

"I'm fine for now. Are you?" I could just see him through the squares separating us.

He nodded but looked worried.

"Jet, those were palace guards. I...they must be taking us back to Cresstalan. Someone must have found out about me wanting to plant the new Tree. I think we've been arrested."

Jet was still. He seemed in disbelief. "But...who did you tell? I thought you were keeping it secret tightly as you could."

"I don't know. I did my best. Perhaps somehow, someone overheard."

Jet said nothing at this, but looked disheartened, which was something for him as he was always full of vigor. Full of life.

"I'm so sorry. Jet, I'm so sorry." I felt deflated. I'd brought him into this. I hadn't honestly thought anyone would find out or suspect what we were doing. At the very least, not until a long time off when the Tree could fend for herself.

What would happen to her now? Without me and Jet to protect her, would she die?

The Garden had barely been started and now it would all have been for nothing.

I looked over to Jet again, he'd somehow moved, though his arms and legs were bound, to the stone grating that separated us.

"Shay...you...you were trying to go and do a good thing. I came along because I believed it to be true. Don't go blaming yourself, eh? There...," he sighed, "There's something I have to tell you, as well."

"Jet." I moved over to him with a series of clumsy thuds, the ropes I was tied with digging into my skin. The stone grate was quite thick so, with our hands and feet tied, we couldn't touch each other, but I felt the smallest bit better by being closer to him.

He met my eyes. "Some of this is my own fault here, Shay."

"How can that be?" I raised a corner of my lip.

He didn't return my smile. "Do you remember when we first met? How Mercully said I'd been searching for you?"

I nodded.

"Since I'd heard you'd had trouble up at the palace, I thought perhaps you wouldn't be so fond of 'em. We'd seen the problems on the other islands for years, and I thought if someone from the palace knew, perhaps something might be done."

I gulped, had Jet been using me this whole time?

"You were in a place of power, I believed, or in a place to talk to those with it." He didn't look away, "I simply wanted to show you what was about. I thought you could change it in ways I'd been unable. But look here, it wasn't Cresstalan's to fix anyway. Their troubles have been done purposely, it seems." He smiled a little now, "I thought we could be friends, but I like you now more than I can say. I don't know what's to come, but I'm glad to have met you. None of this is your fault and I'm sorry for the part of it that's mine."

I lowered my eyes. All of this was so tangled. But no, Jet hadn't used me. I'd wanted to leave Cresstalan. I would have seen the issues with the islands and would have made the same decisions, I was sure.

I looked back to Jet, "It's good you showed me what had been happening. Those people were wrong to do what they've done, whatever their reasons. I'm glad to have met you as well, Jet." I lowered my eyes, unable to look at him when I said, "I like you so much. I guess all we can do now is try to escape."

He laughed, and I looked up to find determination in his eyes once more. "Hopefully they'll bring us some food first, as I'm a bit peckish."

I grinned, "That would be nice." What was to happen to us now?

Thinking negatively wouldn't help anything, but I wasn't sure what to think. We were being taken back to Cresstalan where I'd be punished. There were also people working purposely to destroy the island ring. Where did I fit in?

Letting out a breath, I did the only thing I could think of, and did my best to get into the mindset. It took a few more breaths, but finally I was there.

Jet had been quiet. As I looked over to him now, I saw him gnawing at the ropes around his hands. He looked up from what he was doing and smirked.

"Is that working?"

"Ey, don't worry, it will. What else have I to do?"

I smiled back, then began chewing at my own ropes.

"Tastes a bit like sand, ey?"

I spit a tiny piece I'd broken from the rope and laughed, "Have you tasted a lot of sand?"

Jet spit a piece as well. "O'course. I live on beaches much of the time. Have you not?"

As he asked, I remembered one day I'd been swimming in the ocean with Jevin when we were children. The waves had pulled me under and clouds of water and sand filled my mouth. I fought my way back to the surface, short of breath and frightened.

"Only mixed with sea water," I said.

"Ey, I wouldn't mind a little salt for this. Should enhance the flavor, I'd think. Perhaps I'll go abouts asking the guards to fetch some, ey?"

I laughed, my mouth full of rope, and spoke around it, "Please do."

⌘

We were definitely on a ship, and the next few days were quite uneventful.

There were buckets in the corner of each of our cells so we could relieve ourselves, and we were brought a small amount of food a few times a day at sporadic intervals...whenever we were remembered, it seemed.

We never saw anyone, but guards. I knew a few of the guard's faces from the castle but had never spoken to them. They either avoided my eyes or glared at me outright.

Jet and I concocted a plan to escape, but it went awry. We'd successfully chewed through our ropes and freed ourselves. But whether we'd ever have a chance to try an escape, we weren't sure.

After a time, we realized even if we were able to escape, it would do us no good. We were on a ship in the middle of the ocean and it was full of guards that were apparently charged with keeping us captured. Even if we somehow defeated them, we couldn't run the ship with just the two of us.

"What are we to do then?" Jet asked when we began talking of these issues.

"I don't know where else they would be taking us besides the palace at Cresstalan. All I can think to do is to let them. I don't know, maybe we can find a way for you to escape when we reach the docks."

"And why would I escape, then? Aren't you planning on joining?"

I looked at Jet through the grating that separated us. "Jet. As much as I would love to avoid all of this, I did go against my father's wishes. I don't know how much they know." I looked out of my cell to see if there was anyone around, but we were always left alone. "It's possible I'm just in trouble with the Queen for leaving when I was supposed to be punished, but you shouldn't have to be as well."

"Bu—"

"Jet." I held his eyes and lowered my voice as much as I possibly could, "If you can get away, if you can get back to 'The Sea's Ribbon', you'll be safe. I'll be fine...and if I'm not...perhaps you all can find a way to help me. But I don't think it'll help if you're captured as well." I also wondered how much Cresstalan knew of the people on Fainia.

"Shay, why can't we go on and both escape if we go this far? You'd be welcome aboard the ship. I've told you that, aye?"

"Jet, they went all the way to Fainia to find me and did it in a matter of days from when I left. They'll keep looking. Whatever I'm being arrested for, it's serious. I don't want to get the crew involved either if it can be helped."

"Shay, you're one of the crew." Jet seemed determined about this, but his eyes were wide and seemed to shine with a hint of desperation.

"Don't tell anyone that."

He looked slightly hurt, but I thought he understood. If I was in trouble and they were found helping me, they could all be punished. I had to assess the situation first and find out exactly what was going on.

My heart seemed squeezed inside my chest. "I like you so much, Jet. That's why I need to you to escape."

Jet nodded, slowly at first, and then it seemed he was

decided, "Ey, Shay. I'll escape, fine. But once I do, I'm following along and making sure you stay safe."

"No. Jet!" I lowered my voice again, "How would that even work? You can't do that. If you're caught..."

"I'll go and find a way. Most like, no one will know me at the palace. If something goes wrong, you'll be needing help. If I'm gone, how will I know of danger that comes to you?"

"I'd rather you didn't do that, but let's figure out a way to let you escape first and go from there."

"Fair enough," Jet sighed.

"I'm sure it will be fine."

"'Course."

We continued on our trip, eating little, and not being able to do much.

Jet and I stayed close to each other on either side of the grate. Sometimes we could sleep with our hands held through it.

I woke one morning, my hand still in Jet's from when we'd been talking late into the night. Just about normal things. We'd finally figured out a decent escape plan. Now all we could do was wait.

Jet's cheek was leaning on the shoulder attached to the hand I was holding. His face was slightly squished upwards because of this. He was sound asleep.

I smiled. At least I'd been able to kiss him and spend this time with him. If that was all I got, if I was to be forced to do mind-numbing work at the palace now, perhaps I could always remember this time with Jet and know that, for a short time...such a short time...things had been good.

42
Escape

Finally, we arrived. The guards were shuffling around much more and soon the ship had stopped.

Jet and I clasped hands one more time as we heard feet coming down the stairs.

When the guards had seen that our bonds were removed, they'd just laughed. I wondered if they would tie us up again.

Most of the guards aboard came down the stairs. The cell doors were open, and Jet and I pretended to be tired and unable to struggle. We were getting there. The last few days, with little rest and fitful sleep hadn't been easy, but we were still able to fight. We didn't want to show that just yet though.

As we went along willingly, the guards seemed a little surprised. Seven were assigned to each of us.

This was our reward for going quietly for the moment, our hands were tied behind our backs, but they allowed us to walk and to see. Jet and I snuck looks to each other. So far, our plan would work.

We were walked up to the deck of the ship, and I eagerly drew in the fresh breeze after sitting so long in the stale air of our cells.

We left the ship down the gangplank and entered the market.

I looked over to Jet now, he was looking at me, and I gave him the smallest nod.

The guards' grips had loosened, in fact, I was only being held by four of them. This worked for me. I started with a strong kick to the solar plexus of the guard walking behind me. As he was hunched over, and the other guards were thrown off for a split-second, I jumped up, swinging my tied arms under my feet so my hands were in front of me.

I now had my fists to fight with, though they were bound together. I clasped them and used them, reaching and pummeling every part of the guards around me.

I saw Jet among the chaos. Only one guard was left to watch him as the other ones came to stop me. It was getting harder to move. A couple of the guards had grabbed me and were holding on desperately.

I was actually lucky there were so many guards, not all of them could get to me. The confusion seemed to work to my advantage.

Jet stomped hard on the foot of the guard holding him and was able to wrench himself free. He turned and kicked the guard hard in his middle. And then he was gone.

Just as Jet ran, the throng of guards blocked every view I might have had of him and I felt a blade at my throat.

I smiled and felt tears prick at my eyes. Jet had gotten away.

There was a thump on my head and all went dark.

43
Trap

I woke as I was shaken vigorously. A vision of the throne room and the Queen in front of me, on her throne, met my eyes.

I blinked, trying to bring what I was seeing into focus, but my head pounded, and I couldn't see or think quite straight. I just felt dizzy.

The Queen seemed to be speaking to me, but I couldn't make out what she was trying to say. I tried to tell her I didn't understand but found myself unable to get the words out.

Darkness began to crowd my vision.

I saw the Queen shaking her head and, for a moment my vision and hearing came back into focus, "—her away. I'll speak with her later. Whatever did you do?"

A red sleeve swished as Veler waved for me to be ushered away.

Then everything went black once more.

When I came to, my head hurt, but I was able to think

and see clearly this time. Those guards must have hit my head too hard with whatever they used to knock me out. But Jet had gotten away, at least.

I looked around...as much as I could. I found I was strapped to some sort of reclined chair. My head was restrained as well. I could only see in front of me and what was there wasn't comforting.

There were a number of what looked like lethal devices. Sharp edges and angry shadows surrounded me. There seemed to be a source of light behind be, but it didn't do much to brighten my surroundings.

Where was this? Was I still in the palace? I'd never seen nor heard of any place like it.

I remembered being in the throne room. I'd seen the Queen and she had told the guards to take me away to talk later. That must mean I wasn't too far from the palace.

Seeing if there was any way to get loose from the bonds, I shook my arms and legs and any piece of my body I could move, but it did nothing. I was stuck for now.

Was I supposed to wait here until the Queen came to speak to me? I didn't want to do that. I wanted to find out as soon as I could why exactly I was in trouble.

There didn't seem to be a way anyone could know for sure that I'd planted the Garden...unless of course...had someone overheard me speaking with Jevin? I had expressed all my plans to him. He was trustworthy, or else I wouldn't have gone to him, but the palace was a relatively small place.

There was a chance that someone had overheard what I'd been planning. How else would someone know to search for me on Fainia?

I decided now that I didn't want to be left alone with my thoughts and worries. I wanted some solid answers so I could come up with real solutions to whatever situation I was in.

"Hello?" I yelled as loudly as I could. "Is someone there? Your majesty?" I thought I heard a far-off sound. Perhaps of something dropping, but there was no response.

Though I waited a few more minutes, I realized I didn't know where I was. There was a chance no one could hear me.

My head felt a bit light from yelling even that much. It seemed I'd have to wait for the Queen after all.

There was nothing to do, so I decided to try calming my mind through meditation, at least.

Letting out a shaky breath, I began.

I clicked into the mindset after three breaths and immediately heard a door swing open behind me.

It had to be the Queen. I opened my eyes. I didn't know what was going to happen, what the Queen was going to talk to me about. All I could do was my best. If she asked me about the new Garden I was planting, if she somehow knew, I was going to protect it. Though it might die anyway without me, though I didn't know what that might mean for me, I would protect it for as long as I could.

The Queen appeared in front of me, but someone else was walking behind her. When he came into view, I hopeful. It was my father.

That feeling retreated slightly at the sight of his face. It looked stern and sad.

"Good morning, Shaylite," the Queen spoke coolly.

Morning? Had I slept all night?

"Hello, your majesty. Father," I said to each of them. I tried to be as polite and as casual as I could. Would acting normal help me at all?

I felt distinctly uncomfortable. I was strapped tightly to the chair and both my father and the Queen looked extremely serious.

"Shaylite, enlighten me on something," the Queen said. "I was lenient with your punishment after you severely injured the Crown Prince, was I not?"

I wasn't sure I could think of a worse punishment than what she'd been threatening, but I set myself against exacerbating the situation further, "Yes, your majesty."

"Then," the Queen lowered herself gracefully into a chair my father brought, "please inform me how you expected it to be a good idea to ignore that decision and simply leave Cresstalan altogether."

"I'm sorry, your majesty." I didn't have a reason for it except I thought I would be exceptionally unhappy. I still felt that Fedrid had been in the wrong.

She gave the slightest laugh, just one small, musical, "Ha," and straightened her skirts. "And," she said, "how will you further explain your insistence upon not only leaving, dodging the punishment that was rightfully earned by you, but going along to another island with...stolen seeds of the Great Tree?"

Here it was. They did know. I had to protect the Tree. "I'm not sure what you're talking about, your majesty."

"Hm. Interesting. Because I received word from a guard, who has some quite keen ears, that this was your plan and that you were able to carry it out."

I started to speak, but she held up a hand and continued, "It seems you delivered the seeds to vagrants populating Fainia."

The Queen thought I was in league with Heyda's people? I couldn't support what the people of Queniil were about, but I saw their reasons. For now, I'd protect them too.

"I saw no one on Fainia, your majesty. Its people fled long ago." A thought struck, "Where's Jevin?" my heart started pounding, if Jevin had been punished, had been found out to be involved in this...

"Jevin? He's where he always has been. We questioned him about this, of course, and he said you'd indeed told him of your plan, but that he refused to help you and you somehow broke into the Garden and stole the seeds."

I didn't let out the sigh of relief that I felt in my heart. Good. Jevin was safe. He probably thought they wouldn't be able to find me. He'd stuck the blame to me so he could continue being a Gardener.

Exactly as I would have wished him to do. "I did. I asked him, but he did refuse. I just wanted to make sure you were aware of that."

I looked to my father now. It seemed he hadn't wanted to believe that I'd stolen the seeds. His face had fallen.

Somehow, the Queen knew I'd left Cresstalan with the seeds though. Fine, I would go along with that.

"I did steal the seeds and leave Cresstalan, but I was seasick on the first day aboard the boat. They were in a pouch around my neck, the strap broke, and they fell into the sea without my knowing. They're gone."

"How convenient."

"Shaylite." My father raised his eyes to mine, they looked lost. "How could you steal the seeds of the Great Tree?"

"Father, I'm sorry, but I told you." I looked from him to the Queen, thinking I could convey my case for the new Garden again. "The other islands are suffering. I don't think the Great Tree is protecting them. I thought that if I perhaps planted a new Tree it would help—"

My father rose from his seat and I felt an explosion of pain as he slapped me across the face. My vision was splashed with white light for a moment, and when it was gone, so was my father and the Queen was standing.

"Perhaps," she said, leaving, "in a few days you'll be able to remember that those seeds did not, in fact, fall into the ocean. Maybe then you'll be able to recall where exactly you had the naïve notion to give those seeds to our mortal enemies or worse, plant them."

She was gone. The small swishing of her dress leaving my ears as a door shut decidedly behind me.

I felt tears slide down my cheeks. What was I to do?

44
Pressed

Wherever I was, time was non-existent. There were no windows. I was given no food, no water, and was not even let off of the angled chair to relieve myself. When I had no choice, but to do it as I was still strapped to the table, I was beyond embarrassed. Though I called for anyone for hours, no one had come.

One of the lamps had gone out and, in the flickering light, I thought I saw people and creatures lurking in the room. Then I would blink, and they would vanish away.

I did my best not to cry, to at least conserve water, but once I found myself overwhelmed and did anyway.

This situation was more than I'd expected. Of course, I had never thought I would be caught in my plan and hadn't bothered to imagine what kind of punishment I might receive.

My father had been cold when I left and since even he wasn't helping me, I wondered how broken our relationship was at this point. Clearly, I was of no use to him if I wasn't in the Garden, but didn't being his daughter count for anything? Not really, I reminded myself, thinking back to when I'd first disappointed him long ago. He'd always wished my mother was here instead.

I had more time to think on this than I would have liked.

I'd always known why my father was distant. My mother had died giving birth to me and, whether it was that I reminded him too much of her, or he blamed me for what had happened to her, he had never really wanted me.

Thinking of this, choked, gasping sobs fell from my parched lips.

We'd only ever been close as Master and Apprentice. Now it seemed that since I had, in his eyes, betrayed the Garden, he wanted nothing at all to do with me.

Then I thought of Jevin. He was somewhere in the palace. Did he know I was here as well? Even though we'd fought when I last saw him, I thought he would still be here to help me if he knew. Perhaps though, this place was too heavily guarded.

Of Jet...I tried not think about him. However, during periods where I couldn't sleep or when I began falling into despair, I found myself hoping that he had followed me. Though it would most certainly put him in danger, I didn't want to be kept here. I longed for the easy days Jet and I had together and the small, wonderful things we'd done together. I just wanted to be caught in the rain with him once more.

The periods where I thought like this were brief. I always did the best I could to shake myself as soon as I realized I was spiraling downward. It would do no good.

Either Jet would find a way to get to me, or he wouldn't.

Of course, even if he somehow did, I would just be hunted down again and most likely put through even worse punishments. I never could think of a solution where the ending was good.

For a time, I attempted to concentrate on the interesting things I'd learned. Our ring of islands had indeed once been one continent...and it hadn't been ours.

I wondered what that place might have looked like. How grand had the ruins been before our people had ruined them? Had the sea spires been a massive building in the middle of the land? Were there holes in them to bring air down to the tunnels below? And where did those tunnels end?

Thinking back to Klieton, I remembered the hole Clare had fallen into...with the strange barrier of rock within it. Could that have been one of the tunnels that had collapsed? Or were some intentionally hidden by the people of Queniil?

Even this couldn't distract me for long though, and most of the time, I tried to meditate. It was getting a bit difficult with the distraction of the terrible smell of myself and the hunger that made me feel as if my stomach was attempting to digest itself. Usually though, my efforts ended with me falling asleep, my only reprieve.

One day, during that respite, I lurched awake.

Footsteps, the jingle of a key, and, as I opened my eyes at these things, the demonic blue eyes of Prince Fedrid.

It was all I could do to not burst out crying at that moment. If I had, I would have been broken.

I was not broken though, I was just hungry. And so, I set my face and stared at Fedrid's nose as it wrinkled in distaste.

Keeping my eyes open, I brought him into focus. I wanted to say something clever or something that would at least make him mad if not, ideally, break him instead of me, but my body felt strongly that it wanted to faint.

"Before anything happens here," Fedrid said, raising a key in his hand, "I can't handle this smell."

I felt him unlock the bonds on my feet, my head, my hands.

Though I was loose, I was barely able to move. I gritted my teeth, willing myself to stand, and my immediate urge was to throw a punch at Fedrid.

I couldn't tell you why this was my first thought, besides the various hateful emotions I held towards him, I thought I also might have been half-delirious. At any rate, I wasn't even able to lift my arm high enough to punch him in the face as I'd wanted to. I could barely lift it from my side. The force of the movement I attempted to execute and the failure of it, set me off-balance and I fell face-first to the ground. I was, thankfully, able to lift my arms and use them to stop my face from falling into a puddle of my own urine.

"Disgraceful," I heard Fedrid say as he stood over me. Then I felt pain bloom in my side as he kicked me.

I couldn't even make a sound when he did this. I was glad I didn't.

"Get yourself clean. There's a washroom behind you. Go. Now."

Though I immediately wanted to disobey any order given to me by the Prince, what I wanted more was to be clean. I pushed myself up and made my way, half-hunched, to the washroom.

I felt the faintest surge of surprise as I saw that this washroom was similar to my own. That was short-lived as I spotted a pitcher by a washing basin. I leaped at it and guzzled the water, not even wanting to take breaths between swallows. This led to a lot of sputtering that I forced down with more water. I mourned the drops that squeezed from the sides of my mouth.

Only when I'd sucked the last drop from the pitcher did I set it back down. My stomach felt swollen strangely and my throat hinted at nausea. I let out a breath and relaxed myself purposely, the nausea released a little. Overall, I felt better.

I realized my lips were cracked too and that the water had made them sting, but now I was on to the next task, relieving myself in a basin actually meant for the task. There were soft cloths laid to the side for wiping oneself and I did this.

Taking the rest of the cloths, I soaked them in the steaming bath before me to wipe my whole body thoroughly.

I let out a sigh of relief, a tear dripping down my cheek.

Lowering myself into the pool, I let out a gasp as the warmth seeped into my hollow-feeling body. I washed with soap at the side of the pool and enjoyed every moment I had.

Now though, I began to think of Fedrid out in the next room. So close. What was in store for me after this?

There was even a white robe and pants for me to change into after I finished. I would take advantage of every kindness and use them to strengthen myself for whatever came after this.

I thought for a moment of staying in the washroom. However, I was feeling light-headed from the heat and still so hungry.

Pushing myself, shaking, up from the water, I changed into the clean clothes I'd been given, took some deep breaths to steel myself, and exited into the dark room once more.

The mess I'd made was cleaned, most likely by a guard or servant that had now left, but the smell lingered slightly.

Though a part of myself still wanted to punch Fedrid, I knew it would do me no good. I was trapped here, and I was not in control of my fate.

Fedrid gestured for me to sit on the chair once more.

I did.

"So...who was your friend they captured along with you?"

This was where we were going with the questions today. Well, I would also protect Jet. "I didn't know him. He just happened to be near me when I was captured."

Without warning, Fedrid drew his foot back and kicked me hard in the shin.

"Ah," I let out that much noise, but no more. And I did not look away from him.

"That's interesting," he said, speaking as though he hadn't just done what he had, "because I was told by the guards that you were found holding his hand. On Fainia...which, you claim, is a deserted island."

"They were lying," I said casually.

I saw him draw back his foot this time and I moved my shin out of the way.

Fedrid grimaced but didn't attempt to kick me again. Perhaps he thought I might kick him back at this point. I couldn't have with the guards and the Queen possibly nearby.

It seemed he had another tactic in mind though, for his next sentence sent my heart beating faster.

"Then you won't mind if we kill him? We've just found him, you know. Not very good at escaping, it seems."

At the same time I wanted to launch myself at Fedrid and beat him bloody for even suggesting something like that, I also wanted to plead with him to kill me and free Jet. But I started thinking instead. If they had truly found Jet, they wouldn't kill him.

I looked at Fedrid and found, in a brief sweep of his eyes, that there was a slight glint of fear. He was lying.

"I don't think you should go around killing innocent people if we're getting into it, but apart from that, your killing him won't affect me."

Fedrid shrugged, "I'll let the guards know then."

"Please do." My voice cracked slightly while saying this. Not using it for so long was not helping my discussion skills.

"Where did you plant the seeds?"

"I didn't plant the seeds. They fell into the ocean."

"Where in the ocean?"

"I don't know the ocean well enough to tell you that."

"Damn it. Where are the people you gave them to?" his voice was rising.

"I gave them to no one." I had to keep doing this. I could for now.

Fedrid grabbed my wrist and started to bind me once again, locking me in with the key he held. I let him. If he didn't do it, the guards would, and they would make it much more difficult.

When he finished he said, "I don't believe you for a second."

I shrugged as much as I was able to while bound.

He blew out a heated breath and then punched me in the nose.

Warm blood gushed from it and ran down my lips. It felt as if my head had been split in two.

"To pay you back," he said. It seemed he was going to wait for a response from me. Perhaps he wanted a rise.

I blinked several times and said quietly, but decidedly, my voice affected by blood and what was probably a broken nose, "You deserved it, your highness."

I'd never called him your highness. I wanted to see what he'd do with it.

He lowered his head to my ear and whispered, "And you deserve to die."

In all honesty, I wanted to laugh at that. The boy was deranged. How could I possibly deserve to die only for living as a member of the opposite gender? I had done nothing wrong.

I kept my mouth shut though and, luckily, Fedrid left me.

My stomach growled loudly into the dim room.

45
Torture

There was no waiting this time. Fedrid left and, though I couldn't see it, he must have let in the next person that was to question me.

It was Derrif, the Weapon Master. I tensed slightly when he stood in front of me. The last time I'd seen him, apart from very far away in passing, he had banned me from using the palace weapons.

At first, I was curious why he was here, but it was soon made clear that my silence was about to have consequences.

Derrif's face was twisted in disgust.

"Should have stopped you when I had the chance," he said, reaching into the sack he carried. It was oddly lumpy, and I knew that I didn't want to know what was inside. "First, you try to pass your disgusting-self off as a man, and now here we are. You've committed high crimes."

"There's no proof of that," I said quietly, tasting blood. I had to hold the position that I'd done nothing. Nothing. In my heart I truly believed I had done nothing wrong, so I didn't think it would be impossible, at the very least.

Derrif pulled from the sack a strange-looking tool—a flat, two-inch wide length of metal. "That's why I'm here."

He weighed it in his hand, bouncing it up and down. "Make you sing your sins."

I let out a breath. I didn't know what was about to happen, but I couldn't change it. I would have to endure. I did my best to click into the Garden mindset and hold my tongue.

"Unfortunately," said Derrif now, "I've been instructed not to break anything, or to harm you in a way that will permanently damage you. But there's still plenty within those limits that'll make you tell me exactly what you've done. And it looks like the Prince doesn't have the same restrictions." He grinned at my bloodied nose.

He came toward me with the metal tool. I looked to the ceiling.

"Where did you plant the seeds, filth?"

I said nothing. I concentrated on simply letting my body be. I breathed more slowly and allowed my energy, the little that I had, to flow through me, unimpeded.

"Answer, or else," said Derrif, bringing the tool in front of my eyes so I'd have to look at it.

Instead of closing my eyes, for I knew it was there anyway, I looked, seeing it for what it was. Simply a piece of metal.

He took the tool away from my sight and I didn't see what he was doing, I simply stayed in the mindset.

It came back glowing orange.

I released another breath. I could do nothing to stop this. At least, what I could do, I would not do.

"Where are the seeds?" Derrif asked, his face coming close to my own.

"In the ocean," I whispered.

"Wrong," he said.

My arm rang with pain as if the metal had been shoved through.

Derrif had pressed the fiery length to my forearm.

I was still in the mindset though. I did not scream. My

mouth merely opened and let out a short stream of air, then I returned to my long breaths.

I wasn't going to be okay. I needed to accept that. If I did, perhaps I could continue without breaking. It was the one thing I didn't want to do. So much was being taken from me, but I would not let them have my sanity or my heart. It was a good heart. It wanted to help the world. I focused on its beating as Derrif continued the torture.

He asked me the same question so many times. I didn't answer at all but allowed the hot metal to press into my arm. He never switched to the other arm or anywhere else, and it left a line of red streaks.

After what I thought was four, I felt faint. On the fifth, I did faint.

∞∞∞

This went on for a week, I guessed. Derrif and a few different guards took to torturing me in shifts. About every few hours they'd come. Mostly, I was asked the same questions.

There were times I grew weak and began to deny strongly whatever they accused me of.

Sometimes they were more brutal, trying to scare me into telling exactly what they wanted. They said they had Jet, though they still didn't know his name. I knew if they were hurting him like they said, they would do it in front of me. I ignored them when they talked of him and eventually they gave up the tactic.

Soon I didn't answer at all. They increased the pain of my tortures, holding the metal to my skin for longer periods of time, afterwards leaving wounds angry and open to infection.

I took to trying to meditate as I was tortured, focusing on the Tree of the Fallen, trying to revive that connection I'd felt with her. It helped a little, but I was pulled from the

Garden again and again by the heat pressed to my skin.

I didn't want to be in my body. It hurt so much. It was too painful to be myself.

The more I tried to escape from it though, the more the Trees, both the Tree of the Fallen and the new one I'd planted, were foreign to me. I felt no connection with them, though I tried desperately.

It was after a particularly painful torture session that I realized this.

In trying to leave myself and only exist with the Trees, I was denying the only thing that could protect them. Me.

In only working to protect others, I'd turned away again and again from the fact that I was the one in need.

Just as much as they were hurting, I was hurting. If I didn't help myself, how could I help anything else?

I cleared my mind, gulping, and allowed the pain to exist. I tried to see it as it was. A part of me and, if I denied it, I denied my own body. I felt it deep inside.

It was telling me that my body was in danger, but also that I was doing what I believed was right. If these people were hurting me, they could only hurt others. That was no way to live.

I was in the better position.

∽∞∾

This seemed to work as a method for getting through everything and I kept at it. Acknowledging the pain seemed to make it less potent.

Facing that part of myself though, made others come to light. It seemed I'd been holding feelings down as well.

When waves of pain rolled over me as a guard pressed the hot metal to my thigh, it came with tides of emotion. I felt my face contort into anger and it filled my body where the pain had been. Fear washed that away, and sadness the fear.

I didn't know what was happening. I thought I'd known what those emotions had felt like, but these new sensations made the others feel like I'd been playing pretend when I felt them before.

The strange thing about these emotions too, was that they weren't directed at anyone or anything. They simply washed over me, pure and unbiased.

The fear brought the first tears I'd shed in a torture session, but I was not ashamed of them. I said no words, but simply let the feelings course through me.

When the guard finished the session, I heard his whisper to someone behind me, "Won't be long now."

But I wasn't breaking. I thought I might be mending.

Later, in a state of half-sleep, the Tree of the Fallen appeared before me in a vision.

Then it switched, and I was the Tree.

This time though, the Tree and I were simply melded perfectly. I realized that though I had some connection with the Tree of the Fallen, all but a few times, our connection had been forced by me. I'd wanted it to be real and made myself believe it was.

Now there were no thoughts, there was no desire, no strain. Being one with the Tree in this moment simply meant that I felt in balance. I felt I was connecting the heavens and the earth to each other. I was combining elements and using them to create myself and to grow strong. Most of all, I felt protected and loved. By the air, by the soil, by the water, by the sun, and by my caretakers. I felt truly at peace.

Had I also been playing at the mindset?

Though I felt better for the most-part, I was still tortured, and I felt it all. It dredged up feelings that were so intense, I couldn't place them, and I felt crushed by the emotion that had been locked within me.

I considered resisting it when it came next, but remembered my vision of the Tree, though I thought I'd forgotten part of it. This seemed like the right path within myself.

I accepted that I was afraid. I was sad. I was angry. I had been this whole time and I had pressed it deeper and deeper into myself until I didn't recognize my numbness.

Left alone, I began to overthink though. Instead of letting emotions pass without thought, which had seemed right, I once again placed them with situations.

I was scared they would eventually try to use Jevin against me.

I was angry at Heyda for being with the people hurting the islands, mad at so many more people.

How much did my father know about what was happening? How much did the Queen or the Prince or the Princess know? Were they happy I was being tortured?

One of the sessions had just ended and I felt fear in my stinging wounds.

46
Rescue

I flinched as the door handle twitched. They were back. I grimaced and gritted my teeth.

I let out a long breath, closing my eyes. Afraid. The door handle shook up and down now. Whomever it was seemed to be having an odd amount of trouble opening it.

Upon hearing the ominous scrape of the door as it opened, an unchecked tear slid between my eyelids and down my face.

I opened my eyes and, as I comprehended what I was seeing, the rest of my tears welled-up and spilled down. My voice, so long unused, cracked as I cried, "Jevin!" in relief.

He brought a single finger to his lip and I bit down on my tongue.

In a whisper, he spoke, "Are you alright, Shaylite?"

The corners of my mouth twitched as I shook my head. "When? How?" I rasped, quietly.

"No time. Key?"

I thought for a moment, "I always heard it clink behind me when they brought it out. There might be a hook."

"Mm." Jevin nodded.

I momentarily lost sight of my friend as he stepped behind to get the key.

For a moment, I thought I was dreaming, but this was real. I knew because my whole body still throbbed violently with the pain of my tortures.

Jevin had come. It had been at least a week of relentless questioning, but I'd held out, shown courage far beyond what I had known existed within me, found more of myself as well. The ordeal was finally over.

I heard the small metallic noise and a scoff from Jevin as he found the key. After a moment, he started to unlatch the bonds on my bruised wrists. I winced in pain.

When I was free I slowly moved my limbs up and down, feeling the blood beginning to fill my empty fingers and toes once again.

"Alright, let's go!" Jevin whispered.

I nodded once, trying to stand, but my leg gave way under me, sending me to one knee. I hissed in pain and embarrassment. Jevin faltered back and lifted and steadied me, avoiding the burns on my arm.

I used to be one of the strongest people in the palace; my swordplay could be matched by few. Now I was but a shallow husk of my former self, robbed of that part of myself for the moment.

Finding my footing, I pulled away from Jevin, the thought of being able to walk free bringing strength back and allowing me to move forward, though I limped slightly from my stiff, burned legs.

Jevin led the way. We came out of a tunnel that, when we exited, wasn't far from the Garden entrance. We had been in the palace this whole time. I did not cry, but sadness flowed through me.

Jevin checked the way as we went, making sure it was clear. I didn't know how he had gotten the guards away. We hurried forward. He helped me sometimes as I was so weak, and we made it to his room.

When he opened the door and let me in, keeping lookout as he did so, I saw to my shock and delight that Jet was in the room, sitting on the chair by Jevin's desk.

He looked up as I entered and, before I could stop myself, I hurried forward to him as fast as my injuries would let me and found myself being carefully held in his arms. I had my own grasped tightly around him, not caring that my burns were screaming at the contact, feeling anchored.

"Sha-ay," he said softly, his voice breaking.

I just squeezed him tighter. A new feeling flowing through me that felt warm and bright.

I heard Jevin speaking and though I truly never wanted to let go of Jet, Jevin had been the one who had rescued me from the torture chamber and I wanted to hug him as well.

Reluctantly pulling myself away from Jet, I gave Jevin a tight hug. "Thank you," I whispered to him.

He let go before I did, and I retreated, sitting down onto his bed as exhaustion started to creep in on me.

"Your friend here. Jet, was it?"

Jet picked up a plate of smoked fish and fresh fruit that had been sitting on Jevin's desk. He handed it to me and I immediately picked up a slice of fish and downed it, already picking up the next one. Food. I had food.

Jet nodded to Jevin's question, not taking his eyes from me.

Jevin continued, "He found where you were Shay, he'd been spying around the castle and finally figured it out, it seems."

"I wanted to come and retrieve you myself, o'course," said Jet to this, "but if I'd been captured, you'd surely be in more trouble. I remembered though that you mentioned this one's name." He nodded to Jevin. "I found him, and he figured it all out. How to get you free."

Though my stomach was crying out for more food, I was truly touched, and I swallowed then sat still for a

moment, in awe of what they'd done for me. "Thank you."
It was all I could do to whisper the words.

"Shaylite," said Jevin, "I know that you need rest, but
we probably don't have much time until they figure out
you're gone. I doubt you'll be found if you're here."

I nodded, almost done with the plate of food now and
feeling pulled toward sleep. I did my best to concentrate on
what Jevin was saying, feeling my body finally relaxing a
marginal amount, but with that relaxation came an almost
overwhelming sense of exhaustion. Still, I focused on Jevin.

It hadn't been long since I'd last seen him...when we
had fought, yet he'd saved me, and was acting as if all of
that never happened. I was grateful, but I hoped he was
okay.

He looked the same, but his eyes were tired and
worried, I wondered what he'd expected to find when he
went to rescue me. I wondered how he felt about what he'd
found. Burns on skin and clothes. I had, at least, been
allowed to use the restroom at times, so I hadn't wet myself
again, but I didn't even want to look down to my own body
and see the damage that'd been done.

I shook myself mentally and listened once again to
what Jevin was saying to me.

"Were you able to, Shaylite? Were you able to plant the
seeds?" he was speaking quite low now.

I nodded, tiredness now shadowing my will to eat. I set
the plate of food on the bed, a few slices of fish and fruit
still left. "Jet helped me. We planted the Tree on Fainia.
The other seeds are still hidden in a house there."

"You had him help you?" Jevin turned slightly to Jet
but didn't take his eyes off me.

"I couldn't do it myself. Jet is trustworthy. He did
well."

"And you were able to find a good place for a new
Garden?"

"Mmhmm. Jet helped with that. He knew of a place with ruins...they look so much like the ones here on Cresstalan, Jevin. We made a Garden there. I think it might live...if we can get back to it. If Heyda doesn't find it."

I suddenly felt a sense of urgency in the back of my mind. I had to get back soon to take care of the Tree, but I was so tired. I would have to rest for at least a day before I'd be able to go back. Had Heyda's people found it? And where was 'The Sea's Ribbon'? I almost asked Jet, but I found I wanted to talk as little as possible. I would bring it all up later.

"Shaylite..."

Why did Jevin keep calling me by my full name, the thought crossed my mind fuzzily and then I forgot it.

"Where are the ruins located?"

Now my eyes were getting heavy. "Jevin, I'll tell you...we probably need someone else to know the location of it anyway, but I'm so tired. Jet can tell you."

Jet had hardly looked away from me. I looked back into his eyes and smiled softly. I still wanted to go over to him and hold him and not let go, but for the moment I needed rest.

Jet smiled widely at me, his eyes sparkling, though tinged with a hint of sadness...perhaps for my present state. "Ey, I'll give him the directions. Don't you worry, Shay."

"That will work. Go on and lay down. Rest here for a while." Now Jevin turned to Jet, "Alright, put back on the cap and cloak you were wearing to hide yourself. That will do. Shaylite, if you need us, we'll be in the unused tower room where we trained. Come there after you've rested. I got you clothes to hide yourself. I need to show you something there."

I nodded. Jevin smiled and nodded back.

Jet walked over to me and picked up my hand in his. He squeezed it hard and I felt in my heart and saw in his eyes the same thoughts. I was too tired to decide fully, but with his hand in mine, I felt that maybe I knew what it was to truly love someone.

"Get some rest. I'll see you soon." He smiled and let go, following Jevin out the door.

I inched myself slightly further up onto Jevin's bed and fell to sleep.

47
The End

I woke with a start. By the position of the sun, I didn't think it was much later than when I'd fallen asleep. I looked around, for I was sure something had happened that jolted me from my slumber, but there was nothing amiss.

Though I was still extremely tired, I felt I should go to Jet and Jevin. Throwing on the disguise that Jevin had left for me, I winced when the fabric brushed my pained skin.

I ate a few more hurried bites of the plate of fish and fruit that was still on the bed and spotted a jug of spiel-fruit tea on the desk. Lifting it, I took several long drinks. I found I was thirstier than I'd thought but didn't want to overwhelm myself when I'd eaten and drank so little for the past week.

Leaving the room, I took the jug with me.

I hid my face, my hat low, and looked down as much as possible, but there was hardly anyone in the hallways. I got to the tower room and opened the door.

Jevin was standing there, holding his sword. I didn't immediately see Jet.

"Where's Jet?" I asked, stepping forward into the room and shutting the door behind me. I looked to Jevin questioningly and then stopped as his eyes met mine, his face was detached and slightly manic, "Jev—"

I saw what was behind Jevin, behind a pile of unused blankets on the floor.

My partner in crime all these weeks, someone whom I'd gotten closer to than anyone before, someone I loved...with a bloody hole in his stomach.

All went quiet.

I looked back to Jevin, taking that second to fully understand what the blood-drenched sword in his hand meant.

I did not think; I leapt, ducking the quick swing of Jevin's sword which sliced so close, it knocked off the hat I wore. I got behind him. The only weapon I had was the jug of spiel-fruit tea I'd brought with me. I broke it over Jevin's head and he sank, tea seeping down his face. He was knocked out cold.

Without waiting for Jevin to fully reach the ground, I skidded over to kneel beside Jet. His eyes were closed, but he was still breathing. I squeezed his shoulder, hoping to revive him. His eyes fluttered, and he moaned in pain.

I was desperately making incoherent noises, not even sure what I was trying to say. Why had I never learned how to fix people? If Jet was a plant, I could have helped him. His wound though, looked too bad for me, or anyone, to do anything about.

"Jet," I said, my eyes burning with unshed tears. "I'm sorry. What...you...I didn't...I'm sorry. I can't save you."

I looked over him, calming down a little, wanting to help. I didn't know if I should pick him up.

"I—I'll get help. Just wait. Just wait, Jet."

What sounded remarkably like a laugh escaped him and his mouth curved upwards, even if it was only slightly, into that smile I loved so well. "Shay..." He breathed once. "It'll do no good." He breathed twice. "You're...wonderful. Shay." He breathed a third time, squeezing my hand as a wave of pain seemed to wash over him. I squeezed back. I squeezed back as tightly as I could. But he was gone.

Those tears fell now. I'd hardly any time with him. He had saved me. I brought him here. Jevin—

"I'm sorry, Jet. I'm sorry." I kissed his cheek, my tears splashing onto his still face. I knew he wasn't in his body anymore, but it was all I had of...I glanced back toward Jevin, numb shock still icing over the thoughts of exactly what he'd just done, realizing that Jet had been my only friend. I sat back onto my knees, unable to think and unravel the knotted situation before me. I just stared blankly at the piles of extra blankets lit up by the noonday sun.

48
Why

I sat without thinking for a time, my knees drawn to my chest.

Had Jevin really killed Jet? He hadn't looked like himself when he'd looked at me. And Jet was—gone? How could he be? How was that possible? He was the most alive person I had ever known, by far.

I'd turned away from Jet's body. I couldn't handle looking at it, though that pained me as well.

Should I leave this room? Undoubtedly, I was being searched for.

I felt my breathing begin to quicken and I realized my body, my brain, was trying to process what had just happened. I didn't have time to do that...I didn't have the energy to do that.

I decided to give in the slightest bit, but to think about it as rationally as I could. What had just happened?

Jevin had...killed Jet? Why? WHY? No. Rational.

Was he only against Jet? No. He'd tried to come after me. Jevin was against me. My best friend...was against me? But he'd helped me to steal the seeds. He had helped me get

away with my plan. He thought he'd loved me and had
rescued me. Why?

I looked to Jevin. I thought I saw one of his legs twitch.
Was he reviving? I stood up hastily, feeling panic trying to
rise, and I edged toward the door as quietly as possible.
Where should I go? I had nowhere to go.

The only person I could think of possibly being on my
side was my father...but no. He must have known I was
being tortured and he hadn't come to save me.

'The Sea's Ribbon'. Even if I could find them...Jet...Jet
was...no. I couldn't face them, even if they happened to be
on Cresstalan.

I had nowhere to go and what I wanted most right
now...what I wanted most, that was possible right now, was
an explanation.

Jevin's eyes began to flicker. He was surely about to
wake up. What would he do now?

∾∾

I opened the door silently as I could. Jevin was still not
awake. I snuck around behind him...kept myself from
looking at Jet, and focused on the next step...it was all
I should think about. I got behind a particularly large pile of
blankets and other random items. I hid as well as I could,
pulling a blanket over my head to complete my shelter.

I didn't even have to wait two minutes more for Jevin
to wake. He sat up quickly but held his head as if it pained
him. There was definitely something different about him.

Gone was the easy-going boy I'd known most of my
life. He was tense. From my vantage point, I saw him from
the back and slightly to the side. He still held his sword in
his hand, knuckles bulged as he squeezed the hilt. "Damn
it," he whispered to himself. The stood up, wavering.

He looked around the room once, not even glancing at
Jet's body, and left.

I had to find out where he would go from here. I crept from my hiding spot, grabbed a spare metal rod that might have been broken off something long ago, as spots of rust were all along it, and followed him. He went up the stairs of the tower. I had a weapon just in case...no I would probably have to use it. I saw no way to get out of this, but first I wanted the full story of what exactly Jevin was doing. Could there be some sort of explanation? I would desperately cling to any hope that none of this had happened.

I snuck up the stairs after Jevin and when he exited to the top of the tower, which was level with the rest of the circular roof of the palace, I was able to follow him and hide behind a short wall that separated one part of the roof from another.

Jevin didn't go too much further and I saw why he was there.

I still didn't understand.

49
Revealed

The Court Reader had been sitting on another short wall and stayed seated. Jevin went to him and bowed. The Court Reader nodded and, as the wind was eerily calm today, I heard what they said.

"Did you do it?" the Court Reader asked Jevin.

"I found out where the new Tree was planted by Shaylite and the location of the other seeds. They're all on Fainia. Tarlin's group is there, so we can have them search. The Tree will probably need care soon if we want to keep it alive."

"You said the Master Gardener will join us though, didn't you? He can get us all the seeds we need."

Jevin nodded, "I believe he will, though he only agreed to protect his daughter. I killed the one who gave me this information so that we could keep what we're doing secret for as long as possible."

"You killed the girl?"

Jevin's hand start to shake. "No. The boy who was assisting her with the Garden. He won't be needed in any capacity anyway."

"And the girl?"

"She saw that the boy had been killed. She is well-trained in combat and I was knocked out. She's gone for now, but as I released her from where she was kept, I'd assume there will be many people assigned to finding her. She won't get far, if she gets away at all."

"What of the boy you killed?"

"I left him in a room that I have never seen anyone go into. I believe he won't be found for quite a while."

"We cannot have the girl attempting to stop our plans, she recognized her maid. We must find her. You said she probably wouldn't come to our side, didn't you? Do you still believe there is no chance?"

"Very little. She wanted to plant the Tree in the first place to protect the people of the islands. I think there's little hope she will see our side of things."

The Court Reader seemed angered at this. "These people are the ones to blame. Building up their preposterous nation on the ruins of our people."

"I know, Sentra. We must rid our islands of these imposters. I admit I did question it at times, but they are all brainwashed to believe that it's right for them to have claim over this land."

The Court Reader nodded, "We will finally have the seeds and a way to keep them alive, our forces will use the tunnels, nearly everything is in place, but you must find the girl."

I took a moment to think. Jevin and the Court Reader were with Heyda's people. All this time.

Jevin wanted to kill me. The Queen and her family tortured me. My father...had he truly wanted to protect me? If so, he'd done it by aiding the destruction and slaughter of many people. How could he, when he was sworn to protect?

He was the one who had gone against the code of the Garden.

Jevin and the Court Reader were working together.

This explained how Jevin had gotten the position of Apprentice Gardener so miraculously and perhaps explained why I'd been matched with no one.

So, what to do now? It struck me that I was feeling quite calm about all of this. It's funny how brave you can feel when you're exhausted, the one person who seemed to truly love you has been killed, and your entire life was taken from you. It seemed there was nothing left I could lose.

I gripped the metal rod in my hand, it was about as heavy and long as swords that I used while sparring. Perhaps I could put my skills to use now...I had to do something to help the people of the islands...the ones who didn't know anything, that were simply being punished for no reason. I had to at least try to stop Jevin and the Court Reader. Hinder their plans somewhat.

Perhaps it was reckless. No...it was definitely reckless. Yet still I stood up from the wall I'd been hiding behind and walked forward towards the Court Reader and Jevin. A slight breeze blew, and I felt my burns shudder.

Jevin had been facing away from me and the Court Reader was behind him. They didn't notice me until I was almost fully up to Jevin. The Court Reader leapt up and Jevin turned around just as I raised my rod to attack. He leaped out of the way and drew his sword.

I continued forward and attempted to attack the Court Reader, but Jevin blocked me, stepping between the two of us.

"Go," said Jevin to the Court Reader.

The Court Reader hurried to another tower around the roof and disappeared into it. I did my best to get past Jevin and follow, but he stopped me.

"Oh, no. This is where you and I face each other, Shaylite."

I huffed out a heated breath. "Why do you keep calling me that?"

"It's your name," Jevin said dully.

"You never use my whole name." I went forward but was unable to get past his guard.

Jevin was also trying to attack me, that manic brightness growing once again in his eyes, but I was too good to let him get past me either, even though I only had a metal rod.

Our weapons were crossed and Jevin and I circled, each of us waiting for the other to make the first move.

Looking at him, I thought of all the times we'd dueled each other, having so much fun sparring and practicing drills.

This was not fun though. My body felt as though it'd been ripped in two. Had Jevin ever been my friend? It didn't sound like it. And now, looking at him, I knew he truly wanted to end my life. Right here. Right now.

He broke his sword away from mine and spun to my side, I only just got my blade there in time to stop him sliding it between my ribs. I regained my footing and, once again, we were facing off.

Jevin began to attack, the clang of our weapons rang into my bones. I stepped and whirled, meeting each stroke of Jevin's sword with one of my own. We moved forward and backward along the roof of the palace, the sun shining brightly.

I remembered that going into the mindset of the Garden had helped me in past fights and I attempted to enter into it now, but found I wasn't able to. My tattered body, the clanging of the swords, the sorrow growing in me about losing Jet and about what might happen to the people of the islands, the fact that Jevin was in no way whom I thought he was. I found I could hardly take a deep breath, though fighting in the heat of the day was certainly no help.

I missed one of Jevin's swings and he was able to slice my forearm. I yelled brutally as the burns opened up, letting blood out onto the white stone below me. I had no time to think of that though, for there was murder in Jevin's eyes, sure as anything. He was still coming for me.

"Jevin," I breathed, thinking that perhaps I should try to talk to him, "are you truly going to kill me?"

I felt the adrenaline that had been coursing through my veins since I'd first seen Jet lying on the floor, wavering. My body was still so exhausted. It had definitely been reckless to try to go after Jevin when I was like this. But here I was, and I couldn't turn away now.

"You were only part of the plan," Jevin said. His sword pressed against my metal rod, he was pushing forward with all his strength. "Shaylite, you're not needed."

I admit, I faltered at this. And Jevin almost wrested my weapon from me, but I realized and caught his as well and somehow both weapons flew off in opposite directions, skidding off the roof.

Jevin and I looked at each other, eyes wild, and he came at me with his fists. I ducked and spun around behind him, my breath running ragged now. Jevin reached behind him, finding and taking hold of my throat and turned to face me full-on. His fingers were digging into my neck and I wretched, trying to do something to make him stop. Clawing toward his face, his arms, anything, pummeling him. But I could hardly breathe, and my eyes were going watery.

"You and your stupid plans to save the world...you have no idea what you're trying to save, Shaylite."

I felt his fingers dig deep into my throat and thrust forward. Something that was important in my neck moved as it shouldn't have and, sweat dripping from his dreadlocks, eyes on fire, Jevin ripped out my throat.

I tried to step backwards and fell. In shock. In pain. I felt warmth flow down my front and down the sides of my neck. It must have been blood. I could still breathe, but only just.

Jevin had beaten me and now he would beat Cresstalan. But what did it matter now? It wasn't a place for me anymore. I wished Jet was here.

I was lying face-up. As my vision started pulsing slightly, darkening at the edges, I looked into the perfect blue of the sky and smiled. A few white clouds were crossing it. At least there was something that was good. The sky was there.

Jevin entered my view of the sky, he now had a knife in his hand and was poised over me.

He breathed heavily, beads of sweat running down his face. How much pain he must have been in to do this to me. What had Jevin's true life been?

I felt sadness for him. I felt sadness for the Trees. I remembered that feeling I'd had with them. I was the balance. I was the connection.

A feeling that may have been all the emotions rolled together filled me.

Jevin braced one hand on the ground and the other lifted the dagger high above my chest.

The madcap, yet graceful rise of the dagger scored the air as he pulled it upwards. It hovered above my heart for the longest span of time I'd yet known.

His arm jolted as he tensed it for the strike. If we were sparring, as we had so many times before, I would have already rolled to my left and out of harm's way.

My face winced into a smile and I felt my lips break into a hundred dry cracks. "Do it." My breath bubbled from my chest into my ruined throat. "I have nothi—"

A sun beam flared up from the sharpened metal and it fell towards me. I could see the bright blue sky and pure white clouds reflected in the mirror-like surface.

I thought perhaps I was in the true mindset then, but it didn't matter, for the dagger was at my heart.

50
The Beginning

I opened my eyes to find the sky above dark and somehow different, why did it look so strange?

Sitting up smoothly, I saw moonlight coating a large, grassy plain.

There was a sickly-looking girl standing and staring at me, arms crossed, her pale skin and blotchy face glowing subtly in the dim light.

She gave me half a smile, reaching out a hand as if to help me up, saying, "Don't worry. It wasn't real."

Look forward to

The Locked Series: Book 2
MAGIC ITSELF

Acknowledgements

Thank you to so many wonderful people and things.

To my friends and family who encouraged me through all the years it took to bring this book to life. Though I cannot put all of your names in here, know you are all unceasingly thanked and loved by me!

There are some people who deserve particular shout-outs though.

Firstly, to those who helped me put this book together.

Roma, the graphic design master and my wonderful mother who made the cover of this book become amazing!!! She also is one of the most kind, loving, and non-judgmental people in the world and helped me become what I am. And to Larry too, who is awesome and gave us an extra pair of eyes to know we were doing everything right!

Jessica, for her constant encouragement which helped me to believe in myself and trust I was capable of writing a book. I'm so glad we met and that we can trade books to edit! Thank you for editing this one and for the beautiful artwork between scenes and chapters! You are fantastic!

Melinda, who was the first person to finish reading the full book! Yay! And who volunteered to edit so enthusiastically! You are a beautiful soul and I really appreciated being able to bounce around ideas with you!

To my amazing beta-readers, Kendra (2nd to finish! Thank you!), Britni, Amanda, Carter, Shelly, Joey, etc. Couldn't have done it without your insight!

To Joseph, for asking me to put your name (nickname) in the book which lit the inspiration for one of my favorite characters. Thanks for being awesome in too many ways and for giving me the freedom to let the story take the character where it would.

Rodney, for being my dad, encouraging me to keep going, and for discussing the esoteric intricacies of the universe.

To those of you who bought the first preview chapter in 2015, thank you for your lovely feedback and helping me to know I was on to something.

Now for the things that inspired me.

Though she isn't really a thing, my favorite tree from back in elementary school, Mulberry. I truly began to appreciate trees through you. You are most definitely my Great Tree! I love you!

For that, Ms. Bland deserves a thank you. She showed me the wonders of Mother Nature.

To Bruce Lee whose philosophy of becoming real and inspiring words got me through many hard times.

To Kwon Ji Yong (G-Dragon) and basically all of K-pop. Thank you for getting me through those days that felt so heavy. K-pop, your bright colors, smiles, and flare kept me going. Jiyong, your relentless work to be your very amazing self, no matter what, your unquenchable laughter, your heartfelt music, and your Instagram posts. though it may seem silly, you'd somehow always post something hilarious or uplifting right when I needed it. Truly, you are amazing. Thanks for always being yourself and giving me the strength to do the same.

To Grover, Wilbur, and Kermit. The best cats. You all were so helpful being cute sleeping behind me or in the way, on my lap, while I was writing. I love you all so much! Thanks for the cuddles!

Thank you to all the teachers in my life who encouraged me to read and write and gave me books upon books.

Thanks to Kung Fu and general Eastern philosophy for so many of the important ideas in this book.

To all the books that have inspired me, truly too many, but a few important ones, Harry Potter, Bruce Lee Striking Thoughts: Bruce Lee's Wisdom for Daily Living, Trespassing on Einstein's Lawn, The OZ books, the Throne of Glass Series, The Art of Fear: Why Conquering Fear Won't Work and What to Do Instead, His Dark Materials, and The Chronicles of Narnia: The Last Battle.

That's a lot of thanks and, though I may have forgotten some, one person who I could never forget is Hannah!!! Han-Ban, the endless fun phone calls, the encouragement, the hilarity, and the companionship always. You're my best friend and I'm so glad you've been here for me through all of this! Here's to both of us continuing on to great things! I'll come visit you and Yusuke again soon! I love you!

And beyond all of this, to those out there doing what they can to make this world a better place and always seeking out the beauty there is to find. Thank you.

About the Author

Gemma Lauren Krebs was born in Tucson, Arizona. Her favorite smell (as is the case with most Tucsonans) is creosote in rain and her favorite color is green.

Gemma loves studying philosophies, quantum physics, archaeology, qi, and so many other things, which inspired this series.

Her dreams, besides writing awesome books, are to move someplace with a lot of trees and water, meet Harrison Ford and Kwon Ji Yong, see the Loch Ness Monster, travel the world, fly, and learn more about qi power.

'Nothing Lost' is her debut novel and the first book in 'The Locked Series', which will total four books in all.